Greatness

Thrust

Upon

Us

Pat Robertson Rice

I

ISBN: 978-1-300-74172-5

This book is dedicated to my mother

Jennie Elene Kure

whose parents

gave our family the connection to

Wilmington, NC

and

Kure Beach, NC

ACKNOWLEDGEMENTS

No one could have a better friend than Margie Hall. I thank her from the bottom of my heart for her countless hours of typing and retyping. I'm also indebted to her for her referrals in the publishing process.

For her professional editing of the manuscript, I must thank my good friend, Susan Randall. Without her valuable suggestions and words of encouragement, I may not have sought publication.

To Debbi Zaicko I send many thanks for the fantastic art work she did on the book jacket. The fact that Debbi chose to use actual photos, taken at the Civil War reenactments of the 43rd Virginia Battalion, is a stoke of genius. Being able to see modern day replicas of the actual Confederate uniforms and fashions of the day greatly enhances the reader's ability to visualize the characters in my story. I salute her outstanding creative ability.

To my friends, Mike Williams, Brenda Kintz, and Sue Conway, who were the first people to read the manuscript, I give many, many thanks for believing in me.

Finally, to my "Angel of Inspiration", I thank you for your support!

ACKNOWLEDGEMENTS FOR THE COVER

Special message from Debbi Zaicko…
To the members of the 43rd Va. Battalion of Partisan Rangers:

Thank you all so much for the memories. The pictures that were used brought back a fun time with so many wonderful people. I wish I could have fit everyone on the cover. Special shout out to Stitch, Belle, Harry, Smokey, and Gunner also… to the rest of the illustrious Mosby Rangers…

HURRAH!!

The deepest, most heartfelt shout out and thanks to our Comrades in Arms… Badger and Cooter. May you always know that you are surely missed.

Until we meet again…

Dee

x

PROLOGUE

"Yeah Ahab, but you were the only one of us who got caught with your pants down when the barmaid's father returned home early!" John joked. All four broke into simultaneous laughter as they remembered the events of that night.

Nathan reached in his pocket and tossed some coins on the table to pay for his share of the meal as he commented, "What a night! We could have been killed, you know!"

The others nodded in agreement as they counted out their coins for the bill settlement.

Their farewell dinner had been great, filled with genuine laughter as the four best friends revisited many of their old escapades. Yet, there was a tenseness to their faces that had never been there before. Each man was dreading what came next – the final goodbyes. Men weren't supposed to cry, or so they said.

Darkness engulfed them as soon as they stepped from the boisterousness of the tavern onto the sidewalk outside. A thin sliver of moon was the only illumination in the starless sky. Despite the summer season, there was a slight chill in the air.

John cleared his throat and took charge as usual. "Now do we all agree that exactly thirty days after the official ending of the war, we will meet back here at McGilly's Tavern at noon?" John canvassed the group with his eyes.

"How about you, Thorn?"

Hoping that his voice would not betray his emotion, Thorn spoke, "Come hell or high water I'll be here."

XI

"Nathan, do you agree?"

"You can count on me, John." Nathan affirmed.

"Ahab, are you OK with this?"

Ahab stuck out his chest and took time to hook his thumbs into his overalls before answering. "Now you know I'm a ladies man, John. The women probably won't want to let me go long enough to come to your meeting. But for old time's sake, I guess I'll be there."

Everyone burst into laughter, thankful for the easing of the tension. Ahab could always be counted on for a funny comment.

"Can I take that as a 'yes', Ahab?" John joked back with a smile.

Ahab nodded.

"And I promise that I will be here to celebrate the end of the war with victory for the South," John concluded.

Though the words had not been expressed, each man knew deep in his soul that there was a chance they may never see each other again. Ahab rescued the awkwardness of the situation. "Since I will be staying here, I will be happy to help out with your families in your absence. Never doubt for a minute that I will be praying for you."

Ahab addressed Thorn first. "Travel well, my friend." He engulfed Thorn in a big bear hug and hoped that no one had seen his tears.

Turning to John, he smiled, "I know that you will make us proud at the Confederate Headquarters. Bring our boys back safely."

After hugging John, Ahab moved on to Nathan. "I predict that you will command your own regiment before the war is over." After Nathan's goodbye hug, he turned back to the group. "Now if you will excuse me, I have a lady friend keeping a bed warm for me."

With a quick turn, he gave a final wave of his hand, hoping that their laughter would camouflage his gut wrenching sobs.

The trio placed their hands together in one last gesture of friendship. "May we all return safely," John affirmed.

With one last embrace, each man stepped out of the circle of safety and love and into a future with great uncertainty.

None of them were headed to the same destination that night, but they all shared one thing in common. They wished they could turn the hands of time back to the carefree life they had shared a few months ago before North Carolina seceded from the Union.

Chapter One

"I don't know, Tom, what I would have done without these kids. They have been my life."

"Have you ever thought about how differently things could have turned out if you had been able to have kids of your own?" Tom questioned as he munched on the chicken salad sandwich she had prepared for him. It always struck Tom as odd that fourteen kids could live in the orphanage and that the house could be so quiet at times. The kitchen was cozy and warm with its gingham checked curtains and big, round table where they sat. Outside the old black dog was joyously barking as the children chased him around the yard. Suspended from the trees, the old ropes swayed back and forth as the younger children pumped themselves higher and higher toward the sky.

An old kettle on the stove announced its readiness, and Miss Lizzie jumped up at the whistle. Tom squeezed the lemon slice into the teacup and plopped in a spoonful of sugar before stirring around the hot water that Miss Lizzie added.

"I have thought about my barrenness many times, Tom, and I do think God meant for me to mother other people's kids instead of my own. Yet, the other part of the equation is that if my husband hadn't died, I wouldn't have needed to make a living. The timing is always perfect when God has a plan," she chuckled. Raising the teacup to her lips, she smiled over at Tom Madison, the man whom she had grown to love like a son. "And thanks to wonderful supporters like you, I have been able to keep this orphanage open for thirty years."

"Well, those years have surely kept you young, Miss Lizzie. You're still the prettiest woman in town." Tom's eyes twinkled as he handed out the compliment.

"I'd say Miss Sarah is by far the prettiest woman in town! Why haven't you married her, Tom?" she asked in a loving way.

"She won't have me!" he answered truthfully.

"Well, I guess she has her reasons, but for the life of me, I can't imagine what they would be." She patted Tom on the arm in a motherly way. "Would you like to make a dent in one of my freshly baked peach cobblers?"

"Would I ever!" Tom replied, wetting his lips in anticipation. All sweets were his favorites, but peach cobbler was near the top of the list.

As Tom devoured the dessert, Miss Lizzie added a final thought, "Isn't God strange, the way He works at times, Tom? My two biggest obstacles, the barrenness and the death of my husband, propelled me into the greatest joy of my life."

"Remember the old saying," Tom offered, accentuating his words with his fork. "Every cloud has a silver lining." [1]

Miss Lizzie chuckled in good humor. "Oh, how right you are, Tom, how right you are. God always has a better plan for our lives than we could ever think of, doesn't He?"

Although Tom didn't say anything at the time, he thought back to the tragedy of his own wife's death at a very early age during childbirth. Yet, her death had given Tom and his daughter Angel a very strong relationship -- perhaps much stronger than it might have been if she had had two parents; maybe that was the silver lining. There was no doubt in Tom's

---

[1]

mind that there was always a divine plan, but sometimes it took years to figure out the plan. [2]

On the ride home, Tom thought back to the only major disappointment in his life – Sarah's refusal to marry him when he had asked her six years earlier.

. . . . .

Today was Sarah's birthday, and Tom had taken her to dinner at the Southport Inn. "Come on in the study, and let's have some of your homemade wine before we turn in. I have a surprise for you!"

"Okay. I'll get the glasses."

Tom opened the decanter and poured the wine. "I have a toast for you, Miss Sarah. To the best house manager, best second mother to Angel, and the best friend I've ever had. May all of your wishes come true." The glasses clinked, and together they both savored the wine.

After a minute or so, Tom placed his wineglass down and walked over to Sarah with his hand extended. "Will you please receive this token of love from Angel and me?" The box was beautifully wrapped, and Sarah knew the jeweler well. Nimbly, she tore open the package and pressed open the lid. There lay a perfectly matched strand of pearls – big pearls.

"I don't know what to say, Tom. They're beautiful."

"This one is from Angel." Another box was handed to her. Inside lay the matching pearl earrings.

"Thank you! Thank you so much!" she stammered, touched by his generosity. Moving to the mantle mirror, she removed her ear bobs and replaced them with the pearls.

2

"Let me hook your pearls around your neck."

Sarah gathered up her long, lustrous hair in the back. Tom placed the pearls around her neck and then bent to clasp them.

"Let's have a look!" he ordered and turned her around.

At times Sarah's beauty caught him off guard. In her red dress and pearls she was exquisite.

"The pearls don't adequately say how much you mean to us. Thank you for everything, and here's a birthday greeting from Angel," he managed to stammer.

Sarah laughed as she read the letter quickly.

"Let's get back to our wine, and you can tell me what she said." They settled into two chairs and talked about Angel who was off for her first year at finishing school. The house seemed so empty without her.

An hour or so later, Sarah smiled at Tom. "Thank you for a lovely evening, Tom, and I especially thank you for these extravagant gifts." She meant to kiss her employer on the cheek, but he turned his face, and the kiss landed directly on his mouth. Embarrassed, she pulled back and hurried from the room. The shockwave that had gone through her body scared her. She hadn't kissed a man in a long time.

Once in her room, she read for awhile before turning out the light. A little later, she heard footsteps in the hall. "Sarah," the all familiar voice called, "I couldn't sleep. May I come in?"

"Just a minute. Let me grab my robe." She opened her bedroom door to Tom, and he entered.

"Sarah, tonight when I saw you in that beautiful dress with the pearls, I decided that I would gather my courage. I have wanted to tell you for a long time that I love you, and I would like to ask you to marry me." With that, he put his arms around her and kissed her gently. When she responded, he kissed her more ardently. It seemed natural. It seemed right. It had been way too long for both of them.

"I have loved you for so long, Sarah," Tom confided. As Tom kissed her again, a flood of memories came back to Sarah of what it was like to love and be loved intimately. The wonderful scent of Tom's aftershave permeated her nostrils, and the warmth of his kisses on her neck sent shivers down her spine. "Man was not meant to live alone." Strange that this Bible verse came into her consciousness at a moment like this. Nervously, she responded, "Tom, let's just enjoy being with each other tonight and not rush into anything that we'll regret tomorrow." Her tone was firm, but not threatening. "I want us to take our time. It's been a long time since I have been with a man. Come lie beside me," she invited as she climbed into bed.

Tom pulled his ardor back into check and tumbled in beside her. The moonbeams cast light upon her beautiful face, and with her hair fanned out upon the pillow, she looked almost angelic. "You're right, Sarah. Let's do take it slow."

With that, he began tracing the angles of her face with his fingers very gently. He leaned over and kissed her tenderly upon her lips, and very lightly moved his fingertips across her collarbone and down her shoulder. Every touch on her skin sent more and more awakenings within Sarah that she had denied for so long. Finally, Tom gently caressed the nipple and watched it crest into tightness. Tiny rivulets of desire spread warmth through her and Sarah knew that her body was enjoying its reawakening. Her heart was racing, and she responded passionately to his kisses. It made her happy when she felt his erection next to her, for that meant that he too had become aroused. Tom kissed her again and wrapped his arms around her, pulling her close. They lay in bed for a long time, kissing and touching, like two teenagers who have tasted love for the first time.

Sarah was the first to awaken the next morning. Donning her robe, she softly padded into the kitchen to make the coffee. She paused before the mirror to smooth her hair and pinch her cheeks for a bit of color. She rehearsed and rehearsed what she would say to Tom.

Suddenly, two massive arms engulfed her from behind, and pushing her hair aside, Tom kissed her gently on the neck on the left and then on the right, and finally in the middle. Sarah leaned back into his embrace, reveling in the comfort of his touch. Tom slowly turned her around to face him, taking in her unbelievable natural beauty. With a husky voice, he announced, "We have both loved each other for a long time, Sarah, and we both know that. Now it's time to take that love to a new level and to become man and wife." He peered directly into her eyes as he talked.

"Tom, please sit down and let me have my say." She broke the closeness, afraid that she might back down if she didn't. Settling into the kitchen chair, she reached for his hand across the table. Tom was apprehensive; he wasn't sure what she would say.

"Tom, I too have loved you for a long time -- for being the wonderful father to Angel that you are, for being the wonderful friend to me, for being a wonderful example of leadership for our state, and for being kind and generous with those you love. If we marry, we both know that we will be crossing a line that not all Southerners will tolerate." Her lips trembled a bit, but she fought the tears back and continued on. "Let's be honest, Tom. Angel's place is by your side for your political rallies and your governor aspirations. She shares your love of these political matters, and she will be the one to carry on your legacy. That's her role – not mine.

In some high circles, Tom, having a Creole wife would shut doors for you once the secret was out. And let's face it – secrets always come out and at the worst possible time! I look white, Tom, but the fact is that long generations ago, there was a Negro connection. As we both know, one drop of Negro blood makes you a Negro in the South. I will not have any part in destroying your career, Tom, or of shaming you or Angel with exposure of my mixed heritage. God has given me a gift, Tom. A barren woman was given a child to raise, and I know that I have done a wonderful job in loving, encouraging, and teaching your daughter about life and love. Nothing, I mean nothing, will ever harm my relationship with Angel. We can love each other, Tom, in a very, very special bonding; but I will not marry you. Angel must never know that there will be intimacy between us without marriage."

Seeing the tears in her eyes, Tom rose from the chair and pulled Sarah to her feet. He encircled her in his arms. "Okay," he announced, as he looked into her eyes. "Let's think about what we have said this morning and talk about it tonight." He kissed her gently and then longingly. Sarah was glad when he withdrew, for her resolve was almost gone.

"Could you make me some sandwiches to go? I've got meetings in town today."

"I might even include some of your favorite cookies," she teased as he hurried up the stairs.

Sarah thought about Tom all day as she prepared his favorite dinner. Hoping for an intimate evening, she placed candles in her bedroom and changed the sheets. She rummaged through the schiffarobe for the beautiful nightgown set she had made years ago. Shaking out the wrinkles, she hung the gown in the window to air out. Sarah's bedroom had originally been the guest room, but after Rachel, Tom's wife, had unexpectedly died in childbirth, Tom asked Sarah to sell her house and to move into the main house so that she could be the house manager and nanny for ten year old Angel.

7

Strangely enough, Tom's request had appealed to Sarah, for she had discovered that she was lonely in her big old house now that her husband had died. Moving into Tom's house wouldn't change her lifestyle very much because she worked there as the house manager six days a week anyway. Besides that she couldn't love Angel any more if she had been her own child. Without much hesitation, Sarah had agreed to help Tom out by moving in.

Sarah's exquisite sense of design showed itself in the beautifully made silk panels at the windows and the matching silk spread that she had hand embroidered. The room bespoke the elegance of the person who lived in it. Sarah put on her favorite blue silk dress and made sure that Tom and Angel's pearls were at her throat. The table had been set with flowers and candles. The smells from the kitchen enticingly wafted in the air.

"See you tomorrow, Jake," Tom waved, before opening the door. "I'm home, Sarah," he called and headed toward the kitchen. Sarah intercepted him in the hall.

"I brought you some flowers," he announced and pushed the red roses toward her.

Sarah took a whiff of their heavenly fragrance. "Oh, they're lovely, Tom!" she smiled shyly. "Thank you."

"Not as lovely as you. You look wonderful!" The longing was apparent in their eyes.

"I'll just put these in water," she stammered like a silly school girl. Finding a vase, she filled it with water and lovingly placed the roses stem by stem to achieve the perfect balance.

Tom hung up his coat and then poured a glass of wine for each of them. Carrying the glasses into the kitchen, he offered one to Sarah. "To our future," he proposed. The fine crystal sent a lovely "ting" in the air as the glasses clinked. "I accept your conditions, Sarah," he simply stated.

Tom sat in the kitchen chair and pulled Sarah into his lap. They sipped the wine while Tom told her the news from town. Occasionally, he rubbed her back gently.

Sarah was nervous. "Well, I guess I'd better get supper," she smiled as she jumped up. "I bet you're starved!" Tom grabbed her hand and pulled her to him. He kissed her gently and then passionately. Without hesitation, Sarah matched his passion.

"Can supper wait?" he managed to mumble, and crushed her to him once more.

"Oh, yes," she laughed. "Just give me a second."

Settling things in the kitchen, she grabbed Tom's hand and led him into her candlelit bedroom. The bed had been turned down, inviting in its suggestiveness. "I love you, Sarah," Tom whispered and sank his lips into her creamy skin.

"And, I love you, Tom," Sarah answered. She reached over and unbuttoned Tom's shirt, pushing it from his shoulders. She kissed Tom, allowing her tongue to flame his passion. He unbuttoned her dress and let it drop to the floor. Her dancer thin body enticed him, and the exquisite lace on the black corselet interested him. Tom unzipped his pants, allowing them to fall. Sarah moved to the bed and sat down, opening her arms to invite him. Without hesitation, he rolled onto the right side of the bed. Her corselet snapped in the front, and Tom enjoyed undoing each snap, which revealed more and more creamy skin. Once free, her pink nipples burst from the two soft mounds. Tom pushed Sarah back on the bed; then, following the contours of her body; he kissed her all the way to her toes.

As he retraced his steps back up the body, he settled his intent on the black-laced pantaloons. Gently, he wrapped his fingers on either side and slid them down. Tiny streams of pleasure ran up and down Sarah's body. She was pleased with how skilled Tom was in lovemaking. Taking his fingers, he traced the inside of her thighs slowly and deliberately. In a gentle, but insistent manner, he brought her to arousal. Sarah felt feelings she had not felt in a long time, and a low moan escaped from her lips. She drew Tom on top of her, and he supported his weight on his hands on either side of her. Shockwaves were racing through her body, throwing Sarah out of control. Tiny waves of pleasure edged closer to the brink each time he moved within her until she gasped at the ecstasy of the beginning explosion. At that point, Tom drove deeper and deeper into her and gently brought them both into waves of pleasure.

Exhausted, Tom fell to his side and crushed Sarah to him. They lay there entwined, feeling the ebb and flow of the aftershock. In a few minutes, Tom braced himself on his elbow and looked at Sarah. "Now that's a level of lovemaking I've never been to before!" he confided.

"Nor I," Sarah responded, amazed at what had just happened. It had never been like this with Rufus, her deceased husband. Oh, they had had some marvelous romps in the bed, but their sex had been purely physical. This bonding was much more intimate.

Sarah realized that when you were older, lovemaking was a gift, to be anticipated and enjoyed, and not just rushed into. But whatever it was, she had never been happier.

Tom touched her lips. "A penny for your thoughts, my dear."

"Could I tell you the truth, Tom?"

"Of course!"

10

"I hope that after dinner we can do this again!"

"Why wait for after dinner?"

Tom drew her to him and kissed her passionately. They held each other, talking and kissing for a long time, enjoying their new-found intimacy. Their passion not yet spent, they merged again and again in the shadows of the night.

Chapter Two

The smoke was so thick that you could cut it with a knife. A hazy smoke ring filled the air, drifting gently toward the massive fireplace. The Gentlemen's Club, the organization was called, and Friday nights found thirty or forty of Wilmington's businessmen assiduously concentrating on the cards dealt to them. There were poker chips scattered near each man, and several rounds of drinks had left empty glasses stacked on butler's trays on each side of the room. Some patrons were still sporting a business coat, vest, and tie. However, most of the younger men had thrown their coats across the backs of their chairs. A few had even rolled up their sleeves in anticipation of raking the poker chips in.

John Thompson was a member of the Gentlemen's Club by necessity, for lawyers needed to be seen socially by wealthy patrons. A great deal of business went on after closing time, and The Gentlemen's Club was one of the major places to conduct after-hours business. John's best friends, Nathan Summerville, Thorn McAllister, and Ahab McGee were his Friday night guests once a month for poker night. The four participated in many activities together: hunting, skeet shooting, fishing, and socializing. However, they especially looked forward to poker nights. There was a slightly competitive edge to this night, although none of the four would have ever acknowledged that fact. Suffice it to say, that the winner had bragging rights for a whole month, and those rights were usually exercised to the fullest. No women were ever allowed in the club, as the name indicated. Young teenage boys served as waiters for the ever popular rounds of mint juleps and bourbon and waters. On this particular Friday night, Nathan had the largest pile of chips.

12

Thorn was studying his cards – three jacks and a pair of twos. If he could keep his poker face, he could push the pot higher and then be able to cut his losses. "Well, I'm going to take a chance; I'm going to raise you two and keep the cards I've got."

Ahab, who had a pair of kings, took the bait, "Okay, big boy, I'll see your two and raise you four!"

Nathan wisely folded; he knew his pair of threes was going nowhere. With the pressure on, John rethought his hand. He had two aces, which was usually a winning hand. Discarding three cards, he dropped six chips, "I'm still in!" Ahab dealt him three additional cards. John's expression told them nothing, but the measly two, ten, and four did nothing to help him.

Thorn purposely stalled to make Ahab think he wasn't so sure now about his hand. "Well, I guess I'm still in," Thorn grinned. "I raise you four more, Ahab." *Clink, clink, clink,* the poker chips fell into the expanding pile in the center of the table.

Thinking he had him, Ahab threw in four chips, "And I call you!"

With a slow smile of triumph, Thorn lowered his three jacks and pair of twos. Neither Ahab nor John showed his cards. "Okay, you win," Ahab called good-naturedly, "but I am still the champion with the women!"

"Not tonight!" John announced, making a sweep with his hand of the all male room.

"Why, you don't know what I have waiting for me when I leave you three later tonight!" Ahab teased.

"Oh God, are you back with Widow Douglas?" Nathan inquired with a smile, remembering Ahab's affair earlier in the year.

"Better than that!"

"Let's see," John interjected, "who was widowed in the last month?"

"You're going in the wrong direction!" Ahab cautioned with a grin.

"Okay, who is the new woman in town?" John rephrased the question and started thinking again.

Thorn was too busy stacking his chips and clearing the table space in front of him. Feeling the power of victory, he called, "Okay, back to business. Poker nights aren't for discussions about women!"

John, Ahab, and Nathan burst into laughter. "I didn't think there was any other topic," John joked.

"Guys, have you noticed that people are going crazy over the slavery issue? There's even talk about a war," Nathan added as he picked up his cards.

Thorn was quick to express his dismay. "John, does the federal government have the right to impose laws that will destroy the livelihood of the South?"

"Now, strictly speaking, if Congress passes laws, all states are supposed to abide by these laws. After all, we elected senators and house members to represent our interests," John admonished, draping his coat over the back of his chair.

"Okay, okay, I understand that concept, but when the laws will destroy the livelihood and lifestyle of the South, then I'm not sure that's right!" Thorn argued, somewhat loudly.

"You know what, Thorn? You could always join the Secession Movement. Some political leaders are trying to organize the Southern states to claim states rights and to secede from the Union. What was once talked about in private, behind closed doors, is now being preached in public. If you have an interest in states rights, you should attend one of these rallies," John added.

"Have you ever been to one?" Thorn inquired, handing some of the newly-delivered drinks over to John.

"No, I don't have any crops or any slaves to worry about. However, as a lawyer, I am very interested in the validity of the states rights versus federal rights argument."

"Okay, if you hear of any of these rallies, let me know. I'm curious as to just how far southern farmers are willing to go," Thorn mentioned.

Nathan chimed in, "My father owns a plantation with one hundred slaves. If I want to inherit what my father has worked so hard for, then I have no choice but to be pro-slavery. How could I be anti-slavery? So, what about you, Thorn, how do you feel?"

"Well, to tell you the truth, I don't know how I feel," Thorn began. "I don't own any slaves, but I do run a farm. I can see both sides. Your father and all other men who own slaves have invested a tremendous amount of money to buy them. If the slaves are freed, who is going to give that huge investment back to the plantation owner? On the other hand, what gives someone the right to own someone else? People aren't the same thing as owning a horse or a mule. I don't think they should be bought and sold like cattle."

"Nathan, let me ask you something. Are the slaves treated well on your plantation?" John inquired. "*Uncle Tom's Cabin* painted a dim picture of plantation life."

"None of them have ever tried to run away. Each extended family has a little house to live in, and the older women who can't work anymore take care of the kids and cook while the workers are in the field."

"Who supplies the food?" Thorn asked, very interested now in the conversation.

"Each house has a plot of land to grow vegetables and raise chickens, and Dad supplies a huge ration of food to each family each day."

"Do you ever have to beat 'em?" John inquired, curious now about the inner workings of slavery.

"When I was a small boy, I witnessed our foreman whipping a male slave who had beaten a female slave almost to death. My father was furious with him, and he sold him as soon as possible. That's the only time that I know about that anybody was beaten," Nathan honestly admitted.

Ahab announced, "I don't guess any of you would like to hear my views on the situation in the South, would you?"

"No!" was the loud and simultaneous response, which tickled Ahab to no end.

"Why, men," he replied with feigned hurt, "I am wounded to the core!"

They had all heard Ahab's anti-slavery views over and over and over again. Because of their seven year friendship, political and religious views were not held against each other, merely listened to. Besides, most of the time, they were too busy with sporting events and courting women to worry about current events.

At that moment, a small young man, balancing a huge wooden tray, plopped a corner of his tray onto their poker table. "Here's your dinner."

Oh man, did the food smell good: thick slabs of medium prime rib served on home baked, just-out-of-the-oven bread, along with potato salad, pickles, and a dab of slaw, with hot apple cobbler for dessert. The food at The Gentlemen's Club had a reputation for being delicious. No one had ever bothered to ask if the several rounds of drinks beforehand made it always taste good or if it was indeed just downright good southern cooking. Deftly, the waiter deposited a plate in front of each man, "Shall I place your desserts on a smaller tray for later?"

"Good man!" Ahab smiled, tossing him a poker chip.

"Would you like another round of drinks?" the server inquired before leaving.

"No, we're fine for now," John answered, grabbing for his fork. Total silence prevailed as they reveled in the delicious food.

The guys made short work of the dinner, and Nathan passed around the desserts.

"Now, how about a round of after-dinner drinks on me?" Ahab questioned.

John signaled, and the young man returned to clear the table.

"A round of brandies, please," Ahab ordered.

"Now, shall we get back to our game?" Thorn grinned. "I don't want my winning streak to go cold on me!"

"Lady Luck, smile on me!" Nathan called, as he picked up his new cards; but Lady Luck had smiled on John by the end of the evening.

These four friends had been able to bridge a generational gap that few other young men had ever been able to do in Wilmington's social society. Their college educations admitted them to the after-dinner brandy and cigar conclaves with older men at high society dinners, while their love of fox hunts, turkey shoots, skeet and fishing kept them very active with the younger men in town. Truly, they could hunt, drink, and party with the best of the locals, branding them with the title of being a "man's man". Yet, their love of Southern social life kept them popular season after season with the single women in the constant round of debutante parties, weddings and political rallies that made up Wilmington's social events.

Schooled to perfection in social manners, educated in the best universities, tailored by the finest men's apparel shop, and wealthy enough to support a family, Thorn, John, Ahab and Nathan were more than qualified in all criteria set by the fathers of the eligible debutantes. Behind closed doors, the eligible women called them "The Fabulous Four," and each season the debs vowed to get one of them to propose marriage.

Yet, for some reason seven social seasons had passed without any of them becoming engaged. At twenty eight, they were all happily single.

Indeed, the year of 1860 seemed to show that "The Fabulous Four" had it all, but the hands of fate were soon to change the lives of all Southerners, especially the lives of these four men.

Thorn McAllister's Farm
October 1860

Chapter Three

Finishing up the last of the wash, Bernadette grabbed the laundry basket and headed toward the clothesline. She was halfway there when she spotted Thorn coming up the trail. "Hi, Thorn!" she called when he was in earshot.

"Now, Bernadette, you ought to be in there fixin' my lunch!" he teased good naturedly. Dismounting, Thorn sent his horse to the watering trough. It was then Bernadette noticed that his arm was wrapped in a makeshift bandage. Blood had seeped through the outer covering. "I got in a fight with some barbed wire down on the range, and the wire won," he explained with a smile.

"Come inside. I wanna look at that." Quickly forgotten was the laundry basket still filled with wet clothes.

Once inside, Bernadette put some water on to boil, and then motioned Thorn into a kitchen chair. As she unwound the makeshift shirt he had placed around the wound, she realized that the gash was deep. Thorn winced only when the wound was cleaned; otherwise, he was a model patient. "You're gonna have to wear that arm in a sling for a while to take the pressure off the wound. No range work for you for a couple of days, and I mean it!"

"Oh, I've got some bookwork that I have been putting off, and this will be a good time to work on it. Now, what about that lunch?" Thorn teased.

"Chicken and pastry – your favorite. I made it this morning." Bernadette teasingly opened the lid so that the flavor could fill the room.

19

"Um, um, um! Let me wash up. Thanks, Bernadette, for my nursing." Thorn gave her a hug, and she beamed like a school girl. Bernadette had never regretted coming to work for Thorn after his parents died.

Quickly, she grabbed a bowl and ladled a generous portion. "Hmm, it does smell good!" she thought. Setting the bowl on the table, she waited until Thorn was back to announce, "I need to finish hanging up the clothes, and then I want to ask you something."

"Okay."

Thorn had finished the first bowl and filled another when Bernadette returned. "This may be your best yet," Thorn admitted, and Bernadette smiled.

"Thorn, may I have this Friday off?" she asked, sitting in the chair across from him.

"How could I refuse you after you cooked this wonderful meal?" he teased. "You women always know how to get what you want."

"Fred wants to go to South Carolina to hear some speeches about secession."

Thorn almost choked on his mouthful of pastry. "Oh, I'd like to go, too. I'm interested in hearing about the secession view."

"We are going to catch the morning train, spend the night, and come back the next day."

"Do you have your tickets yet?"

"No, Fred's going to buy them."

Thorn ran to his bedroom and came back with some bills. "Will you ask him to get me a ticket, too? This should cover the cost."

"Why, sure. That will be nice to go together."

"Bernadette, I am going to have to give you a raise. You nurse me, feed me, and keep me abreast of the news!" Thorn tried to give her a hug, but the sling got in the way. They both laughed.

Thorn retreated to the study, and Bernadette returned to her chores. Thorn was beside himself. According to the newspapers, big crowds had been attending the secession rallies. Thorn wanted to experience this moment of history in the making. He didn't want to read about it in the newspaper. He wanted to see it, feel it, and be a part of it; and, thanks to Bernadette, his wish had come true.

"Well, I guess I'd better get on that order," Thorn thought. "I can kill two birds with one stone, since I'll be in Wilmington to catch the train. When I return, I can pick up the supplies." In a few minutes his thoughts of secession had taken a backseat to the orderings for the spring planting.

Friday came soon, and the trio arrived in Camden, South Carolina in the early afternoon. As Thorn, Bernadette, and Fred walked toward the stage, they noted the patriotic banners, heard the stirring music of the band, and dodged the enthusiastic attendees. Children ran to and fro, excited beyond measure by the circus atmosphere. Hawkers called to passersby from their stands where they were selling lemonade, licorice, sour mash, candy and pastry tarts.

An outdoor stage had been draped with festive decorations for the band, and now a speaker stand was being placed in the center. Local dignitaries flanked the speakers who were positioning themselves on the back of the stage. One very distinguished man caught Thorn's attention. This particular speaker sat confidently on the stage waiting his turn. Thorn was amazed that he had no note cards or papers to study. "Must be a smart man to keep all that in his head," he thought. There was nothing outstanding about the man's looks; he had a quiet demeanor and seemed to be in his fifties. However, Thorn could sense that great power resided within this man.

After the recognition of the local dignitaries, the mayor announced, "And now we are proud to host lawyer Tom Madison from Southport, North Carolina, who will speak to us on the options of secession." Great enthusiastic applause came from the large crowd.

Thorn had to laugh at the irony of it all. He had booked a ticket on a train and traveled all the way to South Carolina to hear this well-thought-of speaker, who actually lived only an hour from his home. . .What a joke!

"Thank you so much for coming, my friends. The South is now facing a decision that will be debated in the history books for hundreds of years to come." With that opening statement, Thorn was mesmerized. Everyone in the crowd was silent; not a baby whimpered; not a dog barked; not a person moved. Each was drawn to the words of this man who spoke so eloquently. Thorn was one of the many admirers who stepped forward to shake Tom Madison's hand after the speech. "I'm Thorn McAllister from Wilmington, Mr. Madison, and I thoroughly enjoyed your speech."

Mr. Madison threw his head back and laughed. "Why, you could have just come to Southport to hear this speech!" He slapped Thorn on the back. "We meet the first Sunday afternoon of each month at my home to discuss the latest news, and you're welcome to come. We have a guest house for those who do not wish to return until the next day."

"Well, thank you, Sir!" Thorn muttered. Tom's big hand extended to the next well-wisher, as he continued his warm, personal way of mingling with the crowd. "Right in my back door," Thorn thought. "What luck!" With that done, he made a beeline for the very attractive girl he had spied earlier.

A month later as Thorn was traveling to Tom Madison's Sunday afternoon meeting, he noted that the surrounding forest had been turned into an icy wonderland. Frozen boughs loomed overhead, and even the most trivial weed had been transformed into a majestic shape, cloaked in its sheet of ice. Tiffany's creations could not compare to this handiwork of God. Quiet and hushed it was as they moved through the forest, a frozen picture of exquisiteness. The horses were almost silent as they galloped along, except for occasional snorts of white steam. Marveled though he was at this vignette of icy wonder, Thorn still had an anxious heart.

The driver's whip snapped randomly to keep the steeds on the snowy path. Unconsciously, Thorn pulled his cloak closer to his neck against the deep penetration of the cold, misty air. He had felt compelled to come to this meeting. Thorn wondered if there was a guiding spirit that pushed men toward their destiny. The whole decision to come to Tom's meeting had happened so fast that he hadn't had time to catch his breath. Yet, every fiber of his being knew that this was exactly what he needed to do. "Perfect timing -- was that the chief criterion for the call of fate?" [3] Thorn jerked from his musings as he felt the driver slowing the team. Quickly, he looked ahead; there was a huge house coming into view.

Beautiful gray stones had been lovingly placed, one upon the other, and then mortared between. Smoke drifted from the chimney against the pristinely beautiful blue sky. Even Jack Frost's icy breath could not destroy the outline of the English garden placed in perfect symmetry in front of the house. Welcoming this sight was after the cold ride.

As Thorn was glancing at the garden, the door of the carriage abruptly opened. "Here we are, Sir!" the driver

---

3

23

announced. The horses stomped in their impatience for food and water, and the slightly icy driver hastily pushed a step in front of the carriage door. With confident steps, Thorn bolted from the carriage and moved in the direction of the house. Mission accomplished, the driver led the team to the nearby barn for a well deserved rest.

Glancing quickly at his timepiece, Thorn noted that they had made good time, just under an hour. Not bad, considering last week's weather. Sad thoughts always gripped Thorn when he looked at the timepiece, for it had been his father's prized possession. The loss of his parents was still painful, and the timepiece served both as a treasured heirloom and a constant reminder of his dad's demise.

A heavily coated figure was in front of the stone house, and as Thorn came closer, to his surprise, he realized the figure was a woman. "Hello!" he called. "I'm Thorn McAllister, and I've come for the meeting."

Quickly, Angel turned in the direction of the voice. Leaning upon the shovel, she shielded her eyes with her mittened hand and looked toward the visitor. Her coat was buttoned all the way up to her chin, and Thorn was amused by the long scarf which had been wound around her face, almost as if she had a bad toothache. Rosy patches gleamed on her cheeks, and tiny wisps of beautiful chestnut red hair managed to escape from the tightly wound scarf. "Hi, yourself! I'm Angel. We can't have our visitors falling up the steps today; can we?" In explanation, she waved at the efforts of her shoveling. There was icy frost all over the steps and her coat to attest to her labor.

"Oh, let me help you, Ma'am," Thorn offered gallantly. "A pretty lady shouldn't be doing a man's work."

With that explanation, he grabbed the shovel from her, and within three minutes, the whole walk was clear of last week's freeze.

"Please allow me to offer you some hot coffee and freshly baked cookies in repayment." She bowed formally in thanks. "Come on inside. Sarah," she called loudly, "our first visitor has arrived!"

A tall woman with beautiful dark hair soon appeared, wiping her hands on her apron. She extended her hand in welcome. "Hi, I'm Sarah. Come right this way with me to the kitchen. You will be wanting something hot to drink, I imagine."

The steaming cup of coffee had warmed Thorn up considerably. Soon he deposited his overcoat over the back of the kitchen chair and sampled one of Sarah's cookies. Thorn smiled at her graciousness and noted her exotic beauty.

A few minutes later, Angel returned, and as Thorn turned in the direction of the approaching footsteps, he almost fell out of the kitchen chair. There stood the most beautiful girl he had ever seen. A mass of ringleted curls struggled to escape from the ribbons that tied her hair, and Michelangelo had never chiseled such a perfect face. There was no statue in Europe that could compare to her beauty. Thorn knew at first glance that she was an angel, just like her name implied. Without the bulky coat, her shapely figure became very apparent.

"I see Sarah has taken care of you," she announced cheerily, giving Sarah a big hug. Her hand readily grabbed one of the still hot cookies. "Um, um, um. Chocolate is my favorite!"

In the kitchen light, Angel was able to note how handsome Thorn was. "When you are through eating, Sarah will show you to the library. There is plenty of reading material to keep you busy until the others arrive."

Thorn wondered if there were people who were half-angel and half-human. If so, he knew from the depths of his soul that he had just met one. [4]

As the hour went by, more visitors arrived. Thorn watched Angel darting back and forth to greet people who were attending for the first time and others who were regulars. Thorn wasn't sure if it was appropriate to have sexual attraction for the speaker's daughter, but he could not help noticing the curves beneath her blouse and her long legs. Embarrassed he was when she turned and caught him undressing her with his eyes.

Angel was used to men looking at her; she was even amused by their embarrassment when they were caught in the act. Normally she wasn't the least bit interested in the men who came to her father's talks, but this one was different. There was something about him that piqued her interest. Sure, he was handsome enough, and a muscular chest was easily identifiable under his shirt, yet it wasn't the outer trappings that drew her. She couldn't quite put her finger on what it was, but there was something special about him – she was sure of that.

She realized that she was acting like a silly school girl. Returning to business, she cleared her throat and announced, "I know that many of you have come from a distance for the meeting. Please help yourselves to the refreshments in the next room before we begin in fifteen minutes. There will be plenty of seats for everyone."

The coffee smelled wonderful, and three five-layer cakes beckoned those with a sweet tooth forward. Thorn, however, dived directly into the ham biscuits and chicken salad sandwiches, not realizing until now how hungry he had become. As he looked around, he noticed that he was the youngest person in the room; everyone else was clearly middle-aged. Thorn was also surprised to see women in attendance. Thorn didn't have anything against women; in fact; he had wooed and bedded down more than his share in his twenty-eight years, but he had never met many women who

---

4

were interested in politics. He laughed as he thought of how Angel would affect each of his friends. Oh, Ahab would be interested in Angel's body; John would be intrigued with her political interests; and Nathan would just be interested because she was a girl.

Everyone's sudden departure into the other room brought Thorn back to reality. Grabbing two more ham biscuits, he lumbered into the main room. The library was more than pleasant; a large fireplace with a blazing fire was positioned at one end, while the opposite wall was lined with volume after volume of books. Thorn wondered if Angel had read any of these books. A huge table and several couches couldn't dwarf the immensity of this room. Thorn especially liked the deep crown molding around the room and the Oriental carpets. The beautiful camellia arrangement was the only feminine touch in the otherwise masculine room.

As Tom talked, the afternoon shadows lengthened and then turned to darkness. After the meeting was over, Sarah sought out Thorn. "Our guest house is to the left, and the driver said to tell you that he will be back for you at two o'clock tomorrow afternoon. Breakfast will be at 8:30 tomorrow morning, and you are certainly invited. I hope you sleep well, and I look forward to seeing you in the morning." Sarah's smile was genuine.

Thorn looked around, hoping to see Angel once more, but she was nowhere to be found. Not knowing what else to do, he went out the front door with the last guest and turned left. Pushing open the guest house door, he noted that an elderly gentleman was already settling in the front bedroom, so he walked further back and found the second one. "I am tired," he thought to himself, and the bed looked very inviting. Within minutes, he drifted off, thinking of Angel.

"Good morning, Thorn. Did you sleep well?" Sarah inquired, as she pointed toward the coffee pot stationed in the corner of the kitchen.

"Oh, yes Ma'am, I did. What a beautiful morning; it's amazing how mild the temperature is today after last week's freeze." Thorn added sugar and cream to his coffee and took a large gulp. "Aahhh, there's nothing like morning coffee to get you going," he announced. Sarah noticed that he was looking around, and she assumed he was looking for Angel.

The other guest house resident appeared. "Oh, good morning, Mr. Thompson. I hope you are doing well," Sarah called.

Extending his hand, Thorn remarked, "Hi. I'm Thorn McAllister, Sir. I didn't disturb you last night when I came into the guest house, did I?"

"Oh, no, you did not," Mr. Thompson answered as he shook hands with Thorn. "But I am ready to sample the excellence of your cooking this morning, Miss Sarah!" he teased.

"The coffee is over there, Mr. Thompson."

The entire kitchen seemed to light up all of a sudden, and Thorn turned to find the source. There she stood – a beacon of loveliness in her blue dress.

"Good morning, Angel!" Thorn called and crossed over to her.

"Oh, good morning, Thorn. I didn't see you over there."

Sarah noted the chemistry between them and smiled to herself.

"May I fix you some coffee, Angel?"

"Why, yes. I'd like that very much." Angel's smile was genuine, and it came from the heart.

"Cream and sugar?" he asked smoothly.

"Yes, two sugars please."

"Oh, thank God," Thorn thought, "a real woman – not someone who eats only lettuce leaves so that her figure wouldn't be compromised." Handing her the coffee, Thorn watched as she sipped it carefully.

"Did you sleep okay?" she inquired.

"Yes, the guest house is quite comfortable."

"Angel," Sarah called, as she rounded the kitchen table, "why don't you take Thorn up to the meadow and give him the scenic tour of Southport? I've made the two of you a lunch because his driver won't be back until two. Besides, you two young folks don't want to be stuck with a bunch of old people on this glorious day."

Thorn waited to take his cue from Angel.

"Why, Sarah, what a wonderful idea! It is a beautiful day."

"Thank you, Miss Sarah. I would love to see some of the countryside, and I can't imagine a more beautiful guide than Miss Angel."

Sarah directed Mr. Thompson to the study. "Go on in; I will be back in a moment." Turning to Thorn, she asked, "Would you carry this basket out to the barn for me?"

"I'll grab my sweater," Angel added, excited by this prospect. "Good ole' Sarah," she thought, as she ran upstairs, "she never misses a trick. I love that woman!"

At the barn, Sarah gave directions. "Saddle Angel's horse and tie the basket on the back while I get the lead rope for my horse." Sarah noted that Thorn was quite adept at horses, and that pleased her. In fact, everything about Thorn pleased her: his looks, his manners, his obvious education. Oh, he would make a good catch for Angel. In a few minutes, both horses were saddled, and Thorn hoisted Angel into the side saddle.

"Have a good time," Sarah called as they rode out. Chuckling to herself, she announced under her breath, "And Mr. Wine, work your magic this time!"

Chapter Four

The large oaks spread their branches far and wide offering a pleasant relief from the somewhat humid morning. Only these two grand old dames remained in the meadow, paired as lifelong partners. Here under their boughs, Thorn and Angel decided to have their lunch. Dismounting first, Thorn helped Angel down and then untied the large basket for her, setting it on the ground.

As Thorn surveyed the beauty of this meadow, he spied some little wildflowers. Swooping quickly, he plucked the little treasures for Angel. Everything seemed to be so alive to him now: the pleasure of the sun against his face, the smell of the leather saddles, the soft scent of Angel's perfume, the roughness of the wicker basket. The world seemed more exciting for him this morning. "I have something for you," Thorn announced as he bowed and held out the little beauties.

Angel looked up from unpacking the basket and replied, "Why, thank you, kind Sir; they're lovely." As she reached for the flowers, his hand brushed hers, and an electrified shock ran through her body. Thorn felt it, too, and both looked shyly away. To hide her embarrassment, Angel busied herself with spreading out the blanket and removing the food from the hamper. Fried chicken with the thickest crusting, potato salad, deviled eggs, homemade biscuits, chocolate cake, and a bottle of wine were in the basket. "Wow, Sarah must really want to show off for Thorn. She has never packed wine with lunch before," Angel thought.

"Oh, let me!" Thorn grabbed the wine bottle from Angel and set about removing the cork with his knife. "This is a lunch fit for a king, Miss Angel. Did you help cook it?"

"Oh, no, Thorn. Sarah fixed it up for us this morning."
As she pulled the plates and the forks out, she commented,
"Oh, good Lord, Thorn. Hurry with that wine. I am starving!"
Angel laughed as the delightful aroma of the food drifted to her
nostrils. "What a beautiful day," she mused as she watched the
big, puffy clouds drift over head. Nearby, a meadowlark was
singing, and a busy bee buzzed by. "What a glorious day for
lunch with this handsome man." Angel turned her gaze toward
Thorn, taking in his dark hair and beautiful dark eyes. "I
wonder why some girl hasn't snagged him?" she thought.

"For you, my Angel." Thorn had thrown a napkin over
his hand in jest and was ready to pour the wine. Angel
produced the two glasses, and with a click, they tasted Sarah's
homemade brew. "Um, um, um," they both uttered in unison,
while consuming another big swig. Mellow and tasty the wine
was and deceptive in its ability to intoxicate.

"Now, Miss Angel, can we sample some of that
chicken?" Thorn asked. "My stomach is rumbling." Angel
offered him a plate, and soon it was filled with Sarah's
morning labors in the kitchen. "Oh, my God! This is the best
chicken I have ever eaten," Thorn announced around a
mouthful.

"Wait until you taste her deviled eggs!" Angel teased
with flashing eyes.

"Wow, these eggs are good too," he agreed.

Angel and Thorn chomped their way into ecstasy for
several minutes. Finally, they decided that they would have to
save the multilayered cake until later. Thorn poured more wine
for them, and he settled back against the tree trunk. Angel
busied herself by putting the empty containers back into the
basket, and then she moved over in front of him and spread out
the blanket. The wine had made a flush in Angel's cheeks that
was very becoming. Tiny ringlets had dislodged from her hair
combs and were framing her beautiful face, while the blue

dress she had chosen accentuated her large purple eyes.

"She really is the prettiest girl I have ever seen," Thorn thought to himself. It was a magical moment.

Thorn was first to break the silence. "You have beautiful hair, Miss Angel," he announced as he touched her long curls.

"Oh, I can thank my mother for that. She had lots of hair, too."

"What happened to her?" Thorn asked, before he realized that she might be sensitive about her mother.

Quietly, she answered, "She died in childbirth when I was ten, but I remember everything about her. It's just been Sarah, Dad, and I ever since." Angel surprised herself by speaking so intimately with someone she barely knew, but in truth, it seemed like she had known Thorn forever. It was a strange feeling. She wondered if they had possibly known each other in another life.

"I'm sorry about your mother, Miss Angel. I know she must have been a wonderful person. My parents are gone now, too."

"What happened to yours?" she asked softly.

"Oh, it's a long story," he answered with a slight smile.

Touching the top of his hand, she confessed, "I'm a good listener, Thorn."

He smiled his appreciation. Finally, he gave a long sigh and then a faraway look came in his eyes.

.   .   .   .   .

Clip, clop, clip, clop, clip, clop. . . The shoed horse galloped briskly through the dimly lit cobblestone streets of Wilmington. It was late – way too late – to be in the outskirts of Wilmington's business district in one lonely carriage. Inside the carriage, a blurry-eyed Thorn tried to awaken and focus. *"Emergency at home! Come immediately!"* had been the message delivered at the boarding house. Thorn had been lucky enough to find a late night carriage for hire, and off they sped. "What in the world could have happened back home?" he wondered. It was impossible to sleep on the bumpy ride, but Thorn needed to bounce off the lingering alcohol buzz from the Winter Ball. A good time had been had by all, and Thorn had been glad to see the bed in his boarding house room at 2:00 AM. However, the 5:00 AM message had awakened him abruptly.

"God, I hope Dad hasn't had a heart attack. He isn't really that old, just sixty two, but he does work hard." His mother never seemed to be anything but smiles, so he didn't much believe she could be the emergency.

As the carriage neared his farm, Thorn's heart skipped a beat. The pungent, burning smell reached his nostrils long before the sight came into view. "Oh, my God! There's been a fire!" Hanging his head out the window, Thorn tried to peer further down the road, but to no avail. As they finally drew near, his heart sank to his toes. A smoldering, burning heap of beams lay where the horse barn had once stood. "Oh, my God, what has happened to the horses?"

The carriage careened to a stop as Thorn jumped out, surveying the ruin. His quick eyes took in the fact that nothing was salvageable. Turning to find the foreman among the group gathered there, he saw them – two blankets, side by side. With nausea in his throat, he walked toward them. Without anyone telling him, he knew his parents lay underneath. Hesitating at first, he finally dropped to one knee. Bile rose in his throat as he saw the blackened corpse barely recognizable as his father. His mother's face was recognizable, but the rest of her body was severely burned. Thorn burst into tears, angry at whatever

34

God had allowed this tragedy to happen to two fine people who had never harmed a soul.

A comforting hand patted him on the shoulder. Thorn turned to find Gustav, the foreman, looming above him. "I did what I could, Thorn. I am so sorry." His voice broke, and Thorn found himself rising to comfort the older man. Not holding back his tears either, Thorn and Gustav sobbed in each other's arms.

Both men wiped their tears away, and Thorn questioned, "What happened?"

"I woke up when I heard the horses whinnying in terror, and I ran outside to see the barn on fire. Your father and mother were leading the horses out."

"Take these to safety!" your dad barked at me over the roaring flames.

"I steered the panicked horses over to the corral and put them inside. When I ran back, they were bringing out four more. While I was securing these inside the gate, I heard the falling timbers." His lips started trembling again. "Both of them had been knocked to the ground by the timbers, and they were on fire. I rushed in, grabbed them by the feet, and drug them out one by one." As he gestured, Thorn saw for the first time Gustav's bandaged arms and hands. "They didn't suffer, Thorn. That's one good thing; the timbers killed them instantly. Please believe me, Thorn, I did all I could." A spasm of sobs shook Gustav again.

As they talked, the farmhands were using blankets to slap out the last remnants of the embers. Thorn could not even think straight. What should he do? Finally, he decided he must take his parents to the morgue. "Jose, hook up the wagon for me please and bring it here." He did a quick headcount of the horses in the corral. Twelve. Good, all of them had been rescued; but, my God, at what cost?

35

By now, the sun had risen, but it gave little reassurance to the tattered and burned farm workers. "I want to thank all of you for coming to our aid, especially you, Gustav. I will never forget your acts of heroism where my parents are concerned, and I thank you guys for acting in my behalf while I was gone. Now, would you help me lift my parents into the wagon?" With sad hearts the workers lifted the charred remains into the back. Thorn retrieved the canvas cover from under the seat and hooked it from side to side. At least his parents would be reverently covered on their last journey together.

The little country church was packed to the brim with neighbors and friends on the day of the funeral. Betsy and John McAllister had been greatly loved in the community. Nathan, John, and Ahab sat in the front pew with Thorn, giving him a sense of comfort. Thorn had never even given thought to the fact that he might not have his parents always there. For several days, Thorn had been beating himself up that he had been off partying while his parents were dying.

Ahab, sensing his pain, had made him feel better though. "Time and tide wait for no man, Thorn. When it's your time to go, you go. Only God is in control of when you go and not man." Ahab always had the right words, whether they were for funny or sad occasions. The guys stayed on at the house for three nights with Thorn, using the excuse that he needed some help cleaning up the mess when actually they had stayed to give him support and love. When they prepared to return home, Thorn had tears in his eyes as he thanked them. "You're all I've got now, fellas, as far as family is concerned."

"Well, God help you then, Thorn, if you are stuck with the likes of us!" Ahab quickly retorted and brought the first smile to Thorn's face in four days.

"It is kind of scary to think about, isn't it?" Thorn fired back, laughing.

As they mounted their horses, John called out, "We'll see you for lunch Saturday, Thorn. You'll need a break by then."

"Great idea! I promise I'll be there." Thorn watched as they galloped away into the distance. Gustav and his ranch hands had all promised to remain in Thorn's employ and help him pick up the pieces. "Now, who knows how to build a barn?" Thorn called as soon as his friends left.

"We don't, but Mr. Johnson on the neighboring farm said to tell you he would come when you were ready," Gustav reported.

"Saddle up, Jose, and go ask him when he can come."

"Yes, Sir!" Jose smiled and headed to the corral.

Thorn had been totally amazed by the generous overflow of food and well wishes. His house manager Bernadette had done a wonderful job keeping track of the food and visitor logs and helping him plan the funeral. One night Thorn had broken down in her arms and cried for the second time, and then he was done.

Within days, all of the lumber that Mr. Johnson had requested had been neatly stacked, and Wednesday had been designated as the big day to begin rebuilding the barn. As Thorn was grabbing a quick breakfast, he heard the first rider, then another. Within fifteen minutes, twenty neighbors, bringing saws, hammers and ladders, miraculously appeared. "Thought you might be needin' some help, Son," Mr. Johnson explained.

Bernadette cooked nonstop for the next five days that it took to frame the barn. "Ain't you never heard of a barn raisin', Son?" the neighbors asked. "All we ask in return is a pig-pickin'."

On the last day, Ahab, John, and Nathan brought the pig cooking rig along with two huge pigs. By quitting time, women and children appeared as if by magic, and the pickers and grinners cranked up their banjos and fiddles so the dancing could begin.

Thorn, weary and worn out, had never been as happy in his life. In two weeks time, Thorn had passed the crash course in farm management. Now he knew the meaning of the word "neighbors", and he vowed to himself that he would always be there whenever one of his neighbors needed help. The last of the stragglers left at 11:00 PM. "Let's clean up the rest of the mess tomorrow," Thorn called to his three buddies.

"Fine by us," was their reply in unison. Each fell into a bed and didn't rise until noon the next day.

. . . . .

When Thorn's last words faded away, Angel was silent for a few moments, lost in her own grief. "How old were you then?" Angel gently whispered.

"Twenty seven."

When their eyes met, there was a moment of bonding. Unspoken, but deeply felt.

"We know that your parents are in a wonderful place now called heaven, [5] don't we, Thorn?" The hand he had instinctively used to caress her hair now moved to squeeze her hand.

The same electric shock surged through Thorn, but he managed a reassuring reply, "There's no doubt about that, Angel. There is a God." Thorn had never said that to a living soul. He didn't even know he believed that until now. Here he

---

[5]

was talking intimately to a woman he had just met, but it seemed natural; it seemed right. Every ounce of his virility wanted to kiss her right then as he had done with other girls, but something held him in tow.

"Now, let's talk about you, Miss Priss. How did you get started in politics?" The conversation flowed easily, and they wiled the morning away exchanging their thoughts, ideas, and beliefs. Looking at his timepiece, Thorn announced, "Hmm, I guess we'd better head back. My coach will be here soon." Neither of them wanted to go, but there was no choice. As Thorn lifted the basket onto the horse, Angel took note of his strength. Grabbing her around the waist, he hoisted her back into the saddle, enjoying the feel of her against him. Within minutes, they were headed home.

Their arrival back home did not escape Sarah's alert eyes. She watched happily as Thorn's hands stayed a little longer on her waist as he sat her down on the ground. The easy laughter and banter they exchanged as Angel showed him around the yard pleased Sarah. She clapped her hands together, and looking upward she uttered, "Thank you, God. Angel is gonna fall in love, and it's about time!"

An hour later, Sarah slid her arm around Angel's shoulders as they watched Thorn's carriage leaving. "If he returns for the next meeting, just know it won't be to talk to Tom; it will be to see you!"

"Oh, Sarah, we'll probably never see him again." She passed off Sarah's comments with a shrug. Yet, in her heart, she knew she had met the man that she would one day marry.

Alone in her room that night, Angel brushed her hair, thinking about how taken she had been with Thorn. Laying down her beautiful tortoise shell brush on the dressing table, her mother's framed picture caught her eye. This was the only picture she had of her mother, and she often wondered what her mother would look like now, fourteen years later. She smiled as she gently touched her mother's unruly reddish hair, for she had definitely inherited that from her. Yet, Angel knew that she had her father's eyes and nose.

A few years ago, Sarah had brought her mother's portrait dress out of the cedar chest. She urged Angel to try it on. When Angel pulled it over her head, she realized she was much taller than her mom had been and a little larger, for it wouldn't button all the way around. She remembered the stiff feel of the material in the navy skirt and bodice. For her sixteenth birthday, her dad had given her her mother's favorite garnet and diamond broach visible in that picture. The broach lay in Angel's jewelry box to be passed to the child she would have one day. Angel thought back to the very important conversation she had had with her dad when she was twelve.

·   ·   ·   ·   ·

"Dad, why did Mother have to die?"

"Now, come sit by me, Honey," her father requested as he patted the couch. Angel plopped on the opposite end and turned so that she could see her father's face. "You have asked a very important question about life, and this question deserves a very good answer. You see, Angel, we have a living part of us called the *spirit*, which can never die. Yes, your mother's body failed. The human part of her was pronounced dead, and we buried that part of her in the church graveyard. However, the living part of her -- the spiritual part of her – returned to God. She has been watching over all of us from heaven ever since – over Sarah, over you, and over me. Do you ever dream about your mom?"

"Oh, yes, Dad. She always looks just like she did before she died, all healthy like. She holds my hand, and we usually sit in a field of flowers or rock on the porch."

"How often do you dream about her?" [6]

40

"Oh, ever so often. Not as much though as when she first died," Angel replied.

"The ancient civilizations greatly believed in dreams as direct messages from the gods. In some cultures, dreaming about a deceased relative meant that the relative had actually come to visit with you and to be with you."

"Oh, it feels real when I dream like that, Dad."

"Then trust your heart. Your mom is visiting you because she still loves you and cares for you, despite the fact that she's in the spirit world now. Believe that." He smiled at her and patted her hand.

"Do you dream about her, Dad?"

"Oh, not as much now, but I dreamed about her a lot in the beginning. She probably doesn't worry about me as much because I am grown."

"But why did she die?" Angel questioned again.

"It was just an accident. Do you know how she really died?"

"You told me something about childbirth."

"No, honey, that wasn't it. The baby was turned wrong, and the cord had been wrapped around its neck, choking the baby to death. Nobody knew that the baby had died; and, as a result, an infection invaded your mother's stomach. When the doctor arrived, the only thing he could do was to give her a C-section to take the baby out. By that time, your mom was very weak from the infection. She died because the infection took over."

6

41

"So, she didn't want to leave us?"

"Oh, no! She wanted to stay with us. It wasn't her spirit that gave out, just her body. It was just one of those sad health complications that takes someone's life too early."

Angel scooted over beside her father and nestled her head on his chest. Tom wrapped his right arm around her tightly and kissed her on the head. "She's still around, Angel, watching over you like a guardian angel."

Angel sat up abruptly and turned to look at her father. "Why, that's just the way Sarah explained it to me – as a guardian angel." [7]

"Oh, I'm not surprised. Sarah understands a lot of things." Tom chuckled to himself, thinking it was funny that they had chosen the same symbol.

. . . . .

Angel had never forgotten that conversation with her dad, for it had spawned an intense interest in religion and philosophy at her finishing school. Sarah and Angel often talked about their beliefs in life, death and heaven. They were both voracious readers.

Angel kissed her mom's picture and placed the frame back on the dressing table. Softly, she announced, "Mom, I've just met the man that I'm going to marry!" Angel was never sure if she really saw her mother smile back at her, but she would swear until the day she died that something moved for a second in that picture.

---

[7]

Chapter Five

Sarah had predicted that Thorn would return to Tom's house to see Angel the following month, but Thorn took matters into his own hands sooner than that.

The little bell on the door jingled, indicating that someone had entered the office. Angel quickly marked her place in the ledger and pushed the chair back. Putting on a professional smile, she walked to the front, "Good morning. May I help you?"

"Why, just seeing your pretty face has helped me already!"

"Thorn? What a surprise! How nice to see you." Automatically, her hands went to smooth her dress and to attempt to push her wayward curls back into the bun. "What brings you into town?" she inquired, trying to curtail her excitement.

"Why, I came to see you, Miss Angel!" Thorn was really telling the truth, but he smoothed it over. "I had to come to get a long list of items from the hardware store, so I thought I would stop by to see you and Tom."

Coming around to the front of the counter, Angel motioned toward the reception chairs, "Oh, sit down, Thorn, please." At the political meeting at her home, Thorn had come in his Sunday clothes, but today Angel couldn't help but note how handsome he looked in his jeans and checkered shirt.

"Where's your dad?" he asked, looking around.

"Oh, he has court this morning. I don't expect him back until this afternoon," she answered matter of factly.

"Now, Angel, Thalian Hall is having a wonderful theatrical touring group perform this Friday night, and I wanted to ask if you would like to go with me."

"Oh, Thorn, I would love to go." She could barely contain her excitement, but she spoke calmly, unable to stop her smile.

"Shall I pick you up at your house in Southport?"

"No, actually, I could just stay over at Mrs. Bellamy's. Dad goes home on Thursday nights, and I always stay over to run the office on Friday. Sometimes I even stay over for the entire weekend here in Wilmington if I have plans with my friends."

Thorn was impressed. "You mean Mrs. Bellamy who owns the mansion on Market Street?"

"Yes, Dad and I live there during the week. She is a wonderful person."

"Wow, what nice accommodations!"

"Oh, I know. I just have to pinch myself sometimes to make sure it is real. We are mighty lucky."

"Well, okay. Let's see. . . why don't I pick you up there at 6:00 PM? We'll have a bite to eat and then take in the show."

"That sounds great; I'm looking forward to it."

"Well, I guess I'd better get on over to the hardware store. I will see you Friday night." With that, he opened the door and with a final wave, he was gone.

Angel thought that she would faint. Never in her wildest dreams had she imagined that Thorn would resurface in her life so soon. Then, with true feminine logic, she gasped, "Oh, but what will I wear?" Angel wasn't able to concentrate the rest of the afternoon. Each time the bell rang on the door, she jumped up excitedly, hoping Thorn had returned. "Thank you, God!" She remembered to be grateful and to express her thankfulness over and over again. [8]

Meanwhile, there was more going on at Ahab's hardware store that morning than Thorn realized while he was purchasing his supplies.

"That'll be ten dollars and eighty-five cents, Thorn," Ahab informed him. "Thank you for your business, Buddy." The bills dropped into Ahab's hands, and the cash register acknowledged the input. "Here's your change. Thanks again. Now, Thorn, do you need me to help you load these up?"

"Lord, no! I've got it. You've got other customers. See you Saturday for lunch."

Across the room, a man had been making a study of the galvanized tubs. Checking to see that no one else was in the store, Ahab approached the man. "Is everything on for tonight?" Ahab questioned the overalled farmer.

"Yep, I'll see you at eight sharp," he answered, anxious to be on his way.

"I'll be there," Ahab assured him. The bell above the door jingled again indicating another customer had entered the hardware store. The farmer disappeared as quickly as he had appeared. "Well, Mr. Johnson, how nice to see you again." Ahab extended his hand and gave a robust handshake to his friend. "How can I help you?"

Mr. Johnson produced a list from the inside of his jacket, and placing it on the counter, he called out the items he needed. "Two pounds of nails, two pounds of screws, fifteen feet of rope, and forty feet of wire."

"Yes, Sir!" Ahab smiled. "I will have it in a jiffy."

Jingle, jingle . . . Two more customers trickled in, and Ahab threw up his hand in greeting. The potbelly stove in the back was surrounded by a table and four chairs. A worn checkerboard filled the top of the table and checkers had been pushed to the side. The new customers eased into two of the chairs and squared the board between them. *Clink, clink, clink,* the checkers were arranged in neat stacks by color on the appropriate squares. Ahab's hardware store was the gathering place for locals, and on long, wintry afternoons, checker games were the delight. As the undisputed checkerboard champion, Ahab would cheerfully take on any competitor when he had the time.

"An anvil?" the new customer questioned.

"Oh, yes Sir! Right in the back on the left. Call me if you need any help finding it," Ahab announced as he wrapped and labeled the screws. "Here you are, Mr. Thompson. Three dollars and thirty-five cents."

Pulling the leather coin holder from the pocket of his overalls, Mr. Thompson thrust his large, hairy fingers inside. Fumbling around, he finally produced the necessary coinage. "Thanks, Ahab," he smiled and turned to leave.

The rest of the afternoon wore on, and finally 5:00 PM came. Turning the sign in the window from open to closed, Ahab carefully shut the front door and locked it. Pocketing the key, he headed to the livery stable where he boarded his horse. "Hey, Jake," Ahab called, "I will see you tomorrow." Jake waved at Ahab and returned to shoeing his horse. An accomplished equestrian, Ahab swung easily into the saddle and headed west. Galloping along, his thoughts turned to the nighttime activities that had been carefully planned for the last two months.

Chameleon-like, Ahab had a special gift of blending into his surroundings. Jovial entrepreneur, he played by day in the hardware store; an exceedingly popular bachelor, he played at the social scene on the weekends; and as a sportsman, he competed in all outdoor events. However, unbeknownst to anyone but a privileged few, on certain nights he had a secret life.

Chapter Six

"Sarah, I know that Dad has said in his speeches that the war is not about slavery; that it is about states rights versus federal rights. However, we all know that slavery is quite the issue. So, what do you honestly think about this?" Angel asked one afternoon as they were cooking supper.

"Oh, Angel, I knew we would have to have this conversation one day. Come on, let's sit down and have some tea." Sarah busied herself with the teacups and the sugar cookies while Angel filled the kettle. The ritual was always like this when they talked about intimate matters, sitting in the cozy kitchen, safe from the outside world. "Catnip or dandelion?"

"I will have dandelion," Angel answered. The lemon slices and sugar cubes were placed on the table along with the cookies. When the kettle whistled, Angel poured the water into the porcelain cups while Sarah settled herself into the chair.

"You see, Honey, my heritage is very different from yours." Sarah absentmindedly stirred her cup and seemingly gazed off into space as if to bring the story closer to her memory.

．　．　．　．　．

"New Orleans, where I was raised, was a spirited town. All kinds of people flocked there – white, Negro, mulatto, and Creole. We lived in the Creole part of town. Everyone that we knew was free, and I had never even seen a slave. My momma worked in a dress shop, and she made all the custom orders for the wealthy patrons. At night, she brought the leftover scraps

48

home, and she taught me how to sew. Oh, Angel, I loved the feel of those luxurious fabrics! Anyway, when I was thirteen, she got me a job as her assistant in the same shop, and I enjoyed working there after school and on the weekends. That was when I started designing clothes, hats, and pocketbooks."

"Momma was very strict about three things in my childhood, and I knew better than to cross her. First and foremost, I was to get an education. Lucky for me, there was a neighborhood school run at the church, and I never missed a day. Second, I was to learn to protect myself. Momma gave me a derringer when I was thirteen because I was starting to develop curves. She had a beau of hers to teach me to shoot, and I became very good at hitting the target."

"Do you still have the gun?" Angel asked impulsively.

"Yes, I do, Honey, right by my bed, just where she told me to keep it. Now, the bullets are carefully put away though, because when you were small, I had to be careful that you didn't find them."

"Can I see that gun, Sarah?"

"Well, sure. We can go in my room right now!"

"Finish telling me the story first." The eagerness to hear the rest of the story outweighed the gun curiosity for the moment.

"Now, the third rule was to always keep my birth certificate in a safe place."

"Do you still have it?"

"Oh, yes, Honey. I could put my hands on the paper this minute."

"So, what are you, Sarah?"

"Creole describes me better than anything else, I guess. I have Negro heritage five or six generations back."

"You've always looked white to me, Sarah," Angel innocently stated. "Did your mom look white, too?"

"Oh, yes, Honey. She passed for white many times when she dated. She was very, very, very beautiful, Angel."

"Well," Angel summed it up, "she couldn't have been any prettier than you!"

"Thank you, Honey!" Sarah gave Angel's hand a squeeze. "Now, I never forgot those three rules. The education part was a breeze, but Angel, my mother watched me like a hawk. I was not allowed to have time to run the streets or get involved with boys. I was supposed to get an education first and then explore the world. I was very involved with my church in my childhood, and I loved to sing in the choir. When Momma died I was only eighteen, and I thought that I would die. However, within a few months, I met Rufus at church while he was in New Orleans visiting his cousin. We fell in love over that summer, and after we married, I moved here to North Carolina with him."

"How did you wind up here with us?"

"Your mom and dad were looking for a lady's attendant because she was pregnant. Oh, I loved working for your mom and dad; they treated me like one of the family. I helped Miss Rachel sew the nursery curtains and the linens for your nursery. We even made little dolls. I can remember the night you were born, Angel, like it was yesterday! When I held you in my arms, I felt like I had had a baby, too! I loved you, Angel, from the first second."

"Sarah, did you ever have any children of your own?" Angel inquired.

"No, Honey, I never did."

"You were just waiting for me!" Angel announced, and she squeezed Sarah's hand, changing the mood.

"I guess so, Honey!" Sarah smiled at Angel in return. "When Rufus died, I just stayed on because I didn't know what else to do. Weeks turned into months, and months turned into years, and here we are today!" She smiled after she had finished her reminiscence.

Angel reached across the table and took her hand. "I'm so glad you stayed, Sarah. I wouldn't have had a mother otherwise."

"There was no way I could leave you after your momma died." Sarah's eyes went off into the distance again, and Angel honored her private thoughts. In a few seconds, Sarah snapped back, "Now, let me try to answer your question – how do I feel about slavery? Honestly, Angel, I haven't ever thought much about it. My mom was free when I was growing up and so were all of her friends. Rufus was free and so was all his family. Your mother and dad didn't have any slaves; so to tell you the truth, I have never had to think long and hard about it. Strange, isn't it, for me to say that when I have Negro blood in me?"

"But, Sarah, our Bill of Rights says plainly that all men are guaranteed life, liberty, and the pursuit of happiness. That is certainly against slavery, isn't it?"

"Yes, Honey. Of course, it is." Sarah nodded her confirmation.

"The Northerners freed their slaves, so it must be wrong," Angel proposed.

"Now, Angel, I have lived longer than you; I have read more than you; and I have been blessed with listening to your father's highly-intelligent speeches. Don't put the North on a pedestal. You see, the North is industrialized, and they don't need people to grow crops; they just need people to work in factories. Slaves are expensive – very expensive – to maintain. So many immigrants from Europe, who were willing to work for dirt cheap wages or apprenticeships, invaded the North. The Northern slave owners soon realized that it was cheaper to hire workers than to invest in buying and maintaining slaves. In a way, oddly though, the immigrants became the new 'slave labor', and their working conditions are horrible. Workers die in those factories and coal mines, but progress just continues on."

"Sarah, did you ever read *Uncle Tom's Cabin*?"

"Yes, I did. Your father gave it to me to read as soon as he finished it. If all the slaves in the South are treated that way, I would be surprised. Now, why would any plantation owner pay eight hundred dollars a slave and then beat him to death? That doesn't make sense to me. Oh, Angel, you have stirred me up today with all these questions! I almost feel like a traitor for not taking more interest in the slavery issue."

"I don't think we can avoid it, Sarah. The talk of war is everywhere." The cookies lay between them untouched, like the slavery issue.

Sarah always trusted her gut, and she knew that Angel was right. She needed to start thinking where she personally stood on this issue, for she – like every other Southerner – would be forced to take a stand sooner or later. "Oh, my gosh, look at the time! We need to get back to cooking this supper. Your father will be home soon." Like an automaton, Sarah cleared the table and set the dishes in the sink.

"Angel called, "I'll be in my room sorting out laundry."

After Angel left, Sarah couldn't shake the somber mood; and, unfortunately, a few weeks later, she would have a very important reason to remember this discussion.

Chapter Seven

Saturday afternoon had been a virtual mother load. Forty-four doves had been bagged by "The Fabulous Four" in just two hours. As Nathan, Thorn, and John worked to dress the birds, Ahab, the only cook among them, was rustling up a fish and shrimp stew complete with home-baked cornbread. "Come and get it!" Ahab announced from the campsite about an hour later, and all three came running, pleased by the tempting aroma. "Grab those bowls!" Ahab generously ladled the tasty stew into their tin bowls.

"Man, this smells great," John announced. Each man found a perching spot and began to blow on the bubbling stew. "Oh, my God, this is delicious!" John called, clearly awed at Ahab's culinary skills.

"Man, it is!" Nathan agreed. Thorn was too busy spooning the stew into his mouth to even comment.

John, in true Southern fashion, took the last bite of his cornbread to wipe the remnants of his stew from his bowl. "Um, um, um," he commented, as he popped it into his mouth, "that was some kinda good."

"There's enough for seconds," Ahab called. Almost before he had finished his statement, three bodies rushed past him to the iron pot. Ravenously, they tore into their second helpings. Ahab chuckled to himself at the success of his meal.

"Ahab, hurry and get your second bowl so we can divide what's left," Nathan called, reaching for his next piece of cornbread. "I'm still starving."

"Okay, okay! Don't rush me," Ahab answered moving toward the fire. Ladling out his second serving, Ahab called, "Okay, it's all yours." There was half a bowl left for each of them and a few more cornbread squares.

"Where did you learn to cook like this?" John questioned, as he wiped his mouth with the back of his hand.

"My daddy taught me. I've been going hunting with him since I was a little boy. Over the years, he taught me how to use the shrimp net and the fishing pole. Each time we went out, he would always cook some type of stew."

"Could you teach us how to cook?" Thorn asked with a hopeful look.

"Oh course I could, but I'm not! If I teach you, you may not invite me anymore," Ahab teased back.

The warmth of the fire felt good. The afternoon shadows had lengthened, and the sun was traveling down the western horizon. The men lay lazily sprawled around the fire, enjoying their time away from work. The horses had been fed and watered, and the two retrievers were already sleeping, tired from the afternoon fetching.

"You know," John mused, as he changed positions, "women are cuddly and soft, but there are times like today when I much prefer the company of men."

Throwing another log into the fire, Nathan added, "I think we all feel that way, at least I do. Sometimes I just need to get back to nature and leave behind the complications everyday life offers."

"I don't know about you guys," Ahab sneered, "but there ain't nothing better than a half-clad woman on a soft bed next to me." John, Nathan, and Thorn burst into simultaneous laughter. Ahab was a ladies man through and through, and nobody would deny it.

"I am also glad to be away from the incessant talk of the possibility of war. I am sick of the subject," John grumbled.

"You know, if the war becomes inevitable – and it looks like it will – we will certainly have to call a screeching halt to everything we do for fun. There will be no hunting, no fishing, no partying, no drinking, and no dating," Nathan added, almost as if each word brought home the harsh reality of what possibly lay ahead.

"You know, out of all the talk, there is only one man who has made any sense to me. Tom Madison, the lawyer from down around Southport. He's the one I told you that I went to hear in Camden," Thorn added.

"You never did tell us what he said," Ahab mentioned.

"Tom's main point was, and I quote, 'In order to solve a problem, we need to look at the bigger picture.' Now, I am not going to say this as eloquently as he did, but I would like to mention something amazing that he did bring up. Tom said that God, over many centuries, has always sent teachers to each civilization to deliver His higher teachings. We have all been to college, so who do we remember from history? Who were the greatest teachers in the world?"

Ahab chimed in right away, "I remember studying about Buddha and his Eight Fold Plan for enlightenment."

"Oh, yeah, that's right," John added. "He was some kind of prince who sneaked away from his family to see how life really was, and the Buddhist religion sprang from his teachings after he died."

"Let's not forget the obvious one," Thorn added. "Jesus Christ. He was the most recent leader with the teachings of compassion and unconditional love. The New Testament is centered around his teachings."

"What about Allah? Let's not forget Muhammad and the Muslim faith," John added. "What about Moses. In the Old Testament, he is the one who gave the Jewish faith a much higher code, a much stricter code of living around the Mideast."

"What about Confucius?" Ahab asked. "Was he responsible for any religion?"

"Now you see, guys, this is what I'm talking about. We were listening to our college lectures; weren't we? We do remember that these great enlightened men did show up in various civilizations to give a higher code or a higher teaching to the masses. But, the reason I jogged your memory is that we have never viewed an event that happened right here in our own country as inspired by God."

"What are you referring to, Thorn?" Ahab questioned, with his curiosity greatly piqued.

"Tom said in his speech that he was sure that the most recent men inspired by God to bring higher codes of living were the signers of the Declaration of Independence." A silence ensued for a moment as the guys pondered what Thorn had said.

John broke the silence by blurting, "Yeah, remember how all the members of the Continental Congress were afraid to sign their names to such a bold and brazen decree? Then John Hancock grabbed the Declaration of Independence and signed his name large enough for anyone to see five feet away. You remember that story?"

"You know, I guess they did realize they had taken a higher road – now that you mention it. But what does that have to do with us, Thorn? How does that tie into the talk of war?" Nathan asked.

The signers of the Declaration of Independence stuck their necks out to write the Bill of Rights, and now we are being asked to stick our necks out to test one of those rights.

"What right?" Nathan asked, decidedly interested.

"Life, Liberty, and the pursuit of happiness," Thorn answered. "You see, this is the first time in history this question of liberty has come up to be defined. Our forefathers just wrote the Bill of Rights; they did not define each word.

Do slaves have the right to liberty? The Northerners think they do. Does the South have the right to secede and claim its liberty from Northerner laws that want to change the livelihood of the South? If so, the Southerners will fight to maintain their liberty. In essence, the war won't be about tariffs or slavery, the concept will be defending what the Bill of Rights guarantees us. Unfortunately, each of us must decide that with our hearts and not our heads."

There was another silence – an awkward silence. Finally, Nathan spoke, "This may be too high-brow for me, Thorn, but you have set me to thinking about the war in a different way. I might add, in a more personal way."

"Me, too!" John echoed. Only Ahab was quiet. He had made his decision long ago as to what his conscience had urged him to do.

"I guess we'd better head back to town, guys. Those ladies will be waiting for us at the Mintz's deb party," Ahab announced, rubbing his hands together in anticipation.

"Yep, those birds won't keep forever," Thorn added. Quick work was made of putting out the fire and saddling the horses. Within a few minutes, they were galloping toward Wilmington's Saturday night big event, Natalie Mintz's deb party. However, whether John and Nathan recognized it at the time, a seed of insight had been planted firmly in each man's mind by Thorn.

The highlight of every social season in Wilmington revolved around the debutante parties. Each year, the Terpsichorean Club announced the selection of twelve girls – always from very prominent families – who would make their debut into society. Each girl's family was responsible for giving a "coming out" party for their daughter. After the year of partying had gone by, the grand finale, the Debutante Ball, was held in December.

When they arrived back in Wilmington, Thorn sprinted up the boarding house stairs and opened the door with his key. Grabbing his suitcase, he unpacked the carefully starched shirt. "Good ole' Bernadette, she always knows how to take care of me," he thought. Out came the collar stays, the bowtie, the cummerbund, and the cufflinks from the little black bag she had placed in his suitcase. Thorn did not often wear formal wear, and, in a way, he enjoyed dressing up occasionally. He quickly shaved and washed off before beginning the dressing ritual. Satisfied with his appearance, he grabbed his overcoat in case he didn't come back to the room until the wee hours of the morning.

The huge Mintz mansion lights illuminated the entire city block. Carriage after carriage unloaded in the enormous circular driveway. It seemed that everyone in town had been invited. At the door, a servant took Thorn's overcoat and ushered him into the entrance hall. Much slapping on the back, handshaking, and hello-ing was going on in the hall among the older couples. Thorn, however, was more interested in finding the bar and the hors d'oeuvers.

Two huge, eight-arm silver candelabras flanked each end of the enormous banquet table. Mounds of berries and camellias filled a three-tiered arrangement in the center. At each end of the table, the carving stations had been set up, and uniformed servants were delivering generous portions of ham and prime rib upon the glass plates. Melt-in-your-mouth biscuits were available for the meats. An unbelievable presentation had been accomplished in the beautifully arranged trays. Hour after hour had gone into the making of the sandwich selections: chicken salad, pimento cheese, and egg salad. In addition, ham biscuits filled huge, mammoth silver trays to the brim. Thorn was tossing off his fifth chicken salad sandwich when a soft, sultry voice filled his ear from behind. "Hello, you handsome man." Hastily wiping his mouth, Thorn turned around to find Miss Brenda standing in front of him, on the arm of an unfamiliar fellow.

Remembering his manners, Thorn kissed her extended hand, and then looking up he announced, "I don't know who you are, but you are a lucky man to be escorting Miss Brenda!" With that, he extended his hand.

"Thorn McAllister, meet Addison Steele. Addison, meet Thorn, one of our local bachelors."

"Pleased to meet you."

"Addison is visiting from St. Louis, and he is Natalie's cousin."

"Oh, we're glad to have you visit down South, Addison," Thorn replied. "I hope you will enjoy your stay."

"See you around," Brenda cooed and tucked her arm possessively into Addison's. Thorn was glad to see that she was occupied for the evening. That girl was too determined to get married to suit him. He spotted John at the bar and ambled over to see him. "Is Nathan here yet?"

"No, I haven't seen him. Did you see Miss Brenda?"

"Oh, yeah!" Thorn replied. "Thank God she has a date!"

"Uh oh, here comes trouble!" Mrs. Vandemere, pulling along her ugly-duckling daughter, was heading straight for them.

"Hello, boys!" Mrs. Vandemere bellowed. "I know you want to be the first to sign Sharon's dance card." Embarrassed, the timid Sharon held out the white square.

"Of course we do!" John announced and placed his name on the card.

"May I, please?" Thorn inquired, looking at Sharon. Shyly, Sharon extended the card to Thorn, and he signed it enthusiastically. Bowing to them, Thorn added, "We'll see you when the music starts, Sharon." Mrs. Vandemere lunged ahead, ready to devour her next unsuspecting victim, dragging poor Sharon behind her.

"Look to the right, Thorn." Turning slightly, Thorn spied Nathan gallantly escorting three beautiful ladies toward them.

"May I present our lovely New Bern visitors who are cousins of Natalie." Both John and Thorn bowed quickly and kissed the offered hands. Indicating the girl on his left, Nathan announced, "Susan is studying music at Mary Washington. Charlotte is pursuing a teaching degree," and indicating the girl on his right, "Nora Ellen is beginning a nursing degree."

Turning to the guys, Nathan gestured, "Thorn is a landowner who specializes in raising tobacco and cotton." Then motioning to John, "John is a promising young lawyer here in Wilmington."

"Miss Nora Ellen, may I be the first to sign your dance card?" Thorn asked the striking beauty.

"Oh, I have already beaten you to it!" Nathan beamed.

"Well, could I be second?" Thorn asked. Then he turned to Charlotte and questioned, "May I be third?"

At that point, John spoke up. "What about me? Which dance can I have with you lovelies?" All six broke into laughter. The dance cards were produced, and each man signed his name.

Over the punchbowl, Thorn whispered, "Those are some good looking girls."

"Um, hum," John replied. "This may prove to be an interesting evening." However, John had no idea just how interesting the evening would turn out for him.

An hour later, Brenda asked Thorn to keep Addison company while she powdered her nose during intermission.

"Have you enjoyed your stay here?" Thorn inquired politely.

"Oh, yes. These beautiful trees that are everywhere with those fragrant white flowers, what are they?"

"Magnolias."

"Oh, yes, your countryside is just breathtaking. The cooking is mouth-watering, and the women – wow – quite beautiful. But, Thorn, I must ask you, do you have any slaves?" Addison inquired.

Thorn laughed, "Heavens, no! I am a landowner, not a plantation owner."

"I was amazed at how many slaves my uncle has. We freed our slaves up North long ago. Why don't you free them here?"

Thorn thought for a minute. "First of all, who would plant and harvest the crops for the plantation owners if we freed them? Second, your uncle paid five to eight hundred dollars for each of those slaves. Who is going to give him back his investment if the slaves are freed?"

"But the way they live in those tiny houses," Addison argued.

"Now, I don't mean to be insulting in any way, Addison, but the Southern slaves are treated much better than the North treats the immigrants by forcing them to work in those factories and coal mines. Hundreds of them have died, but you don't hear of any slaves dying down here. By and large, the owners feed them well and take care of them health wise.

"That's not the way *Uncle Tom's Cabin* portrays slave life."

"I'm not sure that Miss Stowe can speak for the entire South." Thorn's words were abruptly stopped by Brenda's return.

"I guess I had better get back to the ballroom." Thorn turned and walked away. For some reason, Addison's words had irked him, but he didn't know why. He certainly didn't own any slaves. As far as he knew, slaves were nicely treated.

"I saw you outside talking to Addison. Man, he needs a course in manners! He lit a cigarette in front of Brenda on the veranda, and he started smoking it until his uncle came over and made him put it out," John gossiped.

"That's nothing. He started attacking the South about slavery. I guess he hasn't heard the rule of never discussing religion and politics in any social situation."

"Well, look at that!" Thorn turned to the left, and there was Nathan, still shepherding the three New Bern girls. It was quite evident that he was in hog heaven with all the attention.

"Don't you think we better help him out?" Thorn laughed and started toward him. About that time, the music changed, signaling the presentation of Natalie, the Mintz's debutante daughter. For months, everything in the Mintz household had been geared toward this important night: the decorations, the gown fittings, and the elaborate cooking. Everything had been in anticipation of this one moment, for Natalie's coming out. Thorn had never been sure if the term "coming out" meant that everyone in town was invited to come out to see her grand entrance, or whether "coming out" meant that Natalie was coming out officially to announce that she was available to be married. Whatever the meaning, the deb party that Mr. Mintz was throwing in honor of his daughter was the most elaborate Thorn had ever attended.

Everyone crowded into the central hall in hushed anticipation while the band played the opening notes of "Pomp and Circumstance". All eyes moved to the top of the stairs. When the two of them appeared, Mr. Mintz, handsome in his formal wear, held tightly to Natalie. The entire audience gasped at her beauty. Her dark hair had been ringleted and swept to the side. A carving on a cameo could not have been more beautiful than her face. Before the grand descent down the staircase, Natalie paused appropriately so that all could see her dress. Beautiful lace appliqué and seed pearls adorned the bodice which dropped to a wide, sweeping skirt.

John signed audibly, "Oh my God, Thorn, she is the most beautiful sight I have ever seen!" Thorn turned to see that John was transfixed, drinking in the sight of Natalie. As she descended the staircase, John did not miss one motion that she made. Finally, John awoke from his stupor. "I'm going to marry her, Thorn. She is the one!"

Shock wasn't an adequate word to express Thorn's reaction. He had never heard John even mention the word "marriage" before. Thorn always trusted his intuition, whether in business or friendship, and his gut told him now that John was serious. [9] Before Thorn could even respond, John sprinted ahead, elbowing his way through the crowd so that he could sign Natalie's dance card. The three New Bern beauties and the one Wilmington beauty, Natalie, presented quite a gorgeous selection for this evening. Knowing that Natalie had been selected by John, Thorn decided to see if he could kidnap one of the New Bern "chicks" from Nathan's "hen house". The night was still young, but Thorn was beginning to see that most of the girls he met at the debutante balls paled in comparison to Angel.

Chapter Eight

Tom Madison often laughed and called himself the luckiest man in the world. He had two lucrative law practices, a passion for politics, a beautiful woman to love, a wonderful daughter who worked with him, and the best accommodations in Wilmington. Tom knew that God had given him many blessings, and he was extremely grateful.

Tom's hometown of Southport was too small to support a full-time law practice. Therefore, Tom had decided to work in Southport only on Mondays, spending Tuesdays, Wednesdays, and Thursdays at his law practice in the larger, nearby town of Wilmington. Angel shared his passion of law and politics, and Tom was lucky that she wanted to work side-by-side with him in managing both offices. Fridays, for Tom, were devoted to helping Jeff, his farm manager, with the many activities involved in running a tenant farm. One of the blessings that Tom often spoke about occurred the first year he practiced law in Wilmington.

· · · · ·

Tap, tap, tap . . . Tom looked up from his desk to see Mrs. Bellamy, one of his favorite clients, at the door. Jumping up quickly, he ran to unlock the door. "Good morning, Mrs. Bellamy. What are you doing out so early this morning? Come in, come in!" Tom ushered her into his office and motioned for her to sit in the chair in front of his desk. "Would you like some tea or coffee?"

"Oh, no thank you, Tom. I've already had breakfast." She smiled and fingered with her white curls nervously before beginning. "I hope that I'm not intruding in your private life.

66

After our conversation last Friday, I have been thinking about something."

"Now, Mrs. Bellamy, I will be happy to help you in any way I can. We can change anything we put on paper last Friday," Tom assured her as he rounded the desk to sit in his chair.

"Oh, no, I am the one that wants to help you!" she announced with a big smile.

"Me?" Tom responded with a confused look.

"Tom, I have been so lonely in that big old house since Charles died last year. All the servants leave after supper, and I don't like to be by myself at night. I started thinking that a nice professional man like you and a lovely girl like Angel shouldn't have to stay in a common old boarding house during the week." She paused again, grabbed onto her pearls, and then plunged in. "So, I would like to rent the upstairs of my house to you all on a year's lease. You can come and go as you please, and I can sleep at night knowing there is somebody else in the house."

"Why, Mrs. Bellamy, what a generous offer! Oh my Lord, we would love that!" Tom broke into a broad grin, and he reached across the desk to shake her hand again and again. "Now, Mrs. Bellamy, how much did you have in mind for rent?"

"How much do you pay at the boarding house?"

"Four dollars a week."

"Then, sixteen dollars a month it will be for your room and board."

"Thank you again, Mrs. Bellamy. I will draw up the lease agreement today." Tom rose from his chair, gathered his papers, and apologized, "I'm so sorry. I have to go to the courthouse now."

"Of course you do, Tom. You and Angel check out of the boarding house and bring your things over tonight – 202 Market. I know you've been there before."

"Oh, yes Ma'am, I know exactly where your house is."

"Okay, good day." With that, Mrs. Bellamy stepped out into the bright morning light a much happier person.

"Thank you, God!" Tom mumbled as he gathered up his papers. Last year, Sarah, Tom, and Angel had been invited to Mrs. Bellamy's annual Christmas party. While he was there, Tom had been struck by the magnificence of the mansion. He particularly loved the architecture and the tastefulness of the fine furnishings. At the time, he had remarked that one day he hoped to live in a house just like that. Now, a year later, God had granted his wish. Tom knew this turn of events was another of his blessings from God, and he was thankful.

As the months wore on, their time in Wilmington became more enriched by getting to know Mrs. Bellamy. Each day, as they opened the front door, weary with clients and bookkeeping, they found that Mrs. Bellamy – or "Mrs. B" as Angel had affectionately nicknamed her – was able to recharge their batteries with her wonderful nurturing and cheerful disposition.

A glass of wine and an hors d'oeuvre preceded the evening meal. When the servants called them to dinner, Tom always escorted Mrs. B into the dining room and held her chair for her before doing the same for Angel. The supper was always superb. Living right near the water, Mrs. Bellamy had access to many fresh seafood items at the local market. Her shrimp scampi was Tom's favorite, while Angel like the fried oysters they sometimes had. The hostess's favorite, however, was the flounder stuffed with crabmeat. Each supper was always completed with a dessert, much to Tom's delight.

Tom always liked to have a cup of coffee in the upstairs sitting room after supper. With the fire crackling away, he would re-read his notes to prepare for his clients the next day. Downstairs, he could hear Mrs. Bellamy and Angel laughing and talking. What a God-send she had been for them, for they had never lived in such luxury. Plush Oriental carpets adorned the floors in each of the bedrooms, and in the upstairs sitting room there was always a bouquet of seasonal flowers.

Heavily-lined floor length drapes were drawn each night by the servants. Each of the upstairs bedrooms had a different color, referred to by the house manager as the "green room, the blue room, the pink room, or the lavender room". Tom stayed in the blue room, and Angel occupied the pink room.

Beautiful oil paintings, by Mrs. Bellamy's sister, depicting Wilmington gardens and river scenes, adorned the walls. Yet, the millenary work was Tom's favorite part of the upstairs. Heavy dentil molding ran across the walls at ceiling level. Tom figured the molding must be at least ten inches deep, and it had all been painted white to contrast with the walls. There was even a shoe molding down toward the floor. Tom was impressed by the craftsmanship, very evident in the woodworking, all over the house.

The furniture was also beautifully handcrafted out of dark mahogany wood; the finely carved details easily revealed the Hepplewhite style. Each bedroom contained a large bed with spindle posts, a chest of drawers, and a long library table with a matching chair for writing purposes. The beds were delightful with their soft, sink-in feather mattresses and finely-starched sheets. A wingback chair with flame stitch patterning completed the room's specific décor. While the room was very functional, it was also exquisitely beautiful, even boasting of an almost unheard of luxury – a closet for hanging clothes and storing linens.

Three nights a week, Tom lived in this luxury, and Angel stayed four. Mrs. Bellamy always told them that she was so blessed to have the two of them in the house. "I get so lonely by myself." However, Tom knew they were the blessed ones.

After tidying up the kitchen, the servants took their leave, and by 8:00 PM, the house was still. Downstairs after supper, Angel loved to run her hands over the cool marble fireplaces that had been imported from France. The ticking of the grandfather clock intrigued her, and she marveled at the rich melody of the chiming on the quarter, half, and whole hours. Like her father's house, the library walls were lined with books that the family had collected.

"Did you read any of these books?" Angel asked one night.

"Heavens, yes! My father always said, 'When you educate a woman, you educate a family.' I have a passion for books. A third of these are my personal ones."

"I feel that way, too," Angel added. "I have started buying books for my own house that I will have one day."

"How old are you now, Angel?" she asked with her eyes twinkling.

"Twenty-four."

"Huh, that's how old I was when I had my first child. Interesting, isn't it, how generations change their outlooks? My mother married at eighteen; I married after finishing school at twenty-one; and, here you are at twenty-four just now talking about the thought of getting married."

A few weeks later, Angel went up to her room to prepare for bed, and she found a beautifully wrapped gift on her bed, so beautiful in fact that she didn't want to disturb the paper or the ribbon. Finally, curiosity got the best of her. She tried to slip the ribbon off the corner so she wouldn't harm the paper. Aahh, success. . .easing the bow off, she gently slid her finger under the expertly creased paper. Mission accomplished, she lifted the paper gently back and pulled out the box. When she opened the box, there was multi-layered tissue paper staring up at her. Gingerly, she lifted the papers to find a card:

'For your trousseau. . .

Love,
Mrs. B'

Beneath the card lay the most luxurious pink silk nightgown. Holding it up, she squealed in delight, noting the exquisite lace, finely crafted rosebuds, and seed pearls scattered across the bodice. "Wow, this is real silk!" Within a second, Angel was downstairs and into Mrs. B's waiting arms.

"Do you think your husband will like you in that?" she teased with a twinkle in her eye.

"But how did you know my size?" Angel asked, amazed at its perfectly proportioned fit.

"Oh, one weekend when you were at home, I grabbed a dress out of your closet and hurried over to my dressmaker. She took the measurements, and we selected the pink silk. I think it turned out rather well, don't you?"

"Oh, it's just fabulous!" Holding the gown against her, she whirled around in front of the hall mirror looking at her reflection. "Oh, thank you so much." Angel hugged the little lady one more time before heading for the stairs. "See you in the morning," Angel called over her shoulder.

Mrs. B. chuckled to herself, "If the gown pleases her that much, I can't wait to see her reaction to the matching robe the dressmaker is working on!" Mrs. B had always loved making other people happy. That was just the way she had been all her life.

Another of the blessings that Tom was especially thankful for was Sarah, the lady whom he loved.

. . . . .

The smell of the sweet spring hyacinths lured Sarah from her cookbook. Stepping outside, she breathed deeply, inhaling the "after the rain" smell in her nostrils. Last year's backbreaking labor was paying off. The English garden that she had painstakingly designed and planted in front of the house could literally be seen coming to life under the kiss of the spring sunshine. Yellow forsythia danced against the white picket fence as the gentle breeze drew across the branches. Multicolored crocuses in purples, whites, and yellows peeked out from under the massive planting of trumpet daffodils, the official heralds of spring. Two cherry trees, which anchored either side of the garden, were budding into tiny pink nodes, soon to blossom into wispy beauty.

In the distance, birds erupted into song as the ecstasy of the earth revealed itself in the new season. Sarah was beside herself with joy. Tom, who noticed every detail of nature, would be thrilled when he returned this afternoon to survey with pride the fence he had put up himself so that Sarah's forsythia could climb.

Thursday nights were Tom and Sarah's special night. With ceremonial precision, Sarah had filled the wine decanter that morning and laid out the fine crystal glasses on the sideboard. Sarah prided herself that the crystal flower vase in the entry hall always showcased whatever flowers or shrubs were in bloom on the farm at that time. With designer precision, Sarah knew just how to juxtapose the large waxy leaves of the magnolia branches to offset the delicacy of the season's flowers. The forsythia branches she had snipped early that morning would be a treat for Tom's eyes when he returned from Wilmington.

Leaving her blooming beauties in the garden, Sarah returned to the kitchen. Great care was always given on Thursday mornings to fixing Tom's favorite dishes for his return dinner. Finishing the food selections, Sarah then turned her attention to her beautification process, for she wanted to be pleasing to Tom, also.

Expertly, she styled her dark, lustrous hair, pulling the ringlets to the side, just like he liked them. After accenting her eyes, she rouged her lips. Stepping back, she eyed herself in the mirror. "Not bad for forty-four!" she mused.

In a few minutes, she heard approaching hoof beats. Jumping into action, she pulled open the front door and stepped out onto the large front porch.

"Pretty as a picture you are, my dear!" Tom called as he dismounted. Taking off the halter, he whacked the horse on the rear, signaling that she was free to feed in the barn.

Sarah rushed down the sidewalk to throw herself into Tom's arms. "Hello, Darling!" she cooed as she kissed his cheek.

Tom enveloped her deeply into his arms and then planted an inviting and meaningful kiss on her lips.

Once inside, Tom removed his coat, and spotting the beautiful floral arrangement, he complimented Sarah. Sarah retrieved the decanter tray and carried it into her bedroom. There Tom poured a glass for each of them.

"To your return," Sarah toasted.
"I couldn't have waited another day," Tom confessed, walking over toward her. "I love you, Miss Sarah, more than you'll ever know."

Sarah smiled and setting down her wine glass, she began unbuttoning Tom's shirt. "I have already drawn your bath, my dear." Gratefully, Tom slid his tired body into the warm, beckoning waters of the elongated tub. Gently, Sarah lathered soap over his chest, and then poured ladle after ladle of warm water over his shoulders and head. She let Tom soak for awhile, and then she gently massaged his neck and shoulders, bringing much-needed relaxation.

Tom had continued to sip his wine as he enjoyed Sarah's pampering. After fifteen minutes, he called, "Okay, I'm ready." Sarah held out the giant velvet bath towel that she had made for him, while Tom stepped carefully out of the tub onto the mat. She encircled him in the towel, motioning for him to sit in the nearby chair.

After bussing his hair, shoulders, and neck of the excess water, she retrieved his robe. "Okay." Sarah held out Tom's navy velvet bathrobe invitingly. Dropping the towel, Tom thrust his right arm into the sleeve and then followed with the left. Pulling one side over the other, he knotted the silk cords in the front.

"And now, my dear, it's your turn." Tom called with a theatrical tone. Sarah giggled like a school girl as Tom unbuttoned her dress in the back. Sarah stepped enticingly out and threw the dress over on the chair. Turning provocatively in a circle, she allowed Tom's eyes to feast on her tiny waist and her bulging bosom. "My God, Sarah, I can't ever get enough of you," he announced as he picked her up in his massive arms.

"Thank God," she laughed, and he deposited her onto the bed.

Thursday night was their time; the rest of the world was far away and of no concern. As they lay there together, Tom skillfully made her body come alive with his strategic kissing and caressing. Sarah purred in pleasure and returned his kisses

74

with ardor. When she thought she couldn't wait any longer, she pushed Tom's robe from his body, and together they pulled off her undergarments so that they could explore their nakedness. Tom always held his ardor in check until he knew Sarah was aroused; and then he lowered himself into her. They enjoyed the pleasures of lovemaking long into the afternoon shadows.

Usually Tom would drift off to sleep after they made love; and Sarah, donning her most beautiful silken robe, would steal into the kitchen to start dinner. When Tom awakened, she would serve dinner in the dining room. For some reason, it was sexually exciting to Sarah to dine in her silken robe with nothing on underneath, while sipping the sparkling wine and basking in the luminescence of the candles. Tom, clothed only in his robe, loved to look across at Sarah's glow after heavy lovemaking and take in the cresting nipples showing demurely through the thin robe. "To a fabulous dinner and to a fabulous lady," Tom proposed.

"Oh, I will accept that compliment," she called with a laugh. At times like this Tom thought his heart would burst with the love he felt for this woman. She was everything a man could want, and he only hoped his gifts and his words told her how much she was treasured. There was nothing on earth that could interfere with their Thursday nights together, for this had become their lovemaking ritual, immensely enjoyed by both of them.

"Oh, I forgot!" Tom called as he rose from the table. "I brought you something." Sarah smiled. Tom was always bringing her something. She contentedly sipped her wine until he returned from the front hall. "Straight from Paris!" he announced, as he thrust the fashion designer magazine into her hands.

"Why, thank you, Tom," she sighed, greedily taking in the dresses on the cover. Holding it to her bosom, she whispered, "Oh, Tom, you spoil me so, and I dearly love you." Tom kissed her on the cheek before returning to his chair.

"Now, about that dessert. . ."

"Yes, Sir!" she mockingly saluted him as she rose to collect the dishes. Putting her salad plate into the dinner plate, she gracefully moved over to Tom's side, and Tom noted the beautiful contours of her body as she moved. As she leaned to gather his plate, he sneaked a look at her cleavage above the robe's fold. Unable to contain himself, Tom gently took the plates from her hands and placed them back on the table. A surprised Sarah looked back at him.

"Now, about that dessert," he mumbled as he rose to kiss her neck and chest gently. Sarah felt her nipples tighten, and that all-too-familiar tingling feeling gather in her groin. Hungrily, they came together in a passionate kiss. Blowing out the candles, Tom pulled her over to the settee. He sat down, positioning her in front of him. Gently, he undid the ties of her robe and dropped it to the floor, silhouetting her statuesque body in the moonlight. Lightly, he traced the contours of her body with his fingers, and then leaning over, he suckled each breast again and again. Sarah stood motionless in the moonlight, immensely enjoying the rivulets of pleasure that ran up and down her body.

"Oh, Tom!" was the passionate reply as he pulled her down onto the couch to make love again. There they slept all night, entwined in each other's arms like age-old lovers, celebrating the intimacies of the body and the sweet slumber of sexual contentment.

Chapter Nine

While Tom was grateful to God for Mrs. Bellamy's accommodations and for his wonderful Sarah, he also considered it a great blessing that he had found a way to be of service to God. One service work that he had chosen was to help Miss Lizzie at the orphanage.

· · · · ·

"Okay, you two better get in high gear," Tom announced one Saturday morning. "I've had one of my premonitions. [10] I believe there is a new child at the orphanage."

"Oh, how wonderful," Sarah answered. "Have you checked with Miss Lizzie yet?"

"Nope, but I'm going to see her today, and I will let you know when I get back."

Tom's premonitions were never wrong, and that meant that Sarah and Angel had plenty of work to do. After breakfast, Sarah checked the flour and the sugar to make sure they had enough for the baking while Angel went to the hen house to collect eggs. When she returned, she sifted through Sarah's recipes and pulled out three.

"Have you ever cooked a ham for the kids?"

"I don't think so," Sarah called as she put the cornmeal back.

---

[10]

"Well, what about a sweet potato dish?"

"No, I don't think we've made that either."

"Okay," Angel proposed, "what about ham, deviled eggs, green beans, corn, and a sweet potato dish?"

"Hmmm, that does sound good, doesn't it?" Sarah nodded approvingly. "You know, those dishes will be easy to cook and easy to transport."

"Now, what birthday cake decorations should we make?" Sarah questioned.

"What about green and yellow since we don't know whether the new arrival is a boy or girl?"

"All right. Great. We can start on the cake this morning. Please find my recipe, call out the ingredients, and we'll begin. Angel, won't there be fourteen now that the new one has come?"

"Yes, I'm pretty sure that's the right number."

"Well, then we can just triple each recipe, and we should be fine."

"Okay. Here is the cake: nine cups of sugar."

Sarah measured out the amount and poured the sugar into the giant mixing bowl.

"Six eggs." *Crunch, crunch, crunch* . . . the eggs dropped into the bowl. By lunchtime, the birthday cake had been completed, and thoughts turned to what to have for supper.

"I was right!" Tom called as he entered the kitchen later that afternoon.

"Boy or girl?" Angel inquired, as she peeled the sweet potatoes.

"Boy named Jacob; he's from Wilmington."

"How old is he, Tom?" Sarah asked, looking up from her biscuit making.

"Eight. Nice looking kid."

"What happened to his parents?" Angel questioned.

"They were killed in a fire."

"Oh, poor thing," Angel remarked.

"Tom, would you like a glass of wine before dinner?" Sarah asked, as she placed the biscuits on top of the stove.

"Are those fried pork chops I see over there?" Tom asked with a smile.

"Yes, Dad, your favorite."

"Then I won't spoil my dinner. Call me when it's ready. I'll be in my study."

Tom ambled off with his stomach growling. For as long as the orphanage had been Tom's service project, a big birthday bash was thrown for each newly-arriving child, marking his or her birth into the orphanage family. The party was always a surprise for the new child, and Tom, Sarah, and Angel supplied mounds of food and lots of presents for all the kids. Sometimes it was hard to tell who had more fun, the adults or the kids.

That next morning, Tom loaded the carefully-packed food into the wagon, and the three of them started in high spirits toward town. Twenty minutes later, the wagon turned onto Main Street, headed toward the orphanage. The white orphanage house with wooden green shutters had a beautiful wide front porch, complete with ferns and flower baskets. Inviting chairs and couches with beautifully made cushions beckoned one to rest from his labors. Huge trees flanked the house, giving much needed shade from the afternoon sun. A little white picket fence with a swinging gate separated the residence from the streets for safety sake. On any given day, there would be a dozen or more children laughing and talking on the porch, playing in the front yard, or having school lessons. Shrubbery had been strategically planted in front of the porch, and the flowerbeds bloomed on either side of the front yard. Several swings hung from the old branches of the trees.

A swirl of naturally curly white hair was Miss Lizzie's most outstanding feature, but second only to her beautiful smile. Tall and thin she stood, surveying her brood, with her hands shielding her eyes from the morning sun. Out back, a few hens clucked in the henhouse, while a docile old cow and a horse completed the backyard menagerie. Out front, a cat curled contentedly on the porch chair, and a huge dog played and frolicked with the kids.

Hearing the wagon, Miss Lizzie turned to see who it was. Her heart leaped with joy; her three favorite people and right on time, she chuckled to herself. How Tom always knew when a new child arrived was beyond her, but he never failed to do his part.

"It's Mr. Tom!" the older boys shouted in recognition. Tom helped Angel and Sarah out of the wagon, and then he went around to the back. Miss Lizzie hugged Sarah, and then Angel, delighted for some adult conversation. Several of the older boys magically appeared and grabbed the crates as Tom passed them down. With happy hearts, the boys carried them inside.

"Oh, you have outdone yourselves!" Miss Lizzie beamed as she surveyed all the goodies.

"If you'll be a good girl, we've brought you something special, too," Tom announced, as he gave Miss Lizzie a hug and a kiss. Arm-in-arm, Tom and Miss Lizzie walked toward the house. It was hard to say whether the adults or the children were more excited about the surprise that was coming.

Once inside, Miss Lizzie gave the command, "Thomas, take all the children on a thirty-minute walk. The little ones must have an older one beside them. Bring back some flowers for Miss Angel and Miss Sarah, but ask first if you can pick them."

"Yes, Ma'am," Thomas agreed with a smile, for he knew what was about to happen.

Amid a snap of cords and an opening of crates, the three revealed the feast that Angel and Sarah had cooked, along with the enormous assortment of presents. A huge ham appeared along with the yams, deviled eggs, green beans, corn, and even homemade biscuits. The toys for the children were quickly arranged on a side table in the dining room. Each present had been wrapped and tied with festive ribbon. The ladies set the table for the kids, while Tom carefully carried the three-tiered birthday cake to a special table, following a tradition established long ago. The cake read, "Happy Birthday Jacob!" The layers were decorated with green leaves and beautifully accented yellow roses. It was truly the crowning touch for the party.

Ten minutes later the gang arrived, each bearing two flowers of some kind. Thomas knew not to spoil the surprise, so he stationed the kids on the porch furniture. A few minutes later Sarah and Angel positioned themselves by the door, and each child presented his flowers: one to Angel, one to Sarah, receiving a mammoth hug from each. Then Miss Lizzie called the newcomer forward.

"Jacob, we are so happy to have you in our family, and today we have a surprise for you. I am going to blindfold you and lead you inside; okay?" With that, Miss Lizzie blindfolded the eight year old child and propelled him toward the dining room. The others automatically fell in behind her. Once in front of the massive cake, the blindfold was removed, and everybody yelled, "Happy Birthday to You!" The smile on Jacob's face was worth more than all the gold in the Southport Bank vault to the adults.

"Okay, find your places at the table; we have a feast that Miss Sarah and Miss Angel have brought." Excitedly, the children scampered into their seats, prayed the blessing, grabbed a spoon, and waited expectantly. Out came the huge platters of food, and the appropriate "ooohs and aahhs" were respectively submitted.

Jacob, the birthday boy, was served first, and Tom was always impressed that the older kids helped the younger kids without being told. The candied yams were met with much enthusiasm, and the beans and creamed corn were also carefully lobbed onto the plates. The deviled eggs disappeared so fast that Sarah had to laugh. Careful to watch their manners, the kids contentedly smacked away for seconds. The enjoyment of the food was worth far more than the time Angel and Sarah had spent in preparation.

Tom stood there watching the scene with his arm around Miss Lizzie, "What's Jacob's story?"

"Well, his family's home was destroyed in a fire, and he was the only survivor. Miraculously, his father got him out and had gone back to get the other children when the roof caved in. The children have been wonderful in helping him get settled this week."

"I love you, Miss Lizzie. You are one in a million!" Tom announced and gave her a kiss on the cheek.

Short work was made of the food, and Angel picked up the empty dinner plates, while Sarah brought the dessert plates over to the table. "Who wants some of Jacob's birthday cake?" Sarah teased with a big smile. Every hand went into the air, and a chorus of "I do's" went up and down the table. "All right, Jacob, come cut the first piece for Miss Lizzie," Sarah announced.

The little boy shyly came forward, and Sarah lifted him up onto a chair. Guiding his hand on the knife, Sarah assisted him in cutting the first piece of cake. "Take this to Miss Lizzie," Sarah directed, as she turned him toward Tom and Lizzie. The sparkle in Jacob's eyes and the happiness of his heart touched Tom deeply.

Miss Lizzie bent down to accept Jacob's gift. "Why, thank you, Jacob, for sharing your birthday cake with us; we love you." Impulsively, the little boy threw his arms around Miss Lizzie, who moved the cake just in time.

"Okay, Jacob, hand these slices out to your new family members," Sarah called from the cake table. Soon each child was licking his lips in delight as they sampled the creamy icing and spongy layers. Seconds had to be served. "What do you say?" Miss Lizzie prompted.

"Thank you, Mr. Tom, Miss Angel, and Miss Sarah."

"Now, would anybody like to open a birthday present?" Tom inquired with a big smile. Fourteen "yeses" chorused in unison.

No one moved, though, until Miss Lizzie gave instructions. "Jacob will receive his present first, and then we will go from the youngest to the oldest. You may go to the front porch and wait for us once you receive your gift, but do not open them." Each child's name was announced, and with great joy they rushed over to Tom, who was handing out the special gifts. Once everyone was assembled on the porch,

Jacob was allowed to open his birthday gift. A wooden truck lay in the box, and Jacob squealed with delight as he clutched his toy to his breast.

"Now, Thomas, you may go," Miss Lizzie directed. Each child had a turn and was thrilled to death. Tom spared no expense in gift giving for Miss Lizzie's children. There were tears of joy and screams of delight, and the adults couldn't have been happier. For the rest of the day, Sarah, Tom, and Angel played games with the children and thoroughly enjoyed themselves.

"Thank you, Miss Lizzie, for allowing us to share in your joy," Angel cried as he hugged her goodbye.

Sarah and Tom finished loading the cases for the return trip. "I love you, Miss Lizzie," Sarah affirmed. "God must have a special place in his heart for you!"

"No more than for you, Miss Sarah," she quickly quipped back. "The food was superb. Tom, what can I say? Your generosity never ceases to amaze me. You are a wonderful credit to our community," she called.

"Let me know if we can help you in any other way," Tom admonished with a goodbye hug. All was quiet as they rode home. Sarah was lost in thoughts of the children's faces; Angel was thinking of how special Miss Lizzie was; and, Tom was thinking of his stillborn child so many years ago.

The three of them had always celebrated the holidays – Valentine's Day, Easter, Thanksgiving, and Christmas – at the orphanage, and they considered that sharing with Miss Lizzie and her kids was what life was really all about. No extravagant present that Tom ever received from Sarah or Angel meant as much to him as the times spent in sharing from the heart with Miss Lizzie and her kids. As far as Tom was concerned, service to others was the best gift he ever gave to himself.

Chapter Ten

While Tom and Angel were interacting with clients in Wilmington the next week, Sarah was having a very different type of interaction in Southport. When Tom and Angel went to Wilmington for Tuesday, Wednesday, and Thursday, part of Sarah was sad, but the other part of her was excited. With the two of them gone, Sarah had the entire house to herself, and it was then that she created her magic. Way up in the attic – where no one ever went – was Sarah's sanctuary. With her expertise in sewing, Sarah had fashioned a painter's smock that she wore on these special occasions. There, in one end of the attic, Sarah's childhood in New Orleans had come to life again.

Canvas after canvas hung on the attic wall. A beautiful kaleidoscopic swirl of strong colors leaped from each of the canvases, beckoning the viewer to sample the spirit of the city. One canvas portrayed the house she grew up in. Another pictured the Creole section with its street musicians and vendors. Her old church had been captured in the majesty of its simplicity. However, Sarah's favorite, which she had worked on feverishly, was the portrait of her mother. The physical beauty of her mother had been easy to capture; yet, her inner beauty, portrayed through the eyes, was a stroke of genius. Sarah gently touched the canvas in an effort to feel the vibration of her mom's exuberant spirit. Ironically, what Sarah hadn't comprehended was the fact that in painting the picture of her mother as she remembered her, she had actually painted a self-portrait. Sarah looked exactly like her mother. This sanctuary was Sarah's private world where she allowed her soul to be free. No one knew of her paintings, not even Angel.

There was a large, swinging ventilation shutter at one end of the attic that was perfect for allowing natural sunlight to flood in. It was here that Sarah had set up her easel. Sometimes she painted for hours on end, but on other days, just an hour or two as it pleased her. Old friends from childhood whose faces she remembered were worked into the scenes, as well as her minister and favorite teacher. Being able to capture the character's strength in their portrayals was her true gift. The pictures captured well the triumphs and the tragedies of the New Orleans' lifestyle.

On this particular winter day, Sarah had been painting all morning, trying to capture her best friend in one of her portraits. Noticing that her shoulders were cramping, Sarah got up from the chair and walked to the sunlit opening. Beautiful countryside greeted her view, and she gazed peacefully around the farm's perimeter.

Suddenly, she noticed a movement, and it distracted her. She focused her eyes. A black man was running from the forest toward the house. As quick as a rabbit, Sarah ran down the two flights of stairs to her bedroom. Grabbing the handles of her underwear drawer, she jerked it open. Reaching for the bullets, she carefully unwrapped them and grabbed six. A jerk on the nightstand drawer revealed the silver, shiny gun. Pumping the bullets into the chamber, she pocketed the extras. She wanted the element of surprise to be her ally.

For a minute, she stood at the backdoor and surveyed the area. The barn to the right was as calm as it could be. The horses placidly drank water from the trough at the corral, but the hens were clucking something fierce. "Okay, buddy, I know where you are," she whispered to herself. Easing out the backdoor, she crossed over to the henhouse. As she quietly pulled the door back, sunlight flooded the one-window room. With forced courage, she called into the silence, "Who's there? I have a gun. I know you're in here, and I'll use it."

"Please, Ma'am. I don't mean no harm. I's not armed; can I shows myself?"

Sarah knew by the trembling in his voice that he was more afraid of her than she was of him. She also knew by his dialect that he was a slave. "For God's sake, you scared me half to death! Now, let me see you this instant!" Sarah tried to quiet her heart and to allow the adrenaline rush to calm down. She had often thought about having another gun hidden outside for instances just like this, but she hadn't done anything about it.

A trembling, old black man began a slow rise. His huge, almond-shaped eyes showed his ultimate terror. His jean pants were tied at the waist, and a faded shirt covered his upper torso. Both hands were straight up in the air in a surrender pose. The only thing missing was a white flag. "Please, Ma'am, let me get goin' now. I jes crawled in here to rest. I's been runnin' all day. I won't be botherin' you no more." The terrified look had not gone away from the slave's eyes.

"Are you running from the law or from your master?" Sarah asked, noticing the scratches on his legs and arms. She saw with shock that he had no shoes.

"Please, Ma'am, they be comin' soon. I needs to go," the man begged, looking anxiously toward the door.

"I repeat, from the law or from your master?" She still had the gun aimed at his heart.

"My mas'er, and I gots to go." He took a step toward the door.

"That would be certain death. They will be searching for you. Come with me. I will hide you in the root cellar. Now be quick." In a flash, Sarah undid the lock on the cellar door and the man jumped in. Locking the door behind her, Sarah sprinted toward the henhouse to tidy up any telltale evidence left on the straw where he had hidden.

Once inside the house, Sarah calmed herself down. In shock, Sarah reflected on what she had done. Harboring a fugitive slave was against the law, but turning a man in who just wanted his freedom was against her moral conscience. It had all happened so fast, she hadn't thought, just reacted. It was only now that the possible repercussions of what might fall on Tom's good name, if the law found that she had harbored a slave, began to sink in. "Oh my God, what have I done? I've betrayed the man I love."

Sarah thought back to the conversation she had had earlier with Angel about slavery. Now here she was, a few weeks later, voluntarily harboring a fugitive slave. Fate had dealt her a swift roll of the dice. She had had to make a decision about slavery whether she was ready to or not.

Sarah readied herself with trembling fingers for Tom's arrival. Two hours later Tom returned, and shortly afterward, Tom heard the horses galloping toward the house. They seldom had company this far out. The other riders stayed on their horses while a middle-aged man made his way toward the door. After knocking on the door, he politely removed his hat. "Good evening, Sir. Are you looking for Mr. Madison?" Sarah inquired as she swung the door open.

"I am right here, Sarah," Tom called as he clambered down the stairs. Sarah turned on her heels to go back in the kitchen, and Tom invited the gentleman inside. The elderly looking gentleman began, "We are looking for a runaway slave. Did you see anyone around here yesterday afternoon or last night?"

"No, no one has come this way that I know of. But in case I do see him, what is your name and how do I get in touch with you?" Tom inquired.

"Grant Simmons is my name, and I am the foreman over on Mr. Townsend's plantation about ten miles from here." Tom offered his hand, and Mr. Simmons shook it. "Do you care if we look around a bit for possible footprints?"

"Why, no, not at all. And good luck to you." Grant tipped his hat and jumped on his horse. The posse slowly circled the house two times and then rode on. Tom and Sarah watched the men from the kitchen window.

"To tell you the truth," Tom blurted out, "I am sorry about the investment that Mr. Townsend has lost in that slave, but I hope they don't find him. You and I both know they will beat him half to death if they do." Tom and Sarah had never talked much about slavery in the intimate way she and Angel had talked. Sarah breathed a sign of relief at Tom's words.

After dinner, Tom retreated to his study. Quickly, Sarah gathered up the leftover biscuits and ham on a plate, and, as an afterthought, she threw in a couple of cake slices. Next, she made two huge sandwiches and grabbed some cookies to put into a sack. In the linen drawer she found an old blanket. Gathering her paraphernalia, she walked down to the root cellar. Opening the lock, she called softly, "It's okay; it's just me. Here is your supper. In this sack are provisions for tomorrow. Rest now. Here is a nice blanket to wrap up in. At 10:00 PM I will unlock the cellar door so that you can continue on. I have risked my job and my relationship with my boss for you. Do not come back here. Do not give this location to anyone else. As far as I am concerned, I have done my duty. Good luck and may God be with you."

"Yes, Ma'am. You's my Angel of Mercy." [11]

With that, Sarah stepped out into the dusk and relocked the root cellar door. Sarah was weak in her knees as she realized what could have happened had the slave been found. Tom would have been fined – or possibly placed in jail – if the judge felt he had aided and abetted. Sarah knew she would not tell Tom or Angel about this incident right now. Down the

---

[11]

road she would have to speak her truth about it, but for now she was keeping the whole thing a secret. At 10:00 PM, she opened the door as planned, and the desperate man slipped out into the darkness. Sarah realized that she had never even asked his name. After locking the door, Sarah breathed a sign of relief before returning to her everyday life, or so she thought.

Chapter Eleven

As Nathan rounded the corner by the livery stable the next Saturday, he was shocked at the number of people in the streets. "Is this an election day?" he asked himself as he shouldered his way through the crowd. "What in the world has happened?" In front of the tavern the congregation was the heaviest. "Excuse me; excuse me," he muttered every other breath, until by some miracle he found himself at the door of McGilly's Tavern.

As he opened the door, the smoke and noise almost knocked him down. He peered across through the dimness, trying to locate his friends. "I hope the guys got our table before the masses arrived," he thought. Finally, Nathan recognized the back of Thorn's head. Pulling his body between the closely-packed tables brimming over with customers, he finally arrived. "My heavens, what is going on in this town?" he screamed above the noise. All three looked up in surprise at the sound of his voice.

"My God, Nathan, haven't you heard?" Ahab asked incredulously.

"Heard what?"

"South Carolina has seceded from the Union. Here, look at the publication for yourself." Thorn slid the proclamation across the table.

Nathan quickly scanned the paper. "Oh my God, it's really happened!" He felt like he was going to faint.

"Sit down, Nathan. Sit down!" John commanded. "The shock affected us all the same way."

"No wonder everyone in the city of Wilmington is downtown. Oh my Lord, I wasn't expecting this." Nathan's mouth still hung open in disbelief.

"Close your mouth, Nathan. You'll let the flies in!" Thorn teased.

Ahab signaled the bartender for a new round. Within a few minutes, Matilda arrived, smiling demurely over at Ahab. Ahab jumped up to make a theatrical bow, complete with a sweep of his hat. "Matilda, I have been waiting for you all of my life!"

"Well, I have been here every Saturday for two years, Ahab!" she teased back. As she served the beers around the table, Thorn noted that she brushed suggestively against Ahab.

Ahab smiled broadly. "If I were a marrying man, I would marry you, Matilda!"

"Yeah, right, Ahab!" she threw back with a hint of sarcasm. However, she winked at Ahab and smiled as she swept off to the next table.

"Ahab, you are such a liar!" John laughed as he held his mug aloft, "To South Carolina."

"Here, Here, Here!" The mugs clinked heavily, and each one savored the strong brew.

John spoke first, "Let me see that proclamation again, Nathan." Dutifully, Nathan passed the paper. "December 20, 1860 – now this will be a day to remember, my friends. From this point on, the South will never be the same again, nor will we. Everything will change whether we like it or not," John observed. "Our fates are out of our hands now."

"I wouldn't say that, John," Thorn butted in. "Perhaps it would be better to say that we will be the ones to decide our fate now."

"Thorn may be more correct, John," Ahab countered. "Every man in the South will now be forced to take a stand. Sitting on the fence will no longer be politically correct. North Carolina will have to vote to join with South Carolina in secession or be forced to side with the Union."

Strangely, all four fell silent at the same moment. Each was lost for a few seconds in the realization of what significance this would be for their personal lives.

"Ahab, I wouldn't want to be in your shoes right now. You are Southern born, but anti-slavery by choice. You're gonna be pushed in a corner," John announced, worried about his friends.

"Don't worry about me, John. I made my choice years ago that I was anti-slavery. You're the lawyer. Answer me this: how can our constitution proclaim freedom and justice for all as our motto when four million slaves are being held in the South, in bondage, against their will?" Ahab's eyes danced with an inner anger, and the skin around his top lip was stretched to whiteness.

"Now, damn it, Ahab. I meant the statement out of concern for you, not a challenge to you," John fired back. "We are not your enemies, Ahab; we are your friends."

"Okay, okay," Ahab responded with the ever-present gallant smile. He held his hand up in the air, "I surrender; I surrender; I took it the wrong way."

Thorn shook his head in disbelief. "Everyone knows not to discuss religion and politics in a public place," he sermonized.

"You'd better tell all these people in this tavern that, Thorn. Look at them!" Nathan challenged.

Thorn surveyed them. Every person in the tavern was either listening intently, talking loudly, or arguing vociferously. Thorn knew they weren't talking religion, just secession. It didn't take a genius to recognize the seriousness of the situation. The gauntlet had been thrown down by South Carolina, and the question was, "Would North Carolina rise to the challenge?"

The four of them had tiptoed around the topic of slavery and the war on many occasions. Ahab was the only one with strong anti-slavery convictions. Nathan's heritage made him decidedly pro-slavery. Up to this point, John and Thorn had been neutral. In general, the four of them had had more pressing concerns of making a living, dating, and hunting in season. Yet, as time would show, each man's destiny would be determined by the piece of paper that lay on the table before them.

Chapter Twelve

After lunch with the boys, Thorn cut out for Southport. He had a date with Angel. Thorn was surprised, however, when he saw Tom waiting for him at the turnoff to his house.

"I've given the girls a phony story. Are you up for a little ride?" Noting Thorn's crestfallen face, Tom added, "Oh, we'll be back in a few hours. They are preparing a late supper for us. You'll get plenty of time with Angel!"

"Yes, okay, sure, Tom," Thorn muttered, embarrassed that Tom had read his feelings so easily.

"I heard in town today that slaves are being smuggled at night near here, and I wanted to check it out. Are you game?"

"Oh, yeah!" Thorn eagerly replied, forgetting about his disappointment.

After riding for five miles, Tom and Thorn dismounted and tied the horses. Camouflaging themselves as best they could, they headed toward the beach. Some nights are dark, but this night turned out to be pitch black. Through the trees, Tom could barely see the torch ahead, and had it not been for that lone light, he would have never found his way. Motioning to Thorn to come closer, he cautioned him by placing his finger to his lips. God forbid that they should be discovered.

The pungent smell of marsh filled their nostrils, and Thorn knew that after the long walk they had finally reached the sea. As they peered through the dense cover of the scrub oaks, a boat revealed itself. Several sets of oars on the boat indicated that it was probably used for hauling cargo up and down the river. Totally nondescript, once out of the shallow water, the boat would blend in with any other night traveling vessel. One man seemed to be giving orders, while three others listened attentively. Their horses had been tethered to the nearby scrub oaks and were contentedly eating from their nose bags.

About thirty minutes later, a birdcall sounded. Tom and Thorn knew instinctively that it was not a bird; it was a signal. They lowered themselves to the ground under the trees to make sure they were totally camouflaged. The man in charge jerked abruptly when he heard the birdcall, and the torch was extinguished.

After a few minutes, Thorn's eyes adjusted to the moonlight. Ten minutes later, nearing 8:00 PM, Tom and Thorn heard the sounds of an approaching wagon. They watched as the wagon rambled toward its destiny. As soon as the wagon reached the marsh, the canvas cover was untied, and six people slid out. Immediately, they were helped into the boat, and each slave positioned himself flat in the bottom.

Thorn thought that he made out two women and four men, but he wasn't sure. The Captain and two men boarded the boat. After spreading the canvas pieces over the cargo, they quickly manned the oars, and off into the night they crept. The entire operation that had taken weeks to plan was completed in four minutes time.

Turning the wagon around, the driver motioned to the only man left behind. Removing the feedbags, he quickly tied the horses to the wagon and jumped in the shotgun side. Into the night they disappeared.

Tom and Thorn remained totally silent until they were sure there was no rear guard. Tom was first to whisper, "Well, we saw it with our own eyes! There are people who smuggle slaves to freedom."

"You're right, seeing is believing!" Thorn answered.

Quietly they began backtracking to the place they had hidden the horses. Mounting easily, they headed toward Tom's house, each lost in his own thoughts of what they had just witnessed.

Is it bravery or stupidity to risk your own life for a cause you believe in?

Both of them were soon to find out the answer. However, there was one thing that Thorn did not tell Tom – he had recognized one of the white men helping the slaves!

That night while Thorn was having dinner with them, Tom was nervous, fiddling with his coffee cup as he made up his mind whether to speak up. Angel and Sarah were used to his "look at the big picture" political speeches during dinner, but Thorn was a guest, and by southern custom he was not to be subjected to political talk at the dinner table.

The flickering fire gave a lovely glow to the dining room, which was still filled with the savory smells of standing rib roast, mashed potatoes, and fried okra, although very few remnants of the meal were left on their plates. The dinner conversation had been light and pleasant. Tom had noted that the candlelight gave a wonderful glow to both of his ladies, and he secretly delighted in the long glances that had been exchanged during dinner between Angel and Thorn. He wondered if Sarah had noticed.

"I beg your pardon, Thorn, if the discussion of politics is offensive to you at the dinner table, but I would like to address Angel's earlier comment about the war, if I may."

In surprise, Thorn looked up at Tom, "Why, no, Sir. I would be honored to hear your opinion!"

Angel looked over at her father, and as Tom began speaking, pinpricks suddenly traveled up and down her spine, and for a moment the room faded away.[12]

·　·　·　·　·

In her vision, the flickering fire was the same, but in this past life that they had shared, Tom was robed, and he had a long beard.　He was speaking of the higher truths to the disciples seated at his feet in the enormous cave in the centuries old fashion of masters teaching students.

·　·　·　·　·

"Deja-vous," the French had named these odd moments of knowing you had been there before.　As suddenly as the scene had appeared, it vanished, leaving Angel with an elevated pulse rate and clammy skin.　She came back to her familiar dining room where her beloved father was speaking.

·　·　·　·　·

"Whether we like it or not, 1860 will mark a pivotal place in the history books of the United States of America.

84 years ago our Founding Fathers wrote the Bill of Rights which states unequivocably that all men are created equal and that they are entitled to life, liberty, and the pursuit of happiness.　Yet, even after writing those beliefs, the Founding Fathers did nothing to enforce those beliefs.

So now we must decide if we will rise to the greatness thrust upon us by the Founding Fathers to put the ideas of freedom to the test.　The next evolutionary shift in thinking is upon our shoulders now.　After all, didn't our forefathers come to this country to escape religious persecution and oppression? Doesn't our Bill of Rights guarantee that this type of religious

------

12

enslavement won't happen again? And yet, have we stopped to think that we are fighting over the question of enslavement all over again?

Are the sweatshops of the North any different than the slave cabins of the South? Each one takes away the freedom of man. No section of the country is without blemish. Those who enslave nine year old boys to work in mines are no better than those who enslave women by denying them the right to vote or buy land. Other sections have enslaved men by the enticement of gold and free land with the appeal to their greed.

In order to define what freedom means we must stand up for our rights. Ultimately, there may be a war, but both sides will be winners in the big scheme of things. If you fight for the truth and the principles of moral conviction, you are on the right side. The North will fight for its beliefs, and the South will fight for its cause."

For Thorn, Sarah, and Angel, it seemed as if time had been suspended. Oblivious to the ticking of the clock and the crackling of the fire, they were drawn only to the echoing finality of Tom's words, "There is a higher purpose at work here."

No one wanted to speak; no one wanted to betray his emotional response to the others. They remained motionless and speechless until Tom spoke again, "But, oh dear God, I fear the price we will have to pay for our higher calling." Tom's voice broke at the end, and the silence was awkward.

Finally, Angel reached across the table and covered Tom's hand with hers. "With men like you, Dad, to lead us, we will be fine." Tom smiled his love back to Angel.

Rising slowly, Sarah finally whispered, "I think some chocolate pie and coffee would taste good right now!"

Attempting to return to normal, Angel and Sarah cleared the plates and silverware just as they did each night, but they all knew that something life changing had happened; the truth had been spoken – and eloquently so. They now understood the Southern Cause.

When the girls had gone, Thorn rose and walked over to Tom. Clearing his throat, he spoke past his emotion, "Thank you, Sir, for giving me my conviction that I do have an important role to play in this and that I will fight for the Southern Cause."

Thorn's extended hand was taken by Tom, and the bond between them was formed that instant, never to be broken. Their destiny to work together in this life was sealed, as it had been in others.

Chapter Thirteen

One Sunday afternoon after sharing another of Sarah's picnic lunches, Thorn leaned against the big oak in their favorite place while Angel rested her head in his lap. Companionable silence that normally only fell to older couples was evident between them.

With her thoughts a thousand miles away, Angel was an easy target for Thorn's eyes. Her creamy skin glowed in the sun in her off-the-shoulder peasant blouse. The interlocking laces of her high-waisted skirt accentuated her slender middle. Always though, Thorn was most drawn to her hair, that unruly chestnut red mass of curls that was somewhat restrained by ribbons.

As Thorn shifted position, Angel sat upward. "What a lovely, lovely day," she offered, gazing fondly at Thorn As if by plan, she scooted over beside him and nestled under his muscular arm. Contentedly, they sat this way until Thorn lifted up her chin toward his face.

"I've often dreamed about this moment," he smiled, and with that, he gently touched her lips with his. Warming to his touch, Angel easily parted her lips for a more passionate exchange. "I love you, Angel – more than you'll ever know." Thorn's heart was beating rapidly, and he felt the all too familiar adrenaline rush in his groin. Glad that he had had experience in lovemaking, he gently pulled her down on the blanket. Leaning over Angel's body, he kissed her again, and then he began tracing the crisscross ribbons on her high-waisted skirt, coming closer and closer to her breasts each time.

Tiny shivers ran up and down Angel's body following the motion of his fingers. Cupping her face, he leaned over again to kiss her gently, and then more passionately. Angel's quick reception pleased him. Pulling her off-the-shoulder blouse down, he kissed her from her arm up to her chest and over onto the other arm. He moved his fingers teasingly across the tops of her breasts at first. Then, using a circular motion, he pushed his fingers down further and further until he was able to encircle her nipples in a very slow, deliberate movement.

Angel lay contentedly with her eyes closed, immensely enjoying the mounting tingling in her body. Every circle he made evoked a tiny spasm, and his gentleness erased any apprehension she may have had. She was sorry when he stopped making the slow, deliberate circles, and she opened her eyes in disappointment.

"Now, do that for me!" he demanded. As if this were the most natural thing in the world, Angel unbuttoned his shirt and pushed it off, exposing his manly chest. With childish delight, she trailed her fingers across his chest and laughed at the goosebumps that the motion had produced. Then, teasingly, she lowered her face toward him and started planting kisses on the contours of his chest in the slow manner that he had taught her.

Stirred now, Thorn rolled up over her and gently slid her blouse completely down, exposing her pink nipples and creamy skin. Using the circular pattern once more, he traced first the left nipple, and then slowly he began tracing the right, working ever so gently. With each spasm of delight, Angel unconsciously arched her neck further back and enjoyed the warm sensations that he was producing. Thorn gently began kissing her breasts and sucking on them, and Angel groaned inwardly.

Stopping, Thorn kissed her gently and then passionately once more and rolled on top of her. Angel circled her arms around him, drinking him in. With his hand, Thorn then pushed her skirt upward, and moving beside her, he began stroking the inside of her right thigh.

Pushing her legs gently apart, he then stroked the left thigh at first with his fingers. When she didn't resist, he moved closer and closer to her passion point. Shivers of delight ran through her body, and Angel was sorry when he stopped.

"Now, do that for me!" he suggested again. With no hesitation, she unbuckled his pants, and together they slipped them off. The bulge in his shorts was quite evident, but Angel was intent on her task. Gently, but hesitantly, she stroked his inner thigh on his right, then moved over to the left. After a few seconds, Thorn easily guided her hand to his manhood, and she stroked it, also.

Now it was Thorn's turn. Pulling her skirt and pantaloons off in one expert tug, he positioned himself between her legs. Slowly, and with great care, he stimulated her until he knew that she was ready. Positioning himself totally above her and balancing his weight on each hand, he kissed her passionately again, and she arched up toward his body.

Waiting no more, Thorn gently lowered himself into her. Shudders ran through Angel's body of such exquisite nature, she thought she would die. Wave after wave of pleasure wracked her body, and she openly moaned with delight.

Delighting in her arousal, Thorn pumped a little deeper; finally unable to resist any more, he exploded inside her. Once spent, he pulled her beside him on the blanket in a protective manner, for she was still in the aftermath of orgasm, and her breathing was erratic. Never before had he experienced such intense sexual feelings, so fulfilling, so satisfactory, and so long-lasting.

Having had numerous affairs, Thorn knew that what he had had with Angel this afternoon was very different. He had gone to a whole new level in lovemaking. He had been contemplating asking her to marry him, and this unbelievable experience had cinched his decision. Thorn now knew that he was ready to ask Angel to marry him.

"I have been with a lot of women, Angel, but I've never created a feeling as wonderful as this."

"Oh, God, Thorn, I've never felt anything like that in my whole life, and the tinglings are still going on!" she laughed in childish delight.

He drew her close to him, feeling the beating of her heart, and they rested like this, content in each other's arms, saying nothing and needing nothing but each other. Later, Angel pulled away and looked at Thorn with great love. She whispered almost shyly, "Thorn, can we do that again?"

"Oh, we'll do that many, many times, my dear!" he laughed, mistaking what she meant.

Putting his hands on her breast, she muttered, "Please, Thorn, start the fireworks again!"

"Your wish is my command, my dear!" he delighted in saying.

Chapter Fourteen

One Wednesday morning, Sarah was immersed in her painting of a New Orleans scene. Sometimes it was hard to tell who had more paint, her smock or her painting! She was touching up the face of a friend of hers when she heard the horses whinnying. "Something has spooked them," she thought. Throwing her brush down, she mumbled, "Oh, dear God, it must be another runaway slave. No one ever comes out this far."

Remembering that she was alone, Sarah threw off her smock and dashed down the attic stairs to the first floor. Flying into her room, she jerked open the drawer and deftly loaded her gun, placing extra shells in her pocket. Then she raced to the back door. That was her horse whinnying loudly, and instantly, she knew that someone was in the corral!

When she rounded the barn, a slave was trying to slap the lead rope onto Betsy's halter. "That's my horse! Take your hands off her!" Sarah demanded.

"I's a dead man without this here horse," he sneered. "Ain't no white woman gonna stop me."

"I said take your hands off the halter, Mister!" The black man paid no attention to her words. PING, the bullet landed perfectly beside his foot, sending a little puff of dirt up into the air. Shock registered on the slave's face and then anger.

When he started toward Sarah, the bullet deliberately and expertly entered the fleshy part of his right shoulder. "Back off or the next one goes to your heart!"

The slave knew she meant it, and he froze in place. Holding the gun steady with her right hand, she reached into her pocket with her left and threw a gold coin between them in the dirt. Plunk! "Take this coin to help you buy passage to safety, but never try to take what doesn't belong to you again. Pick it up and get out of here before I change my mind."

The poor man was hesitant, not knowing how to read this crazy woman who had shot him one minute and had thrown gold at him the other! Suddenly, he lunged for the coin. Grabbing it quickly, he ran as fast as he could away from her.

Only when he had disappeared from sight did Sarah's hands shake. Huge tears of indignation welled up in her eyes. Moving toward Betsy, she reassured her horse with a pat and led her toward the barn. Sarah poured a ration of oats for her as a special afternoon snack and then turned toward the house.

Once in the kitchen, she sank down into the chair; huge, wracking sobs engulfed her. She cried for the pain of the plantation slaves; she cried for the pain of the slavery issue; and, she cried for the disillusionment of her once perfectly filed belief system.

"God, did I pass the test? Did I really help my fellow man by rewarding him for doing wrong?"

This was twice now that the slavery issue had come full circle. The last slave's action of trying to steal her horse had left a bad taste in her mouth. Sarah wondered in her heart, though, what she would do in his shoes. How desperate a measure would she take to stay alive? If her two experiences with slaves were a tiny snapshot of what was to come, they were all in for a rough ride.

Knowing that she couldn't focus on painting any more, Sarah dutifully trudged up the flights of stairs to pull the ventilation shutter closed in case of rain. As she passed her mother's portrait, she gave a mock salute, "Thanks, Momma! You literally saved my life today. A woman does need to know how to protect herself."

In her heart, Sarah knew that the time had come to tell Tom about both incidences with the runaway slaves. That night, Sarah carefully locked up the house. She knew that that particular slave was long gone, but she wasn't sure who would be coming behind him. Her gun, for the first time, was placed openly on the nightstand. As she cut out the lantern, her last thought was about getting a big dog that barks very loudly. Finally, she drifted off into a fitful sleep.

Chapter Fifteen

Thorn was always excited on Saturday mornings when he came into Wilmington to meet the guys because the waterfront was a fascinating place.

On this morning, his gaze took in monkeys in cages, wondrous smelling coffee in burlap bundles, parrots on perches, huge bunches of bananas, enormous steamer trunks, heavy wooden armament crates, and sweating sailors. Lots of spectators milled around the waterfront on the weekends, curious as he was, as to what exotic wonders from the West Indies they might see.

Thorn was not surprised when he saw the stretchers come off the newly-docked ship. Wilmington had a hospital for sick sailors right on Front and Dock Streets, called Siemen's Bethel. A little more centrally located in the city was Walker U.S. Marine Hospital for ailing sailors. "Thank God I'm not one!" Thorn muttered to himself, because the poor sailors looked a little green. The familiar sound, "*toot, toot, toot*" of the railroad engine was heard in the distance.

The Weldon-to-Wilmington railroad connection was one of the longest in the south, and much of this cargo that he was looking at would be shipped out tomorrow on the train. Leaving the waterfront, Thorn turned down the busy side street toward McGilly's Tavern, but he was quite unprepared for what he was about to hear. As Thorn approached the table, he called good-naturedly, "I can see that I am way behind you guys!"

Ahab turned first to see who it was, and then jumped up to extend his hand. "Well, hello, Thorn. We thought the

108

clutches of love had beckoned you to Southport!"

"Hi, Ahab. I'm glad to see you, too!" Thorn shook Ahab's hand, and then, in turn, with John and Nathan. Ahab signaled the waitress for a beer, and she nodded, giving him a big smile.

"Well, catch us up on the news, Ahab; what's her name this week?" Thorn inquired, giving a wink to the other guys.

"Here you are, honey!" The barmaid plopped down a fresh brew from her full tray. "Haven't seen you in here lately!" she teased.

"But Rebecca, I'm still saving myself just for you!" Ahab placed his hands over his heart and made a theatrical sweep of a kiss.

"Yeah, right!" Rebecca tossed back and turned to the next table.

"Aahh, Ahab, some of the ladies are finally catching on to your lies!" Nathan laughed.

"All right, guys. All right! John, what's the latest with you and Natalie?" Ahab turned his head closer toward John to catch his response over the loud noise in the popular place.

"I can successfully say that you can give up on thinking about dating her, Ahab. I have asked her to marry me!" John answered with great pride.

There was a moment of silence, and Nathan was the first to speak, "Marry you?"

Diplomatically, Ahab rose to the occasion. "Congratulations, John. We are all happy for you!" He slapped him on the back, "To John and Natalie!" Thorn and

Nathan jumped up quickly to clink their steins with John and Ahab's, "Here, Here, Here!"

"When are you planning to get married?" Thorn questioned as he took a big sip of his beer, shocked at the news.

"Now, of course, I'm asking all of you to be my groomsmen. Will you help me out?"

"Of course we will!" Thorn assured him.

"But, when?" Nathan queried.

"As soon as possible. Natalie and I are afraid everything will be too topsy-turvy if North Carolina secedes -- so we hope within the next six weeks. She and her mom have been working on the details for the last two weeks," John concluded.

They sipped on their beers for awhile before John spoke again. "Have you been reading the news lately? My God, it looks like we're really headed toward war!" He hit the side of the table in disbelief.

"Can you believe that Mississippi, Florida, Alabama, Georgia, Louisiana, and Texas could move that fast to pass their secession decrees, too?" Thorn added. "This whole thing is moving way too fast for me. So, what are our options? I guess North Carolina will be next."

"Oh, I read the answer to that in the paper today," John piped in. "It's pretty simple. One choice is to do nothing and continue on with your life until our state officially secedes. The second choice is to volunteer right now for either a three-month or a one-year hitch to show your patriotism."

"So what happens if we volunteer?" Thorn inquired.

"As I understand it, each county will form a volunteer militia unit which officially offers its service to the state governor. The various militia units around the state will then be formed into one big regiment for fighting the enemy."

"Will the volunteers be paid?" Nathan interrupted.

"Yeah, a hundred and fifty-six dollars for the one-year sign-up. I'm not sure about the three-month hitch."

"Does North Carolina have a militia unit starting to form?" Thorn inquired.

"Now, that I don't know," John replied.

Buried deep in private thoughts for a minute, no one said anything. Thorn broke the silence. To no one in particular he announced, "When I enlist, I'm going to join the cavalry."

"The cavalry!" Nathan shot back.

"I've really been thinking about it, and I'd rather have a horse under me when the going gets tough. I'd rather be on the offensive team than the defensive team any day!"

"You know, Thorn, I think you've got something there. I may just join up with you in the same unit!" Nathan added.

"Well, that would be great!" Thorn flashed a big grin at Nathan.

"And, I, my friends," John announced, "have decided to write to Jefferson Davis to see if he could use my lawyering skills in drawing up dispatches and writing edicts rather than enlisting in the army."

"Good thinking, John. You won't die as quickly in an office as you will on a battlefield!" Thorn was quick to add.

"What have you been thinking, Ahab?" John asked, knowing his friend's deep-seated anti-slavery beliefs.

"I'm not gonna do anything but run my hardware store. War or not, every town has to have a hardware store. I will just take my chances with the conscription – if it comes to that."

As they were leaving the tavern after lunch, Thorn fell into step next to Ahab, "Ahab, I don't know quite how to say this, but I'm worried about you."

"What do you mean?" Ahab asked.

"Are you working for the Abolitionist Movement?" Thorn inquired, looking him straight in the eye.

"Why do you ask?"

"Because two weekends ago, I recognized you at the marsh near Southport where a wagonload of escaping slaves were loaded onto a boat."

"How did you hear about that Freedom Ride?" Ahab asked, obviously surprised that anyone had been watching.

"Angel's father heard about it. We rode out to see if the slaves were really being sent to freedom by white people. I recognized you – even in the dark – because of your height."

"My God, Thorn, you could have been killed!" Ahab argued, exasperated that he had been caught red-handed.

Grabbing Ahab's arm, Thorn admonished him, "You are like a brother to me, Ahab, and I don't want you to be killed over some cause."

"I've not been in danger; we plan these things very carefully."

"I respect your anti-slavery feelings, Ahab, but I don't think it's worth your life."

Ahab put his arm around Thorn, "Thanks for your concern. I truly appreciate that, my friend. Soon every Southerner will have to make a life-changing decision for himself. Brother may have to fight against brother over this secession issue. We may have to die for what we believe in. Stay away, Thorn. Don't go to another Freedom Ride out of curiosity. Too many people hate the Abolitionists. Fighting could break out; it has happened in other parts of the country," Ahab informed him with a stern tone in his voice. "Now, let's change the topic," Ahab smiled. "Tell me about this girl you're in love with!" He raised his eyebrows in a theatrical fashion and made Thorn laugh.

"Oh, no. I'm not telling you about her because you'll try to grab her for yourself!" Thorn teased back.

"How did you meet her?" Ahab smiled as they started walking in unison again.

"Believe it or not, through her father."

"Her father? Now, that's a good one!" Ahab chuckled.

"I attended a secession meeting at his house, and I met Angel that afternoon.

"Aahh, she's an angel, huh?" Ahab ribbed back.

"In more ways than one!"

"Here's my street. I'll see you tonight at the dance about 8:00 PM," Ahab called.

"Okay, see ya." Thorn called after him as he turned toward the boarding house, but Ahab never made it to the dance; he had a change of plans.

Chapter Sixteen

A month later, "The Fabulous Four" were nervously waiting in the Pastor's study for the arrival of John's father, who was his best man.

"I must say, you three dress up pretty well!" John announced, as he surveyed his handsome friends in their formal wear. "I'm sorry to be breaking up the foursome, but Natalie probably won't trust me to be with eligible bachelors every Saturday night."

"Where will you go on your honeymoon?" Thorn inquired, thinking about where he might take Angel when they got married.

"We're going on a two-week sweep through New York, Boston, and Richmond. I can't wait because I've never been to New York or Boston!"

"Oh, you're going to love Boston," Thorn added.

At that moment, the door opened, and Mr. Thompson entered, "There you are, boys! Some of the first carriages will be arriving soon, so I guess you better hurry on down to the entrance."

Each groomsman stopped to hug John before leaving. Although nothing had been said, Thorn knew that an era was ending for each of them. No more all night partying, sporting, and tavern hopping on Saturdays and Sundays. The last seven years had been a great experience. After his parents had died, Thorn was glad to have had his buddies as his second family. Yet, Ahab was seldom there anymore, John had been busy working on wedding plans, while Nathan and Thorn had been harvesting crops. "The Fabulous Four", unfortunately it seemed, had cycled out.

St. James Episcopal Church could easily hold two hundred people, but on this day of the wedding, the pews were filled to capacity. Some latecomers even had to stand in the back of the church.

Thorn was to escort down the aisle a pretty young thing from South Carolina, Susan Conway, who was one of Natalie's cousins. Ahab, because of his height, had been selected to escort Cynthia, Natalie's sister. Nathan escorted Elaine, Natalie's other sister. Thorn noted that John seemed nervous and a little pale as they stood at the altar, but Mr. Thompson beamed at the thought of a new daughter-in-law!

With the beginning cords of "Here Comes the Bride", everyone stood in honor as the bride appeared at the back of the church on the arm of her father. Thorn's first thought was that she was floating on a cloud of white, her dress was so full and beautiful. Natalie's dark hair had been ringleted, and it served as the perfect contract for the heavenly vision of white netting. Around her neck was the dazzling diamond pendant that John had given to her as a wedding gift.

Certain that everyone had had sufficient time to see her dress, Natalie and her father began the long walk down the center aisle. Thorn glanced over at John, who was beaming from head to toe as he looked at his soon-to-be bride. As splendid as she looked at that moment, Thorn completely agreed with John's comment the moment he laid eyes on her at her coming out party. "She's the most beautiful thing I've ever seen!"

Mrs. Mintz was already dabbing her eyes with her handkerchief, for it wasn't every day that her firstborn got married.

"Dearly beloved, we are gathered here today. . ."

No expense had been spared for the reception, which was held downtown at the Greystone Inn, a mere walk from the church. As soon as the doors of the reception hall opened, beautiful chamber music flowed out onto the sidewalk. Several doormen were positioned to check wraps, and champagne flutes were ready for the taking from the huge butler trays. Several bars had been set up in the mahogany reading room, and the backroom beckoned everyone to sample the cuisine. Huge scallops, crab cakes, and shrimp were heaped on the beautifully carved silver serving trays at one end of the table. On the opposite end of the twenty-foot table, carving stations had been set up for ham, turkey, and roast beef samplings. In the center of the table, a huge spray of flowers had been placed, falling gently down to lend their natural perfumes. Assorted sandwiches and sweet delicacies anchored the middle of the massive table.

In the far corner was the non-alcoholic punch for the ladies. Thorn grabbed three cups for the bridesmaids in hopes that Ahab was at the first bar getting drinks for the groomsmen. Ahab wasn't hard to spot; he was a head taller than anyone else in the room, and yes, thank God, he was at the bar! A photographer was setting up his equipment, and women were grouped all over the hall talking behind their hands, which meant that gossip was being exchanged. The finest jewelry was on display today: bracelets, hairpins, necklaces, and rings. The dazzle of the bright gems reminded Thorn of a firefly display. Not one thing had been left undone – fine music, wonderful food, beautiful flower arrangements, and, most important of all, beautiful women!

Were it not for his love of Angel, the girl in that green silk dress would have already been flirted with and tagged for future reference. Thorn was sad that Angel was out of town, for neither John, Ahab, nor Nathan had ever met her. This wedding would have been a wonderful time for introductions; however, Thorn knew that his responsibility as a groomsman was to see that the bridesmaids were taken care of at the reception. Catching Susan's eye, Thorn ambled over to her with the cups of punch. "Where are the other bridesmaids, Miss Susan?" Thorn inquired, looking around.

"Off to powder their noses, I think," she replied.

"Here you are, my friend, bourbon and water – just like you like it!" Ahab announced.

"A little heavy on the bourbon; isn't it?" Thorn laughed, looking at the brown colored highballs.

"It's gonna be a long night, my friend!" Ahab laughed, and then toasted. "To John and Natalie." The three glasses clinked, and the party began.

Chapter Seventeen

Thorn had not seen the Wilmington streets this crowded since that day South Carolina had seceded. "Good Lord, I need to be a contortionist just to get through this crowd," he thought. At long last, Thorn found himself at the door of McGilly's Tavern. "Excuse me. Excuse me," he uttered over and over again, trying to move toward their regular table. "What in the world is going on?" Thorn yelled over the noise.

"Haven't you heard? Beauregard fired on Fort Sumpter!"

"I don't believe it!"

"It's true," John affirmed, pulling him closer to the table, where Ahab was reading to them.

"It seems," Ahab continued, "that Beauregard demanded that Major Anderson of the U.S. Army evacuate the fort since South Carolina was no longer a part of the United States government. Anderson agreed to do so on April the 15th, at 3:30 PM, unless he heard otherwise; but Beauregard wasn't satisfied with that response. So, this note was delivered:

> *We have the honor to notify you that Beauregard will open fire one hour from this time.*

When Anderson didn't evacuate, Beauregard fired red-hot cannonballs designed to catch the wooden fort on fire. The siege continued all through the night."

"Was the fort located on land?" Nathan interrupted.

"No, the fort was three miles out in the Charleston Harbor."

"Go on, Ahab," Thorn urged.

"At noon on the 13th of April, a white flag went up. The U.S. Army left on the 14th, and the Southerners entered the fort and ran up the new Confederate flag."

"Wow! This must be an exciting time to live in Charleston. Just think, South Carolina was the first to secede and the first to fire the opening shot of the war!" Thorn announced.

"Let's hear it for South Carolina! Hip-Hip-Hooray!" The mugs clicked.

Nathan yelled, "Does the newspaper tell how many men fired on Fort Sumter?"

Ahab held up his hand, signaling that he had heard the question and looked for the answer. "It only says, and I quote, 'a small crowd'."

"Wow, talk about the Northerners folding like a two-dollar suitcase. Hope the rest of the war is that quick and that easy!"

All around the room, the articles were being read aloud by one member at the table while the others listened intently. History had been made, and the Southerners were reveling in the results.

If the excitement that was in the bar was any sign, the South would have no lack of men volunteering to fight.

"Here's to that small crowd!" Nathan toasted.

That was it. The die had been cast. There was no turning back now. North Carolina had to secede.

Chapter Eighteen

One fine Wednesday morning when the first ray of the morning sun hit Sarah's face, so did the adrenaline rush. She knew instantly what she had to do. This insistent energy was the same energy that had taken hold of her when she was painting her mother's portrait. In a second, she bolted from the bed and dashed into the kitchen. Grabbing the coffee, she filled the teakettle and reached for the porcelain cup. Hastily, she assembled two sandwiches and grabbed a couple of cookies. Readying herself with a quick brush of her teeth and hair, she jumped into her clothes. After all, the call from the "Angel of Inspiration" did not come every day.[13]

Up two flights of stairs and into her inner sanctum, she ran. Donning her artist smock, she grabbed a canvas and set it upon the easel. After opening the ventilation shutter, she breathed a silent prayer, "Okay, God, I'm ready for you to work through my hands!" As she always did, she paused a second and closed her eyes, and usually the image that she was to paint would appear. As she closed her eyelids together, she recognized it was not to be a New Orleans scene, but a portrait of Tom. Tears crowded against her eyelids, and she settled back in the chair, reaching over for the pencil to start sketching.

Three hours later the first hunger pang hit her. Sarah grimaced at the taste of the cold coffee, but munched happily into the chicken sandwich. Standing away as she nibbled her sandwich, she reflected on her sketch of Tom. Dressed in his normal vested suit, Tom looked straight ahead from an upper body position. His faithful Bible was clutched under his left

---

[13]

arm, and a slight smile played across his lips, as if he knew a secret.

With the "Angel of Inspiration" still holding tightly to her, she surrendered her hands once more, not to the pencil again, but to the oils. Deftly, she shadowed, filled, contoured, and lined. Within three hours, Tom was beginning to come alive, and so was her bladder. Racing down the stairs, she relieved herself, grabbed more cookies and water, and sprinted back. Only a few more good hours of sunlight remained. Diligently, she worked until she finally had the eyes – those all important eyes – just right.

Sarah was never sure how this power worked. She knew exactly when it arrived, and she knew that this was a relentless energy that ran through every vein. She also knew that every time it came, she lost track of time. Everything was oblivious to her when the fingers of inspiration took hold. She was their puppet, and they were her master.

At last, as the sunlight diminished, she closed the shutter soundly and paused to touch her mother's picture lovingly before leaving. She was tired, bone tired. She trudged to her room to lie down for just a minute; she never even felt the sleep overtake her.

The week passed by without another visit from the Angel of Inspiration. Soon it was Saturday again.

In Wilmington on Saturday, the guys met as usual at McGilly's Tavern.

"Well, it looks like you lucked out, John, my boy," Thorn offered looking at the confirmation sheet. "The old age factor is sure working on your side! Congratulations!"

"Yeah, most lawyers are way too old to enlist, so you, my friend, have been able to write your own ticket -- right into

Confederate Headquarters in Richmond." Nathan added, as he finished reading the sheet.

"Working for Jefferson Davis, all the way to the top of the Confederacy. What a political coup for you, John," Ahab added, turning around to signal for more beer.

"Or political disaster!" John added, with a sinister laugh. "If the South doesn't win the war, I will be put in jail for political treason, along with Mr. Davis."

"Oh, the South is going to win the war!" Nathan declared. "We're motivated; we're knowledgeable about the land; we're expert horsemen; and we're willing to fight. Just look what happened at Fort Sumpter. Did you know that up North a man can pay three hundred dollars and not even have to enlist?" Nathan asked incredulously.

"Yeah, that's why they are calling it the rich man's war," Ahab chimed in.

After they finished lunch at McGilly's Tavern, "The Fabulous Four" broke up, each going in a different direction. Thorn had decided that today was the day he would make his move. Pushing open the heavy wooden door, Thorn grimaced at the loud bell that rang overhead, signaling his presence in the jewelry store.

Mr. Kingoff came rushing from the back, wiping his hands upon his leather apron. "How are you this fine afternoon?" Mr. Kingoff smiled genuinely, sensing the discomfort in his young visitor. Thorn met Mr. Kingoff's extended hand with a big shake.

"And how may I be of assistance?" Mr. Kingoff asked, intuitively knowing that engagement rings would be the topic of conversation. A young man never came into a jewelry store by choice, only when driven by the call of love.

"Do you know her size?" Mr. Kingoff challenged with a smile. "We'll need to know that first."

Thorn broke into laughter, and the nervousness left him. "No, Sir, I don't. But I do want to discuss a ring with you!"

"I thought so. Come back into my office where we can talk privately."

Thorn sighed in relief, realizing that no one would accidentally see him if he were in the back office. Opening the swivel gate, Mr. Kingoff pointed to the left, and Thorn walked behind the counter. Sitting in the office seat, Thorn dug into his shirt pocket, producing a ring box. He could still hear his mother's voice, "This is my engagement ring, and one day it will be yours when you find the right girl!" The sparkle of the diamond was not hindered in the dim office lighting.

"That's a nice stone," the jeweler commented. Pulling out his eyeglasses, he announced, "A very nice stone."

"Sir, I want to add some stones on either side so that this ring will be special for my girl. A new, especially created engagement ring."

"Well, that won't be a problem at all, except for the sizing. Now, what stones does she like?"

"I don't know; I want it to be a surprise."

"Oh, well, in that case, may I suggest either emeralds, sapphires or rubies. Let me get some loose stones to show you."

Thorn slid back into the seat, comfortable at last. When Mr. Kingoff returned, he set the stones one by one on either side of the diamond. Immediately, Thorn knew that he wanted emeralds.

"All right, now the next question is what size emeralds. I will be right back with several sizes."

Thorn wondered if he should ask the price of the different size stones, but he decided that only the best would do for Angel. With the jeweler's help, Thorn decided on the medium-sized stones.

"Platinum or gold setting?"

"Platinum."

"Okay, all we need now is her ring size," Mr. Kingoff concluded, smiling at the nice young man.

"How can I find that out if this is supposed to be a surprise?" Thorn was stumped on that one.

"Well, here is some clay. Press one of her rings into it when she isn't looking, and then bring the clay back. I can figure out the sizing from that."

"Okay!" Thorn smiled in relief. That hadn't been bad at all.

"I'll put your mom's ring and the loose stones in the safe until you return."

"I'll see her this weekend, and I'll bring the clay back in Monday. Now, how much do I owe you?" Thorn asked.

"I'll need half the cost down, and then you can pay for the rest when I see how much labor it involves. Now, when do you need this?"

"As soon as possible," Thorn beamed, becoming more excited about the proposal.

"Oh, I understand!" Mr. Kingoff nodded. "That won't be a problem. Okay, I'll see you back on Monday." The two men shook hands to complete the deal, and Thorn paid him. Walking out into the bright sunlight, he ambled down the cobblestone streets to get his horse. He was happy to be heading to Southport.

The early spring months brought special blessings to the earth in the South. The air was a little fresher, the pines a little greener, and the berries more pungent. The winds of March had cleared the air, and the rain had provided the necessary communication for the deeply-entrenched underground bulbs to awaken. Such was the splendor of the countryside as Thorn headed toward Southport. He was glad to be alive and glad to be heading to see his girl.

Thorn couldn't imagine life without her now and there was no doubt that he wanted to spend the rest of his life with her. "But," he thought, "the war has changed everything. Should they try to be married like John and Natalie before he enlisted in the army or should they wait to be married until he returned home?" Pondering those questions, he headed happily into the afternoon sun.

Chapter Nineteen

The sweet smell of the honeysuckle vine wafted gently through the side window of Tom Madison's office. In town for supplies, Thorn gave Angel a surprise visit.

After a quick hug, Angel, who was unable to control the excitement in her voice, exclaimed, "I'm so glad that you will be able to spend Easter weekend with us!"

"I'm looking forward to it, my love. What does your family do to celebrate Easter?" Thorn inquired, hoping home cooked food would be a big part of it.

"Well, let's see. On Friday night we go to church, Saturday we take the Easter Bunny gifts to the orphanage, Saturday night we go to the Community Festival and Sunday the Easter Bunny visits us."

"Wow! That's a lot of activity for one weekend!" Thorn acknowledged. "Now, Angel! Don't you know that you are too old for the Easter Bunny to visit you?" He teased, giving her hand a squeeze. He loved to tease her.

Motioning for Thorn to sit in the reception chairs, Angel asked, "Do you have time for me to tell you the truth about Easter?"

"All the time in the world."

"Easter is very special to me because this holiday involves something of my mother's. When I was little, my father made a huge wooden Easter basket for me and also lots of wooden eggs.

Lovingly, my mother painted the basket pastel green, and then she painted little bunny scenes all around. Once she finished, she and I spent many days painting the eggs pastel colors.

Some of the eggs were designed with hinges on them, and this is where the Easter Bunny would hide my Easter gifts."

Angel paused for a second, "But here's the best part!" Her eyes jumped with excitement. "Thorn, Mother painted Dad's name, her name, my name, and Sarah's name on four of the eggs. So I have her handwriting preserved, too! I wouldn't take anything for that basket."

"Wow! What a wonderful heirloom. I'm so happy for you!" Impulsively, Thorn jumped up to give Angel a big hug.

Sitting back down, Thorn suddenly became serious. "Angel, will I be included in the gift giving on Easter Sunday?"

Angel teased, "Have you been good enough for the Easter Bunny to bring you a gift?"

Thorn laughed. "I think so."

"It will be fun for all of us to exchange gifts," Angel smiled.

"I know that your father would like some of his favorite brandy, but I don't think that will fit in an egg!"

Angel laughed, "I'm sorry, I should have told you this part. Sometimes we put a note in the egg telling the recipient to look in a certain spot in the dining room to find his gift."

"Whew! That makes it easier for me! So I'll get brandy for your dad and what about a designer magazine for Sarah?"

"Oh! She would love that!" Angel agreed.

"And what for you, my sweet Angel? What can the Easter Bunny bring you?"

"Honestly, Thorn, the only thing I can think of is more time with you. That old war just gets closer and closer all the time."

Thorn was touched, but he pushed past his emotion. "I know just what the Easter Bunny can bring you!"

Before he left, Thorn gave Angel a lingering kiss. Then he dashed out the door to his wagon, loaded with supplies.

"Oh Lord! I just love that man," Angel thought as she walked back to her desk to tackle a stack of business receipts. His visit had been a pleasant interlude to a boring morning.

The two weeks passed quickly – finally the weekend before Easter arrived. On Saturday morning, Sarah had just added another log to the stove when the kitchen door burst open. Tom called excitedly as he stacked two boxes beside the door. "Here they are!"

"Tom. Let me get you some coffee."

Tom plopped into the kitchen chair to begin pulling off his boots. Sarah retrieved his moccasins from the study, and Tom gratefully slid his feet into their comfort.

"I've made your favorite pancakes, fried some sausage, and fixed some eggs because I knew you would be starved to death."

"I am hungry, I can tell you that for sure!"

Sarah's breakfast plate looked quite inviting, and he dived right in, savoring the tangy taste of the sausage and the sweetness of the syrup. As he was eating, Sarah looked across at the man she loved.

No other man loved tradition quite like Tom. Every holiday was celebrated to the max.

A few minutes later, Angel yawned her way into the kitchen. Immediately she spied the boxes.

"Oh, Dad! You brought the boxes from the barn!"

Excitedly, she tore into the top box. "Oh! Look Sarah, it's the paper streamer we made last year." They had worked for days to make a green, pink, and yellow garland that would adorn the dining room windows.

"Why, here are the Easter bunnies," Sarah cried. "I had forgotten that we made them!" Two years earlier, Sarah had taught Angel to tat, and they had created twenty colorful designs to hang in the windows.

Angel placed the first box on the floor beside her; kneeling down, she carefully lifted the top of the second box. Reverently, she lifted out the pastel green basket.

Tears welled in her eyes as she caressed the hand painted designs. Tom and Sarah stood quietly as she tiptoed back into her childhood memories.

Happiness filled Angel's eyes as she called, "Let's unwrap the eggs!"

Simultaneously, all three grabbed for the tissue wrapped treasures.

"I found yours, Tom!" Sarah called happily.

More tissue rattled; then Angel yelled. "I found Mom's." Lovingly, she traced the golden letters spelling out her mother's name – R-A-C-H-E-L.

In a few minutes all the multicolored eggs had been unwrapped and displayed proudly inside the basket.

"Oh, me!" Angel gasped suddenly. "We need to put Thorn's name on an egg. He'll be here for the Easter Bunny brunch."

"Good idea, Honey!" Tom answered, "I'll go get the paint from the barn."

Within a few minutes, brightly colored Easter bunnies adorned the windows, and the multicolored garland graced the triple window. Easter truly came alive when Angel placed the finishing touch on the dining room table – her mother's Easter basket. Inside lay five special hinged eggs. Angel smiled as she ran her fingers over the egg with T-H-O-R-N.

"I can't wait for next weekend to come!" she thought, and then ran upstairs to get dressed. She still had some painting to do on the gifts for the orphanage kids.

Chapter Twenty

The whole town turned out for Southport's Easter festivities. The local inn sponsored a wonderful pig picking with all the trimmings. After the pig picking, the fiddling began. Everyone danced like there was no tomorrow -- grandmothers, kids, couples, teenagers, and lovers.

Angel was greatly surprised that night to find out that Thorn was quite a dancer, and she loved him even more when he made a special point to dance with Miss Lizzie, Sarah, and other old ladies from the church congregation. All the teenage girls flirted with Thorn unabashedly. Tom made sure that he danced with the widows from the church, and Sarah and Angel followed suit by dancing with the widowers.

At 9:00 PM, the fireworks began, and children and grownups alike were lost in the beauty of the geometric figures catapulted into the night sky.

Thorn stood with his arm around Angel, surveying the bursts of light. Two other people were observing the couple standing there so contentedly.

"How long before he asks her to marry him, Tom?" Sarah asked, smiling up into his face.

"Dunno, but when he comes to ask my permission, I'll be a happy man. He'll make a great husband for her."

"I couldn't agree with you more," Sarah answered back with a nod.

The next morning, the smell of coffee had been teasing Thorn's senses for a while, and eventually he stretched and strained his muscles and climbed out of bed. He doused the water on his face and brushed his teeth. Then raking his hands through his hair, he jumped into his clothes, feeling carefully to make sure that he had the package in the right place. That done, he strode to the main house.

"Good morning, Miss Sarah," he announced, looking around for Angel.

"Well, Miss Sleepyhead should be down in a minute, but I guess you could use a cup of coffee, huh?" she asked with a smile.

"Oh, I'll get it, Sarah." Grabbing one of the cups, Thorn poured the coffee and dropped in two sugar cubes.

"That was a nice evening last night; wasn't it, Sarah?"

"Did you see how some of those ole' geezers can still dance? I thought Mr. Briarhopper would dance my legs off!" Sarah laughed at how breathless she had gotten after the fourth dance.

"He can't hold a candle to Miss Lizzie. I'll bet she was something in her day," Thorn announced.

"They say she was the most beautiful woman in the county," Sarah braggingly added.

"Well, all I can say is that title now belongs to you, Sarah."

"Well," a new voice blurted out, "what about me?"

Quickly, Thorn turned and smoothly added, "You, my dear, are the most beautiful girl. You're not old enough to be in 'the woman' category yet," Thorn explained, kissing her on her forehead.

Sarah laughed to herself at the lovebirds. She wondered if what was so obvious to everyone else had registered with them. They were definitely heading closer to the aisle.

"I am as hungry as a bear!" Tom announced coming into the kitchen.

"Be ashamed of yourself, Tom! You had four plates of barbecue last night," Sarah admonished.

"And just who ate half of every plate I got?" Tom teased.

All four of them laughed in unison.

"Angel, if you will take over the bacon, I'll scramble the eggs. Here's your coffee, Tom." When Sarah uncovered the bread pan, a wonderful whiff of cinnamon filled the room.

Like a child, Tom asked expectantly, "Oh, Sarah, did you make the cinnamon buns this morning?"

"Oh, yeah. With lots of glaze and raisins -- just like you like 'em. Now, you boys go relax in the library, and we'll have this ready in a jiffy."

Sarah had outdone herself for the Easter brunch: baked apples, grits, bacon, ham, cinnamon buns and eggs. The chaffing dishes were piled high with food.

"Okay, guys, we're ready," Angel called in a few minutes.

No one needed to be called twice, for Thorn and Tom arrived quickly to pull back the chairs for the ladies. Grace was said, and each person began filling his plate with the mouthwatering selections.

"Sarah, these stewed apples are the best! I'd rather have them than even eat candy."

"But have you tried the cinnamon buns?" Tom inquired.

"Nope, I'm saving them for dessert. This red-eye gravy is to die for!" Angel added, as she wiped her lips.

"Can you cook like this, Angel?" Thorn asked suddenly.

"Sarah has been teaching me."

"She's doing very well, I may say," Sarah fired back in defense of Angel.

With the meal over, the guys retreated to the library again while the girls cleaned up the table.

"Let's not forget the wine," Sarah added. "You know how your father likes tradition."

Four wineglasses and the decanter were placed on a tray and carried into the dining room. Angel moved the large Easter basket back into the center of the table and Sarah positioned her wrapped gifts on the sideboard. Then Angel completed her gift giving.

"Okay, guys! We're ready!" Sarah called invitingly. "We'll step into the kitchen while you place your gifts!"

Tom and Thorn strategically placed their gifts, and then they put slips of paper into the appropriate eggs.

"Girls! Come back. We're ready," Tom called. Tom pointed with pride to the eggs, "Did Angel tell you about these eggs from long ago, Thorn?"

"Yes sir, she showed me the basket and eggs when I arrived Friday night. How wonderful that you have carried on this tradition, and I appreciate your letting me play Easter Bunny, too!" Thorn concluded, with a big smile.

"Did you notice the egg with your name on it?" Sarah teased.

"Oh! I noticed that egg the first thing," Thorn replied, producing a laugh from the three of them.

"Since you are our guest, we want you to have the honor of going first," Tom directed, handing him the purple egg with his name on it.

When Thorn carefully opened the hinge of the egg, he found slips of paper inside directing him to the sideboard where three wrapped gifts awaited his opening.

As soon as Thorn undid the first package, a delicious aroma wafted upward and filled the room.

"Your favorites," Sarah called. "Two dozen lemon, two dozen chocolate, and two dozen oatmeal."

"You do know the way to a man's heart, don't you, Sarah? Thanks so much."

The next gift was square shaped. Tom's voice boomed, "For you and your buddies to use at the Gentleman's Club." Inside the wrapping was a very expensive box of cigars.

"My friends will like these. Thanks Tom."

Angel's eyes sparkled as Thorn reached for her gift. A black jeweler's box revealed a pair of cufflinks. "Oh Angel! You had them engraved. Why I'll wear them today! Thank you very much."

"Now, it's your turn, Angel," her father announced.

Carefully, Angel opened the hinge on the pastel pink egg. Inside lay two slips of paper, directing her to the chair in the corner.

Quickly, Angel tore off the ribbon on the first present and slipped the paper away. Inside lay a gold compact, encrusted with pearls on its diameter. The small hinge opened to reveal a mirror inside. Angel remembered admiring this in a shop window when she and Sarah were in Wilmington.

"Only the best for my girl!" Sarah beamed as she gave Angel a hug.

The next gift was oddly heavy. With nimble fingers she released the paper to reveal a handcrafted silver box.

"Press the switch," Tom urged.

Beautiful resounding notes filled the room. "Oh Dad!" It's a music box; I have always wanted one. For a few more seconds they stood spellbound listening to the lovely tones, filling the room.

Thorn could not stand it any longer. He walked over to Angel and pulled the jewelry box from his pocket. Bending down on one knee, he spoke past the lump in his throat, "Will you marry me, Angel?" The beautiful diamond ring sparkled in the sunlight as he offered it to her.

Throwing her arms around his neck, she cried, "Oh yes, Thorn! Oh yes!"

In a second, she turned toward her father, and he drew her in his arms. "I couldn't be happier for you two. I gave my permission to Thorn this morning."

Sarah was waiting with her arms wide open, and the two held each other tightly. Separating finally, Sarah quipped as she wiped the tears away. "I guess we'd better learn how to sew a wedding gown now."

Tom uncapped the wine and poured four glasses. Proudly he toasted, "To the best Easter I've ever had." All four clinked simultaneously, and each took a big swig.

Looking back at the ring, Angel stammered, "When did you buy this beautiful ring?"

"Two weeks ago. The center stone is from my mother's wedding ring, and I selected the emeralds for either side so that it would be very special." I had planned to propose this weekend, and the Easter Bunny gifting provided the perfect opportunity."

An hour after Sarah and Tom had opened their gifts, Sarah announced, "Tom, we'd better get to the orphanage." Sarah gave Tom a meaningful look.

"Oh, yeah, the orphanage," he responded, knowing full well that they hadn't planned on going to the orphanage.

A little while later, Tom pulled the wagon around, and Sarah called, "You two lovebirds enjoy the afternoon. We'll be home about five o'clock tonight." Tom helped Sarah into the wagon and then jumped into the driver's side.

"How long do you reckon it'll be before they tumble in that guest room bed?" Sarah questioned and then chuckled to herself.
"About thirteen seconds," Tom responded and joined her laughter. They were silent for awhile, and then Tom

announced, "Sarah, I wish we had a bed to tumble into."

"So do I, Tom. So do I." She scooted over beside him to lay her head on his shoulder as he placed his arm around her. Sometimes she was sorry she couldn't marry Tom, and this was one of them.

Chapter Twenty-One

Sarah could not believe it -- twice in one month? Placing the dishtowel down, she stood very still for a minute to make sure. There was no doubt the "Angel of Inspiration" was back. Resolutely, she closed down the kitchen, making sure that nothing could catch fire.

Grabbing some fruit and a glass of water, she headed for the attic. As she opened the shutter to let in the warm sunlight, she uttered her usual prayer. "Okay, God. I'm ready for you to work through my fingers again."

As soon as she positioned the canvas in place, she closed her eyes. Within a minute, a portrait of Angel appeared in her inner vision. "Oh, so it's to be Angel this time." The thought warmed her heart and brought a smile to her lips. Picking up her pencil, she began the sketching from the outside in. She tamed the wild, unruly chestnut hair a bit and lovingly drew in those vibrant eyes. After fringing the eyes with heavy, dark eyelashes, she sketched her delicate nose and beautiful, full lips. Angel's favorite dress was quickly drawn in loosely around her neck and shoulders.

Sarah had always thought it was so odd that when the fingers of inspiration held her captive, she made no mistakes in her sketching. Yet, when she just sketched by herself, she often erased and redrew, and sometimes even changed her mind in midstream and started over. With these portraits, it seemed that some power worked through her. She wondered if any other painters had ever experienced this same thing.

Satisfied, she stood back to get her perspective. "Wow! Everything is perfect!" Dabbing seven colors on her palette, she started with the oils. Confidently, she set in on the background, illuminating, shadowing, and blending, little by little. Hours went by, and soon the natural light began to fail her. She was surprised when she saw pink hues interlaced with the purple clouds of sunset through the opening. Standing, she stretched her back and then muttered, "Goodbye, my loves. I'll see you tomorrow." She blew a kiss to Tom and to her mother. "And you too, my Angel," she smiled.

Sarah thought it was odd that her back and shoulders never bothered her when she was painting along with the Angel of Inspiration. Sometimes as she painted on her own, she would have a backache for several days after a day of painting.

Downstairs she scraped a little dinner together and thought how happy she would be when Tom returned home in a couple of days. Before she lay down, she said, "Now, Mr. Inspiration, don't forget to come for me tomorrow. Angel's portrait isn't finished." Pulling the covers up, she planned to read a while, but she was tired, and sleep came very quickly.

About eight o'clock the next morning, Sarah felt herself being gently raised into a type of consciousness, easing away the subconscious hold that had held her tightly all night.

"Whew, I slept like a log!" Sarah thought to herself. She yawned and then yawned again. "Well, I guess I'd better get up." Bathing quickly, she dressed and entered the kitchen, longing for her morning coffee. Two eggs over light and some oatmeal with a generous dollop of molasses satisfied her hunger.

"Well, thank God I got to eat before you came," she announced, for she felt the all too familiar presence of the Angel of Inspiration.

"Well, I'm glad you're back, Sir," she called. "I couldn't leave my baby, Angel, half-painted now; could I?" Sarah laughed out loud. What a wonderful way for God to touch her life.

Taking her coffee along, she entered her creative place. Pausing a minute, she opened the shutter and waited to greet the sun, observing the beauty of a spring day. "Okay, God. I'm ready for you to work through me again." With that, she squeezed new paints onto the palette and started mixing them together. The power took her to Angel's eyes first. Expertly, the perfect color of blue purple was blended with just a few strokes and then applied to the canvas. Tiny dots of white were added to form the whites of the eyes. With a quick black dot, the pupil appeared. Angel's entire enthusiasm about life had been captured in those few brush strokes.

Carefully, Sarah worked with delicate strokes, hollowing the cheeks, tinting the lips, and shading the hairline. The Power knew exactly how to expertly fill in the details, and Sarah just surrendered herself to the process. She was surprised when the afternoon sunrays arrived in the room. Standing, she walked a few steps back. What she saw caused her to gasp. "My God!" Angel had jumped right off the canvas into her heart. Sarah was amazed at how magnificently Angel's soul essence had been captured. "Thank you, God," she whispered, and huge tears spilled down her cheeks in gratitude.

"The picture is perfect," Sarah decided. She knew better than to try to improve on it. Turning slightly towards Tom's portrait, she asked, "Do you like it, Tom?"

Was it the lighting, or did Tom actually wink back at her? Sarah laughed at the thought. Satisfied, she closed the shutter, and then waving to all three of her loves, she closed up shop. After a snack, she flopped across her bed and fell directly into the arms of her dreams.

Chapter Twenty-Two

All day Saturday had been exceptionally busy for Thorn and Angel. Their once animated conversation had finally dwindled down to a comfortable silence as they sat huddled closely on the buckboard seat of the wagon. Everything Thorn was taking with him to the training camp had been carefully packed in the confines of the wagon. Snuggling closer, Angel wound her hand through his shirt so she could link her arm in his.

"I'm so glad you agreed to stay with us this last week, Thorn."

"Shoot, it was generous of your dad to invite me. I was kind of surprised last weekend when he made the offer. Did you put him up to it?" Thorn looked over at Angel to catch her eye.

"No, Thorn. Cross my heart and hope to die. We had never discussed it. I was as surprised as you." Her wide-eyed look of innocence told him that Angel was telling the truth.

"I guess it must have been Sarah's influence then," Thorn chuckled to himself. "Sarah has been scheming to get us together for a year, Angel."

Angel laughed. "Oh, how well I know. She has been giving me pep talks since the day after I first met you."

"Well, they must have worked, because here we are...engaged to be married."

Thorn smiled at her in genuine delight. "She is so beautiful," he thought to himself as he took in Angel's cheekbone structure and flawless skin. "I hope we'll be able to have some private time together, Angel," Thorn voiced his concern.

"Oh, Dad will be in Wilmington working all week. Sarah's always sewing and cooking. I think I'll have plenty of time to sneak over to the guesthouse," Angel added with a big smile.

"Or we could always go on another picnic," Thorn offered with a big grin on his face.

"Oh, now that's a great idea!" Angel commented, nodding her head in agreement. Angel still had every moment of that famous picnic afternoon etched in her brain. Even now, just thinking about the sensuality of the day made shivers go up and down her spine. Without thinking, she moved closer to Thorn.

"Uh huh. What's this? Trying to seduce me again?" Thorn teased.

"Me? I wasn't the one who seduced you, Thorn! You seduced me!" Angel replied in mock indignation.

"Right! I did seduce you, Angel, and I thoroughly enjoyed every second of that afternoon." Thorn laughed. "As I recall, I really didn't get a lot of opposition."

Angel threw her head back and laughed long and hard. "You're right, Thorn. I was enjoying every touch and thrust."

"Wow! What an afternoon." Their laughter echoed through the trees and down into the hollow. Two lovers, just doing what lovers always do, seizing the moment so that they could have their memories to hold onto forever.

144

Thorn would be leaving to join his volunteer regiment in a week, and neither of the two knew when they would see each other again, if ever. All they had was this precious little time to make a whole lifetime of memories.

The wagon rumbled down the path, steadily nearing Angel's home. Lost in thought, each of them drifted back to the magical afternoon picnic when their passions had had their way, and their lovemaking had left them both shaken to the core. The whinnying of the horse broke the blissful memory as she hastened her step in recognition of her road home.

"We're here at last!" Angel announced. "Home sweet home."

"I hope Sarah has something wonderful to eat," Thorn mused.

"Oh, you men! All you think about is eating!" Angel retorted with laughter.

"You're wrong there! There's one other thing we think about a lot, especially when there's a beautiful girl next to us." Thorn put his arm around her to pull her closer. "Make no mistake about this. I love you, Miss Angel." With that, he planted a kiss on her cheek. Angel smiled back at him.

"Let's make these last days wonderful ones."

"I agree," Thorn stated. He turned his attention toward making the turn into the guest house driveway.

"Hey, you two!" Tom called from the front porch. "Sarah's fixed a wonderful supper for us. Come on over and eat and then we'll unload the wagon later. Just unharness Winnie and send her to the barn."

"Okay, Dad."

"Okay, Sir. We'll be right over."

"See, you got your wish, Thorn. Sarah's done some cooking."

"Oh, thank God. I'm starved!"

Soon Winnie was on her way to the barn for a much-needed rest, and hand in hand, Angel and Thorn strolled toward the homestead. A whiff of savory stew filled their nostrils.

"Ah, it's her Brunswick stew!" Angel announced, with a grin.

"I love Brunswick stew," Thorn replied with an anticipatory look.

Lifting her nostrils upward, Angel announced after one big sniff, "And a seven-layer chocolate cake, too!"

"Ah, I've just died and gone to heaven," Thorn concluded.

Holding the door for Angel, they headed to the kitchen. Sarah, apron-clad, had tendrils escaping from the ponytail that she had hastily concocted that morning. Tom was relaxing with a glass of wine at the kitchen table, watching Sarah put the finishing touches on the meal.

"Garden salad first, then the stew, and finally the cake," she announced invitingly as she hugged Angel first and then Thorn. "Welcome, Thorn. We're glad to have you stay with us. I'll do my best to fatten you up before you leave."

"Glass of wine?" Tom offered as he shook Thorn's hand in welcome.

"Don't mind if I do, Sir."

"Come into the dining room with me, and I'll fix you right up," Tom commanded.

Angel slipped her arm around Sarah's waist. "Thanks, Sarah, for your wonderful gestures of love."

"Oh, you're my girl. You know that, Angel. There's nothing I wouldn't do for you." With that announcement, Sarah kissed Angel's forehead. With a twinkle in her eye, Sarah whispered, "There's something else I'm going to do for you."

"What?" Angel mumbled.

"Disappear a lot these next few days!" Both women howled in laughter, and Angel blushed.

"What's so funny?" Tom inquired, as the guys returned.

"Nothing," Angel answered quickly. "What can I do to help you, Sarah?"

"Get the chaffing dishes from the dining room."

"When do you ship out, Thorn?" Tom inquired.

"One week from today."

"Hmm. That's not much time, Son."

"I know. Angel and I were talking about that riding home today. I want to take this opportunity to thank you for allowing me to stay in the guest house so that I don't have to ride back and forth each day to see Angel."

"Glad for you to stay. Who's tending to your farm?"

"My house manager and her husband will tend to the animals and keep the home fires burning." Thorn smiled back at him. "I have complete trust in Bernadette and Fred."

"You're a lucky young man in many ways, Thorn, yet I've always said that we tend to make our own luck." [14]

"Okay, boys, let's eat," Sarah called from the dining room. Both men immediately jumped to attention and rushed there. Fresh pink napkins, gathered in silver napkin rings, lay across the flowered china. Large goblets held fresh-brewed sweet tea with a sprig of mint from Sarah's herb garden. The garden salads were to the left of the plates, awaiting the sweet and sour dressing. Homemade rolls, delicate and fluffy, just invited the application of the honey butter, Angel's favorite.

Thorn and Tom helped the ladies into their chairs before sliding into theirs. Tom offered the blessing, and the meal began. Crunch, crunch, crunch -- the salad, fresh and crisp, was mouthwateringly good, with its mix of tomatoes, carrots, cucumbers, hardboiled eggs, slivers of onion and fresh bacon. The dressing was just short of heaven.

"Every time I think the food just can't get any better, it does!" Thorn concluded between bites.

"Just wait till you get to the stew. I sampled it before ya'll got home. Just delicious! My compliments to the chef."

Sarah held her tea glass in salute and laughed at Tom's compliments. Short order was made of the salad course. Angel quickly cleared the plates, and handed each person a soup bowl from the sideboard.

"You first, Son." Tom bowed aside, motioning him ahead to the chaffing dish. "And now, ladies." Sarah and Angel fell in line behind Thorn, and Tom pulled up the rear. Thorn ladled a generous helping into his bowl and passed it out

---

[14]

to Angel. Then, he filled Sarah's bowl, Tom's, and finally his own.

"Well, you have outdone yourself. This is the best Brunswick stew you have ever made!" Angel declared, eagerly spooning in another bite.

"Do you have that recipe, Angel?" Thorn called. "I want you to know how to make this!"

"Angel knows how to make all my recipes, Thorn. She'll be a great cook when ya'll get married." With great pride, she made the announcement, "Angel and I have been cooking together since she was nine years old." It was a unanimous vote to reserve the chocolate cake for later that night, along with coffee, since everyone was so full.

"Well, Son, let's get you unloaded while the ladies do the dishes," Tom suggested as he pushed back his dining room chair.

Angel and Sarah were still straightening the kitchen when the guys returned. "Are you through already?" Sarah questioned in disbelief.

"Yes," Tom answered. "Now let's see what kind of poker player you are, Thorn. Sarah beats me every time, but I still keep trying."

Soon the four of them were positioned around the table, chips in front of them, waiting for Sarah to deal. Thorn looked around the room. Darkness had fallen and the lit kerosene lanterns cast a lovely glow on the ladies' faces. The house still smelled of Brunswick stew, and fresh flowers adorned the hutch. Tom and Angel made theatrically scowling faces at their dealt cards, while Sarah's laughter filled every corner.

"There's nowhere else on earth I'd rather be than right here in a family of love," Thorn realized. He was looking forward to his week's stay with them. Perhaps this intimacy would quiet his ever-growing fear that he might lose his life, fighting for a cause.

Chapter Twenty-Three

On Wednesday night before they shipped out, the four friends met for the last time at McGilly's Tavern.

"Yeah Ahab, but you were the only one of us who got caught with your pants down when the barmaid's father returned home early!" John joked. All four broke into simultaneous laughter as they remembered the events of that night.

Nathan reached in his pocket and tossed some coins on the table to pay for his share of the meal as he commented, "What a night! We could have been killed, you know!"

The others nodded in agreement as they counted out their coins for the bill settlement.

Their farewell dinner had been great, filled with genuine laughter as the four best friends revisited many of their old escapades. Yet, there was a tenseness to their faces that had never been there before. Each man was dreading what came next – the final goodbyes. Men weren't supposed to cry, or so they said.

Darkness engulfed them as soon as they stepped from the boisterousness of the tavern onto the sidewalk outside. A thin sliver of moon was the only illumination in the starless sky. Despite the summer season, there was a slight chill in the air.

John cleared his throat and took charge as usual. "Now do we all agree that exactly thirty days after the official ending of the war, we will meet back here at McGilly's Tavern at noon?" John canvassed the group with his eyes.

"How about you, Thorn?"

Hoping that his voice would not betray his emotion, Thorn spoke, "Come hell or high water I'll be here."

"Nathan, do you agree?"

"You can count on me, John." Nathan affirmed.

"Ahab, are you OK with this?"

Ahab stuck out his chest and took time to hook his thumbs into his overalls before answering. "Now you know I'm a ladies man, John. The women probably won't want to let me go long enough to come to your meeting. But for old time's sake, I guess I'll be there."

Everyone burst into laughter, thankful for the easing of the tension. Ahab could always be counted on for a funny comment.

"Can I take that as a 'yes', Ahab?" John joked back with a smile.

Ahab nodded.

"And I promise that I will be here to celebrate the end of the war with victory for the South," John concluded.

Though the words had not been expressed, each man knew deep in his soul that there was a chance they may never see each other again. Ahab rescued the awkwardness of the situation. "Since I will be staying here, I will be happy to help out with your families in your absence. Never doubt for a minute that I will be praying for you."

Ahab addressed Thorn first. "Travel well, my friend." He engulfed Thorn in a big bear hug and hoped that no one had seen his tears.

Turning to John, he smiled, "I know that you will make us proud at the Confederate Headquarters. Bring our boys back safely."

After hugging John, Ahab moved on to Nathan. "I predict that you will command your own regiment before the war is over." After Nathan's goodbye hug, he turned back to the group. "Now if you will excuse me, I have a lady friend keeping a bed warm for me."

With a quick turn, he gave a final wave of his hand, hoping that their laughter would camouflage his gut wrenching sobs.

The trio placed their hands together in one last gesture of friendship. "May we all return safely," John affirmed.

With one last embrace, each man stepped out of the circle of safety and love and into a future with great uncertainty.

None of them were headed to the same destination that night, but they all shared one thing in common. They wished they could turn the hands of time back to the carefree life they had shared a few months ago before North Carolina seceded from the Union.

Thorn thought that the farewell dinner at McGilly's this week with his three best friends had been the most gut wrenching sadness he had ever experienced, but now, the emotional family farewells were proving to be even worse. Sarah, barely choking back her tears, handed over a huge sack loaded with home-cooked goodies that she had made for his trip. Tom presented Thorn with an initialed, leather bound journal and a box of pencils. With their final well wishes and goodbye hugs, Sarah and Tom retreated inside.

Cupping her face in his hands, Thorn confided, "I want you to know that I love you, Angel, and I will carry your memory with me everyday. Don't worry, I'll come back, I promise, and we'll grow old together."

"Oh, Thorn!" Angel flung herself into his arms and cried like a baby. "I love you so, and I'll pray for your safety everyday."

With one more passionate kiss, Thorn mounted his horse and headed west. At the turn, he looked back with a final wave, and then moved closer to his destiny.

In Wilmington, on the same day, John was saying his farewells. "Thank you, Mother Mintz, for allowing Natalie to move back in with you while I'm gone," John spoke with barely veiled emotion.

"Oh, John! I pray for all of you who have answered the call. I know that you will be safer in Richmond, but at some point, the Yankees will try to take over our new seat of government, and I worry about that." She dabbed her eyes with her freshly-starched handkerchief. With a last kiss on John's cheek, she discretely withdrew to the back of the platform, so that John and Natalie could say their goodbyes.

Natalie threw herself into John's arms. "Oh, John," she sobbed, "what will I do without you?"

"Now, now, Natalie, I've promised you that I will come home to you!" John spoke with certainty that he didn't feel inside. He knew what the price of war could be. "I'll telegram you as soon as I reach Headquarters. I love you with all my heart!"

One more kiss sealed his love. Grabbing his suitcase, he rushed to jump on the train which was slowly chugging forward.

As the train pulled away, John committed to memory the picture of Natalie waving goodbye, so beautiful and proud, even in despair. After all, John had great reason to return home, Natalie thought that she was pregnant.

At Nathan's plantation, the emotions were running high, also.

"Now, you write me as often as you can!" his mother urged, as she handed the food she had cooked to Nathan.

"I've asked God to watch over you, Son!" Mr. Summerfield added, as he shook hands with Nathan.

"I'll be back! Don't worry!" Nathan called, as he turned his horse's head to the west.

"Thank God, Thorn will be there with me," Nathan thought. "Otherwise, I'd be a lot more scared."

In just three hours, John arrived in Richmond, Virginia where he took a buggy from the train station to the Confederate Headquarters.

Jefferson Davis's Richmond headquarters wasn't as elaborate as John had expected, but the man himself was larger than life. As they were introduced, John noticed his direct eye-to-eye contact, as if he were genuinely interested in every word John had to say.

"Sit down, John." The President lifted his hand toward a large chair across from his desk. Even on this sultry day, his aristocratic apparel was impeccable. He cut a handsome figure with his silver gray hair and beard and his slender frame. His desk -- bare except for a lantern, quill pen, and a few papers -- openly declared his insistence on neatness and swift action.

"What I need is a man of your caliber to draw up documents and declarations within the hour. The wording must be in legal correctness, but it also must be written in clear, concise language. I have no problem knowing exactly what I want to say or do, but I don't have the time for the proper presentation. This is where you could come in. Could you become my right-hand man in this way?"

"I am both honored to be of service and dedicated to the Cause, Sir," John responded with truth.

"One caution," Mr. Davis's tone became more commanding, "never assume you know what I want to say. Ask me if you are hesitant about the wording. Is that clear?" His eyes bore directly into John.

"Yes, Sir. I will do my best." John felt like saluting as he answered, but he was still a civilian.

Calling to the lieutenant stationed outside the door, Mr. Davis announced, "Take Mr. Thompson to Supply for his uniform and swearing in.

John rose and extended his hand. "Thank you, Sir.....ah...for this opportunity to serve."

"Welcome to the Confederate Army." With that, Mr. Davis sat down, grabbing the paper waiting on his desk for his perusal. The lieutenant, crisp and official in his uniform, ushered John from the room with military precision.

In three minutes flat, John's life took a three hundred and sixty degree turn, from civilian to enlisted man. John had privately wondered if his decision to work for Jefferson Davis was the right choice, but it was too late now. He was an official member of the Confederate Army.

Volunteer Army Training Camp
July 1861

Chapter Twenty-Four

Huge clouds of dust particles were being kicked up from the dry, sandy path as each enlistee reached the designated spot. Twenty-five men were already in various stages of settling in as more trickled in from all directions. Squatters Ridge was central to New Hanover and Brunswick Counties, and it had been designated as the location for the newly-forming North Carolina volunteer militia. Hitching posts had been positioned all around the large pasture for convenient tie-ups. As Thorn was dismounting, he was surprised to see tents off in the distance. They were strange looking tents, almost similar to a teepee with what he guessed was a twelve-foot high mast in the center.

Thorn watered his horse and put a feedbag on her before looking around to find Nathan. They were to meet here around noon. Unbeknownst to Thorn, in one of those larger tents, the cook was putting his finishing touches on his headquarters.

"Throw me those bags of flour from the wagon, Tom." The huge slave easily hoisted a fifty-pound bag on each shoulder and deposited them in the corner of the tent. Next, came the rice bundles, followed by the cornmeal. Enormous caldrons had been stacked outside the tent in the fire pit area that the slave had dug earlier. A huge pig was being slow-cooked over the fire. Bowls, plates, cups and utensils were stacked in yet another corner of the tent. The scene resembled that of a jigsaw puzzle with lots of puzzle pieces, but soon each piece would fit perfectly, and by suppertime, a mess hall would magically appear to feed the growing number of men.

In another tent, medical supplies were being logged in. Unguents, ointments, salves, chloroforms, bandages, gauze, alcohol, iodine, and splints covered two long tables. Five steamer trunks with lift-out shelving were ready to house the supplies once they were categorized and labeled. Lieutenant Gage figured that it was better to be safe than sorry, even in the training camps at times there were broken bones or appendectomies.

One of his friends, Fred Dickinson, a retired doctor, had volunteered to help out during the two-week training sessions. Popup cots were being assembled inside the tent for any first-aid emergency.

"I thought I had retired you," Doc Dickinson lovingly uttered as he found his tattered, black medical bag that he had carried for thirty long years. Carefully, he repacked his bag with the necessities in case there was an on-the-spot emergency.

"Feels good to be useful again," Doc thought to himself, and he was glad that he had let Lieutenant Gage talk him into helping with the training camp. Gage and his two assistants had been readying the camp for two weeks before the enlistees arrived. Not a fan of confusion, Gage wanted everything to work like clockwork for his volunteers. "Get them trained right from day one" was his motto.

Twelve men would be able to sleep in each Sibley tent, but the commander knew that most of the men, especially the hunters, would prefer to stretch out on a blanket under the stars. Either way, he planned to work them hard all day so that there would not be any complaints about turning in early.

The smell of the newly sprouting grass on the open field permeated the air, while the bees buzzed lazily around the scattering of wild flowers. Thorn shifted uneasily from one foot to the other; waiting had never been one of his virtues. Nathan was in avid conversation with a friend across the way.

Suddenly, a tall, rugged looking man briskly strode toward the assembled group. This was the first time Thorn had seen the complete Confederate Calvary uniform. Steel blue it was with gold buttons on the coat which had red trimming on the outside of the placard. A cap completed the look with its decorated bill. Noting the sweat on the commander's face, Thorn wondered if the material was appropriate for the somewhat warm afternoon.

"Morning, men. I'm Lieutenant Gage. I'd like to welcome each of you to my regiment. This will be called the Sixty-fourth Regiment, and I suspect most of us live in or around the New Hanover and Brunswick area; am I right?" He looked over the crowd, finding one lone hand. "You, sir?" he inquired of the youngish looking boy.

"Dave Addison, Sir, from Richmond, Virginia. I came down so that me and my cousin could fight together," he responded with pride.

"Well, you're mighty welcome, young man," the lieutenant smiled genuinely. "I guess you know that for now you must supply your own horse and your own traveling gear. You may use your own knives and pistols, but we will be issued rifles, horses, and uniforms by the Confederate Government at a later date. Now, just when we'll receive those things, I don't rightly know; however, we're all here today to learn some basic military tactics, both on foot and in the saddle."

Looking down at his list, the lieutenant added as an afterthought, "Might not be a bad idea to buy up some provisions for the trip, cause I don't know when we'll meet up with the main line. Best prepare ourselves this month while we're not too far from home. That being said, Tommy here will be around to get your name and other pertinent information for our roster. You guys, (he pointed to his left, making a sweeping motion) mount up so I can see what kind of horsemen you are."

Thorn untethered his horse, Star, and effortlessly mounted, trotting behind the others. The troop assembled quickly. The lieutenant's wiry eyes didn't miss a trick. He knew instantly that his men were well heeled in horseback riding.

"Okay, we got two men who'll need a little extra time, but the rest of you look seasoned. We'll go through a few basic commands and maneuvers so your horses can get used to bugles and drums from day one. Stay five abreast." From out of nowhere, a man on horseback appeared blowing the first blasts on the trumpet, while another began a steady drum beat.

Thorn patted his horse's flank. "It's okay, girl. It's okay," he uttered, as she apprehensively nodded her head up and down.

"Forward!" the lieutenant commanded and set the pace toward the west. Each man had to pull back on his bridle, for the horses were used to galloping everywhere they went.

"Easy, girl. Easy, girl," Thorn whispered.

Within three minutes, the horses had quieted down despite much snorting and head bobbing, and they trotted easily as the riders tried to maneuver into rows of five across. The lieutenant detached himself from the unit and pulled to the side so that he could watch the men.

"Not bad! Not bad at all," he mused. The fact that practically every Southern man owned a horse and was skilled at riding was the one thing the commander had counted on.

"All right, left turn," he commanded, as he resumed his place in front. All thirty men turned left on command, but there was much confusion with so many horses in one small place.

"Okay, halt. Get back into straight lines again. I'll show you how to make a proper turn. This time, only the front row will turn."

"Left turn," he commanded again. "Now, second row, don't ever begin your turn until you see that the first row has straightened itself out; okay?"

"Second row. . .third. . .fourth." This time there was no jumble. Spacing the turns a little did seem to be the best way to avoid confusion.

Once more, the lieutenant appeared in front. "All right, right turn!" The first row executed the turn perfectly, followed by each succeeding row. Satisfied, the lieutenant led them back to the original starting place.

"All right, guys, good job. Dismount and give Tommy your information while I work with the next group."

Thorn felt funny being called "Mister Thorn", but Tommy was eager to be respectful to these men who had chosen to fight for the South. Too young to legally enlist, Tommy had signed on to be the lieutenant's right-hand man.

As they waited in line, following Southern social courtesy, each man introduced himself to the nearby men, and soon they were engaged in lively conversations about women and hunting.

Thorn looked around for Nathan and spotted him in the third row of the new unit that was practicing. He was glad to have a personal friend in the regiment because he knew deep down that this was going to be a long, hard journey.

In a short while, the lieutenant returned with the second group. "Now, tie up your horses. We're going to practice on foot. I want rows of eight across with an arm's width between

161

you." After some arm measuring, the group was assembled in neat rows.

"Make a note, Tommy, forty men accounted for."

"Yes, Sir!"

"First row, fall out to the side." Mechanically, eight men responded as commanded and moved away from the formation.

"I'm going to alphabetize you now by your last name so that you will always know your muster spot. Any A's?" Two hands shot up.

"Up front," lieutenant commanded. "Names?"

"Adams," the first man responded.

"Addison," the second replied.

"All right. Spots one and two in row one."

"Tommy, tend to the numbering, placing the number beside each man's name as we complete them alphabetically."

"Yes, Sir!" Tommy eagerly responded.

"Any B's? No? How 'bout C's?" Two men moved forward. Thorn figured that McAllister would land him straight in the middle row, and he was right.

When the task was completed, the lieutenant proudly stated, "I know that Regiment Sixty-four will fight bravely and will also return safely home once we've licked the Yanks. Here's to a short war!"

"Here, here!" were the enthusiastic responses.

"Now, turn to the man on your left and meet him. Look him in the eyes and memorize his name, for he may save your life one day. I want you to know three facts about him, and you have four minutes to talk. Go!"

The lieutenant paused while the conversation buzzed back and forth animatedly. At the end of four minutes, the lieutenant's voice boomed, "Wiley?"

"Yes, Sir!" a tall man answered from the back row.

"Name three facts about the man on your left."

"He's married, Sir, with two children, and he enlisted from Delco."

"Good, Wiley. You passed with flying colors. I'm proud of you. Now, everyone turn to the man on your right and memorize his name, including three facts about him." The second conversation ended precisely four minutes later.

"Mr. Latham?"

"Yes, Sir!"

"Name three facts about the man on your right."

"Sir, he's not married, he's twenty-eight years old, he's engaged to a girl named Angel."

"Very good, Mr. Latham. You passed your test."

"Men, you must know everyone's name in this regiment by Friday. Regiments that know each other and watch out for each other survive. It's just that simple. We'll march a little bit now. Try to follow the cadence set by the drummer."

As the bugle sounded, and the drum rolls started, Lieutenant Gage gave the command, "Forward! March!. . .Left, right, left, right, left, right." After a few, quick steps, each man fell easily into the cadence and marched in somewhat good formation.

"Left turn!" came Gage's command. Most of them executed the turn nicely, but a few on the outer perimeter of the line had to quickstep twice to stay abreast. Gage was pleased. There wasn't an idiot in the lot.

"Right turn!" A few stumbles, but the lines evened out quickly.

"Regiment, halt! Now men, continue to meet each other over lunch. Try to associate a fact about each person with the person's name. Drink plenty of water, for we'll continue to practice all day long. Dismissed!"

Thorn liked Lieutenant Gage. He was a no-nonsense, get-the-job-done guy, but with a nice attitude. In his innocence about soldiering, Thorn never knew that not all commanders were as good as Lieutenant Gage. New Hanover and Brunswick County guys had been blessed, and they didn't even know it.

Thorn also had no idea how accurately Lieutenant Gage had predicted his future. The man on his left, Dan Latham, would indeed one day, literally, save his life.

A varied group they were: some old, some young; some rich, some dirt poor; some businessmen, some farmers; some married, some single; but what they all had in common was that they loved the South, and they did not want their way of life destroyed.

As the first days turned into a week, Thorn found himself enjoying the camaraderie of the men. As an only child, Thorn had not grown up with brothers under foot, and for that reason, he found the leisure hours before and after dinner to be both entertaining and educational.

Chapter Twenty-Five

Dumping the large bolts on her bed, Sarah deposited the two other bags on the floor. Her luminous eyes danced with the excitement of her brand new project. Grabbing the French publication with the latest styles, Sarah leafed back through the pages, impatiently looking for Angel's dress. There it was; beautiful beyond description! Seed pearls and bugle beads encrusted the round neckline and banded the tips of the long, pointed sleeves. White satin composed the tightly fitting bodice, which was decorated with hand-sewn pearls. A simple straight skirt emerged from the bodice, while a sweeping long train snapped onto the back and both sides. Scattered pearls decorated the entire length of the train, which was banded with the same patterning of the neckline. No other bride in the whole South would have a wedding dress as exquisite and style setting as this one would be. The creation of this wedding gown was to be Sarah's love gift for Angel. The completed wedding dress would be a total surprise for Angel, who had gone to visit her college roommate.

After Thorn left, Angel had been quite despondent and Tom surprised her by suggesting that she take some time off from work to visit her finishing school friend. Before she left, Angel had seen this dress in a bridal publication and had had a fit over it.

"Oh, my God! Sarah, come see this dress!" she screamed from the den.

Quickly, Sarah put down the recipe she was scanning and raced to Angel. The settee and floor were covered with magazines turned back to specific wedding dress pictures. The two of them had talked of nothing else but the wedding ever since Thorn's proposal.

"We don't have to look any further; this is it!" Angel announced, jumping off the couch like a singed cat.

"Wow, this dress is beautiful!" Sarah surmised, as she took in the details, noting exactly the page and the publication name. "When you return home from Richmond, we will get to work in locating that dress." Sarah lied through her teeth. She knew right then that she would make the dress for Angel. A store bought dress would never do for that special day.

As soon as the Richmond train pulled out of the station with Angel on board, Sarah marched straight to the cloth shop where she purchased the white satin material and decorative trimmings. She even found a beautiful tiara style headband from which she could fashion a lovely bridal veil.

Back home, she poured herself a glass of tea and sat at her desk to begin sketching the pattern pieces she would need. Lost in thought, she jumped when she heard someone at the front door. "Sarah, are you home?" Tom's familiar voice called.

"Oh, yes, I'm coming, Tom!" she answered, running for the hall.

"Hello, my dear!" Tom planted a kiss on her forehead and then hugged her tightly. Pulling away, Sarah tugged on his hand.

"I have something to show you in my bedroom!" Sarah smiled.

Tom raised his eyebrows theatrically, "In your bedroom, huh? I bet you are going to try and seduce me!"

"No, Tom, it's not that – this time!" She teased back at him. Once in the bedroom she handed him the picture of the wedding gown.

"Oh, my God, how much is that going to cost me?" Tom muttered, taking in the high fashion.

"Not one thing. It's my wedding gift to Angel, but it's a surprise so don't you dare breathe a word to her. Promise me you won't say anything!" she admonished, looking him straight in the eyes. Involuntarily, Sarah's hands had gone to her hips, and Tom had to laugh at her schoolmarm stance.

"Okay, okay, I promise!" he answered quickly. "I guess there won't be any food around here with you sewing all the time." He summoned up his poor little boy face and Sarah died laughing at his constant theatrics. Good-naturedly, she announced, "All right, let me pour you a glass of wine, and we will make some dinner together!" Arm in arm they walked into the kitchen.

"Thank you for loving my daughter, Sarah. You've done a great job with her."

Sarah's eyes misted over, "She's easy to love, Tom. You're right; I couldn't love her more if she were my own flesh and blood."

"Strange, isn't it," Tom mused, "that God gave you a daughter to raise despite your barrenness."

"Maybe it's not so strange at all. Perhaps the three of us planned to wind up together long before we were born," Sarah added.

"I have never doubted that there is divine guidance that shapes the lives of men, as you well know," Tom remarked and kissed her on the cheek.

"Well, whoever or however, I am glad we found each other, Tom!" They both smiled, content in the bond that they had formed.

Bringing them back to reality, Sarah asked, "Leftover stew and garden salad or an omelet and homemade biscuits?"

"One of your omelets sounds wonderful!"

"Okay, hand me the eggs, and I will show you how to make a good one!" Tom loved to cook with Sarah; it was such a low key change from his hectic law practice. Even when he was a little boy, he had always loved the intimacy and coziness of the kitchen.

Soon Sarah had the kettle whistling and the vegetables out to chop, while Tom cracked the eggs into a bowl. Life with Sarah was so pleasant in a thousand ways, and he hoped to participate in one of his favorite pleasantries that night. Smiling at that thought, he turned his attention back to the eggs. Tom was a lucky man to have a woman like Sarah, and he knew it. He hoped she knew how much he loved her.

Chapter Twenty-Six

Even though there had been only one quick letter from the training camp, Tom, Sarah, and Angel weren't really worried. The newspaper carried daily reports about the war and the early victories for the South.

When the office bell jingled that afternoon, Angel stood up quickly, thinking it was a customer.

"Well, Hi, Dad! You're back from court early."

"I finished the case, thank God." Tom crossed to his desk to place down an armful of papers. With a smile, Tom turned toward Angel. "I thought you'd want to see this!" He held out an envelope.

Leaping with excitement, she grabbed the envelope with great anticipation. "Oh, my heavens! It's from Thorn!" Eagerly, she tore open the envelope and pulled out the piece of white paper.

July 9, 1861

My dear Angel,

So far, so good. We didn't lose a single man in our regiment at the Battle of Bull Run. That's the first real action we've seen. Lieutenant Gage has eyes in the back of his head, and he keeps us safe.

Camp life can be fun at times. We play cards, wash clothes, and cook. One guy

169

brought his slave. Can you believe that? My buddy, Freddie, can play the harmonica like you wouldn't believe. Around the campfire at night, the storytellers really shine.

I have heard about the biggest fish, the biggest dove, the biggest fox, and one guy even shot a bear.

One scout told us that one regiment had had three men die because they contracted measles. Crazy, isn't it? I thought measles only affected children.

We're leaving tomorrow morning for a new assignment. I'll write as often as I can.

Angel, I miss you so much. Tell Sarah I miss her cooking and give my regards to your father.

I dream of you at night, and your beautiful face stays with me all the time in my memory.

I love you deeply,
Thorn

Angel's eyes misted over as she folded the paper. Tom gave Angel a quick hug. "He's gonna be fine, Honey. We're all praying for his safety."

Later that night as Angel and Tom were working on some gifts for the orphanage kids, Angel suddenly asked, "Dad, why have you always been so interested in the orphanage?"

"Oh, Honey, I have been so blessed by God that I feel the need to give back to my community. God has blessed me many times over with monetary rewards, and I think it's because I keep the money circulating to help my fellow man. You see, money is just a means, or a tool, to use as one method of help. Some men don't have money to give, so they give of their time in labor; such as building, roofing, fencing or plumbing where the church is concerned. I have the money but not the time so I give contributions to church. I think each person should select one or two community projects to give whenever or whatever they can. Early on I asked myself what two organizations in Southport were doing the most to help their fellow man. I quickly realized the answer was the orphanage and the church. Therefore, I have dedicated my time to those causes."

"Wow, that is something I should start thinking about now that Thorn is gone, and I have so much time on my hands. I need to be doing something worthwhile, too," Angel answered, more to herself.

Tom went on painting the wooden train, but then he thought of something else he wanted to say. "You know, Angel, God has given each of us a gift. Part of our job is to find out what our gift is and then use it in service to God. A gift is something you don't have to work for; it's just inside you. Some people are born with the gift of singing, some are born with the gift of playing the piano, some are born with the gift of painting, and some people are born with the gift of designing buildings. Yet, I will tell you this; you will never find more joy in life than when you are using your God given gift to help others."

"What's your gift, Dad?"

"Mine is a mental gift. I have the ability to make speeches in the courtroom, in the church, and in political gatherings that help people understand the truth."

Angel blurted out, "Oh, I know Sarah's gifts; obviously hers are creative ones: cooking and sewing. She is never happier than when she has a project. She gets all excited about the church projects and the orphanage projects; doesn't she, Dad?"

"Yes, she does, Honey. However, there is something else to think about concerning gifts; God works in mysterious ways. Some people aren't born with a loving heart like Sarah. But through a service project, sometimes they find their gift, and that changes them forever. Do you remember old man Warner at the church?"

"Who could forget him, he is there every time the doors open."

Tom chuckled, "Angel, it wasn't always that way. Old man Warner married a whiskey bottle after his wife died in childbirth. He would show up half drunk at church on Christmas or Easter, and that was all. One year, I got the bright idea to ask him to make some flower boxes, since he had all of those scraps of wood at the lumber yard, so that we could sell them at the bazaar. When he brought them, I realized that those flower boxes were beautifully made. I had no idea that he was that skilled as a carpenter. Those boxes sold for high prices.

The next year, I took him a Chippendale pattern and asked him to put the pattern on the flower boxes to sort of change them up. When he delivered the flower boxes, six ladies bought the boxes off the back of the wagon, and eight people gave him orders for more! People started going by the lumber yard to view his work and to place additional orders when they realized he could also make arbors, decorative fences, and bird houses. It seemed that with these new creations, he seemed to value himself again, and he drank less and less. Finally, I commissioned him to make those beautiful boxes; you know the ones on Main Street?

When he delivered them, they were planted with lovely seasonal flowers and greens. It turned out that he knew right much about plants, too. Anyway, the point I am making is that once Mr. Warner started using his gift of woodworking, he was filled with joy again; and that joy spilled over into lots of service work for the church and the community. If you ever need anything, go see old man Warner; he can create magic, and I guarantee that he will be happy to help you!"

Unable to stand it any longer, Angel blurted out, "Dad, what's my gift?"

Tom thought for a moment and said, "Honestly, Angel, you have many gifts, but I would advise you to use your mental gifts. Ask yourself, What do I know that this town really needs, and then go out and do something about giving it to the town."

Angel was quiet after that, and Tom returned to painting the train. Admittedly, he had more paint on himself than on the train he was painting, but he was very happy being of service through the gifts for the kids.

A few minutes later, Angel commented, "Dad, can I have the orphanage as a service project, too? I just love to go there."

"Of course, Honey. That's a wonderful idea because when I die, someone will need to carry that on, and I would be so proud if you would continue the legacy."

"What do you mean, 'When you die?' I am not giving you up yet, am I?" Angel teased back.

His heart felt happy with her response.

"Now, what else can I do?" Angel thought. "What else does this town need?" She sat for several moments in silence.

"That's it! She snapped her fingers in delight. "Dad, I know what I am going to do. I am going to create a park or a type of playground adjacent to the school. There is nothing at my old grammar school but worn out grass patches. Those kids deserve much more than that!" Excitement gleamed in her eyes and happiness filled her heart. After all, she did have her father's genes, and he loved those projects. "Oh, Dad, what is the first thing that I need to do?" She grabbed a piece of paper.

"Well, let's see. Point one, access the needs."

"They need swings, a see-saw, several jump ropes, several balls, and some outside benches." Angel listed each item carefully.

"All right," Tom said, "Point two: go talk to the teacher to see what she thinks they need and see how that stacks up with your list. Then, Point three: go by the hardware store and get the cost of the wood to build the structure, the cost of the chain for the swing, and the cost of the equipment. Finally, Point four, make an appeal to old man Warner while you are in the hardware store."

"Wow, projects are easy when you think about them in a logical way; aren't they?" Angel said.

"Now, the most important point is," and Tom broke into a smile, "how will you pay for the project?"

"Well, I have saved up some money, and I bet I know someone who just may match my funds!"

"And, who would that be?" Tom teased back.

"Me!" Both turned in surprise as Sarah entered the room, "I would like to help by making a monetary contribution, my dear."

Angel jumped up to give Sarah a big hug. "She is just wonderful; isn't she, Dad?"

"Oh yes!" Tom quickly answered with a big smile.

Whatever Angel chose to do, it seemed that Sarah always had a helping hand in it.

Chapter Twenty-Seven

"Hi, Miss Angel!" Mrs. Terrell acknowledged as she opened the school house door. "What brings you to school today?" Pulling the door closed, she stepped outside onto the porch.

"I wanted to talk to you about some playground equipment."

"Playground equipment?" Mrs. Terrell wrinkled her brow in confusion. "We don't have any." She looked quickly at Angel, not understanding the implications. "Excuse me a minute." Mrs. Terrell pushed the door open. "All right. School's out. Little ones first."

Angel chuckled as she heard the quick shuffle to leave the room. In ten seconds flat the room was empty.

Motioning her in, the teacher absentmindedly picked up a doll, a book, and a piece of chalk before turning back to Angel. "These stools may be the most comfortable for us. I can't sit in those little desks." Angel quickly positioned her rump on the stool. After crossing her legs, she hooked her heel in the lower rung and turned toward Mrs. Terrell. Mrs. Terrell's much larger rump didn't fit as comfortably on the stool, but she took the weight off her feet by straddling the seat in a sidesaddle manner.

Without hesitation, Angel plunged directly to the heart of the matter. "We would like to supply some outside toys and some playground equipment for the school children to use at recess. Do you have any suggestions of what they would like?"

Mrs. Terrell was caught off guard, and her eyes misted over. "Why, you are an Angel, just like your name! You are the answer to my prayers. Why, yes! I have lots of suggestions."

Angel retrieved a piece of paper from her left pocket. Spreading her folded paper out, she grabbed a nearby book to bear down on. "Okay, what do you need?"

"For rainy days, a checkerboard and some small decks of assorted cards. I would love to have some dress-up clothes. For outside, some swings, rolling tubes, seesaw, balls, jump ropes, and wagons." The pencil lead moved furiously across the paper.

"Anything else?" Angel asked with a grin.

"Not that I can think of." Mrs. Terrell's voice trailed off as she tried hard to remember items the kids had wished for.

Jumping down from the stool, Angel extended her hand. "Thank you, Mrs. Terrell, for your time. I'll get right to work on this list."

Dumbfounded, Mrs. Terrell managed to mutter, "Who's helping you with this?"

"Miss Sarah."

"Well, thank you again, Angel. This is such a surprise!"

"My dad is teaching me about the importance of service and giving back to the community. This is my first project!" she proudly announced. [15]

15

"Well, you couldn't have chosen a better one!" Mrs. Terrell nodded.

With brisk steps, Angel moved toward the door. After calling a quick good-bye, she hurried outside. She couldn't wait to see the kids' faces when she delivered the new equipment. Unhitching her horse, she headed home to tell Sarah.

Hearing the backdoor slam, Sarah threw the skirt she was hemming aside.

"Hi, Angel," she called. "I'm in the library." In a few seconds, Angel plopped onto the couch beside Sarah.

"Do you have the list?"

"Yes, and it's not bad! Most of it we can buy in Wilmington."

"Good. What's left then?"

"Swings, wagons, seesaw, and dress-up clothes."

"Why, I can make the dress-up clothes from scraps that I have here," Sarah announced, happy to have another project.

"You know, Sarah, I bet some of the men at church would help build the swings and seesaw if we supplied the wood and rope."

"I bet they would!" Sarah's eyes danced with excitement.

"Do you think Dad would help us figure out how much rope and wood we'll need?" Angel questioned.

"Shoot! Old man Warner at the lumberyard can tell us exactly what we'll need to know."

"Okay, let's go into Wilmington tomorrow and buy the small stuff. When we see how much money we have left, we can let Mr. Warner figure out what we can purchase with the remaining funds," Angel suggested.

"Great idea!" Sarah answered, excited by the whole thing. "And while we're there, we might look at some material for a few new outfits for the bride-to-be."

"Oh, Sarah, you're the best." Angel threw her arms around her in a big bear hug.

"Let's make a list of play clothes, and I'll see what scraps I have," Sarah urged.

"Hmmm, we could make the costumes to fit fairytales and seasonal tales so that the older kids could portray the stories for the younger kids."

"Great idea," Sarah affirmed.

Grabbing a piece of paper, Angel recorded the seasonal characters: the Easter Bunny, Santa Claus, and the Thanksgiving Turkey. The more they listed, the more they laughed.

"But, Angel, we could also go over with some surprises for the kids on holidays, like cupcakes and cake, and...just little things for them."

"Wow, that would be great, too, Sarah."

"Okay, what's going on in here?" Tom's booming voice startled the two. The afternoon had flown by as they made their plans.

"Oh, Dad, I never knew a service project could make me so happy!" Angel threw her arms around her dad, as she had done as a much smaller child.

"For a minute, with all this cackling, I thought you two had been in the wine pretty heavy," Tom joked.

"Tom, you know better than that!" Sarah scolded.

"Fill Tom in on the details, Angel, and I'll scramble up some supper for us."

With that Sarah headed to the kitchen where she grabbed her apron. As Sarah's fingers pulled out the sweet potato pie she had made that morning, her mind raced ahead with the fun of creating character costumes. "Thank you, God," she uttered, "for this wonderful, new project."

"Oh, Angel! I almost forgot! I have something for you. This came in the mail today," Tom announced with a smile.

Angel squealed with delight, "Oh, thank you, God! It's a letter from Thorn!" Quickly she tore open the envelope.

January 10, 1862

My dear Angel,

> *I hope that you, Tom, and Sarah are all doing well. Tell Sarah that I sure do miss her good home cooking. Our rations of salt pork and hardtack leave a lot to be desired. Occasionally, we can shoot a turkey or rabbit to spice up our meals.*
> *We're on the road a lot to fortify different regiments. Lieutenant Gage is still the best commander to serve under, that's for sure.*
> *I hope to be able to get a furlough soon because I miss you and love you so much.*
> *Please tell Tom and Sarah that I miss them, too.*

179

With all my love,
Thorn

While Angel read her letter, Tom went to the kitchen where Sarah was.

"Oh Tom, I forgot to ask you about something I heard at my meeting at the church today."

Tom sat in the kitchen chair. "What did you hear?"

"Do we have a new commander for the Army?"

Tom gave a short laugh. "Yes, his name is Robert Edward Lee, but do you know something really strange? He had been commanding in the US Army for thirty two years. When Lincoln told Lee to attack Virginia, his home state, he refused and turned in his resignation."

"What in the world?" Sarah gasped as she kneaded the biscuit dough.

"They say he graduated as a top cadet from West Point and that he's a brilliant tactician. Jefferson Davis snapped him right up."

"Wow, that's a strange turn of events, isn't it?"

"Call me when supper's ready; I'm going to my study."

Chapter Twenty-Eight

"Now, let's see how many gingerbread boys I have." Sarah's finger pointed in the air over each one as she counted. "Twenty-four. Good enough." Grabbing her piping bag, she expertly outlined each one with a white icing line. "I'll leave the nose, eyes, and mouth for Angel to do when she comes home," she thought. "Now, to mix the lemon tarts." Using a measuring cup, Sarah dumped the proper amount of flour, lard, and butter in a bowl. In a few turns around the bowl, the mixture for the crust was ready. After greasing the baking tin, she plopped the dough into each hole. A silver tart maker was secured from her baking bag. Quick as a wink, she mashed into each ball with the tart maker, leaving the imprints of a crinkled shell. In no time at all, she stuffed the tart shells and began squeezing the lemons. Consulting her recipe, she measured out the necessary sugar and cornstarch and set it aside.

A short while later, she retrieved the shells and left them to cool. With the baking complete, she grabbed some iced tea and headed to the dining room where one long table was laden with the costumes. The Big Bad Wolf had been selected as the first costume to be made. Red satin had created the lining of the cape for Little Red Riding Hood, while leftover gray flannel had created the torso for the bad boy himself.

This morning's job was to cut out the facial features for Mr. Wolf so that Angel could sew them on when she came home. Some black cloth furnished the whiskers and the pupil of the wolf's eyes. White scraps created the eyeball and rows of teeth, and an old pink tablecloth was deftly cut to yield the long tongue and insides of his ears.

"Oh, gosh! Eyebrows!" She had forgotten those and the ears. Snip, snip, snip. In no time at all, the two were created. At the sewing machine, Sarah sewed all of the materials inside out, and then turned them to the correct side. "Oh, my Lord, what a menacing tongue that is," she thought to herself." Happily, she pedaled the machine until all eight facial features had been created. Afterwards, Sarah combed Tom's closet for an old nightshirt for the wolf. Angel's closet yielded an outgrown skirt and blouse that would look great with Red Riding Hood's cape. Satisfied, she folded everything neatly for Angel's return.

Sarah and Angel worked feverishly all weekend because Monday morning had been selected as the day to deliver the new equipment to the school playground. Tom, Sarah, and Angel left Southport that morning, loaded down with costumes, games, and refreshments to rendezvous with Mr. Warner who had loaded up the wooden equipment. Mrs. Terrell was to keep the students inside until 10:30 AM so that there would be plenty of time to set up everything outside.

Mr. Warner arrived first, and he began to unload the seesaw and the swings. As he was pulling the ladder from the back of the truck, the Madisons arrived.

"Hi, Tom! Hi, Sarah! Hi, Angel!" he called cheerily.

"Hi, Mr. Warner!" they chimed in unison.

"What's that thing in the wagon with the sheet over it?" Sarah inquired.

"Oh, that's my gift to the schoolhouse. Come, look at it," he beamed with pride. When the sheet was yanked off, the three of them were shocked at its size.

"What is it?" Tom asked, intrigued by its construction.

"I call it a 'climb-about'. The kids can climb on it, through it, around it, or over it."

Made out of wood, the configuration was dome shaped with horizontal bars running all the way around.

"Climb up in the wagon, Tom, and help me push this thing out, please." They pushed and pushed until the edge tilted down to the ground.

"Now, Miss Angel, lead the horse slowly forward, and we'll guide the 'climb-about' to the ground."

Boom! The heavy piece settled itself in its new home.

"You've outdone yourself, Mr. Warner. The kids will love that!" Sarah exclaimed.

"Now, Tom, help me with the ladder so we can bolt these swings to the tree limbs." As the men started on the assembling, Sarah and Angel began stacking the boxes near the schoolhouse door.

Out came the jump ropes, horseshoes, and balls.

"Tom, can you and Mr. Warner hammer in this spike for the horseshoes when you have time?"

"Sure, we're almost finished."

At exactly 10:30, the front door opened and excited children burst through the door for recess. Ironically, they all stopped dead in their tracks, awestruck by the transformation in the schoolyard. The other children came running out and bumped into their transfixed friends.

Mrs. Terrell spoke through her tears, "Students, this is Mr. Warner, Mr. Madison, Mrs. Royster, and Miss Madison. They have provided you with these wonderful gifts."

"Thank you! Thank you! Thank you!" the kids yelled.

"Now, go enjoy yourselves!" Mrs. Terrell called.

The joy on their faces was worth more than any gift Angel or Sarah had ever received.

"I'll never be able to thank you enough!" Mrs. Terrell dabbed her eyes with her hankie and gave them a huge smile.

The adults took great pleasure in watching the excited children having the time of their lives. The "climb-about" was a big hit!

No one took notice when Sarah and Angel sneaked inside the schoolhouse with the boxes. Safe inside, away from prying eyes, Sarah and Angel began the transformation. A beautiful green linen cloth covered the library table. Soon plates of assorted luncheon goodies were produced: deviled eggs, sandwiches, tea cakes, cookies and gingerbread men with each child's name on them.

Angel ran out back to fill two containers with water from the well. She and Sarah had cut up the lemons and measured out the sugar early in the morning. The lemonade was quickly created. Quick as a wink, the costumes were placed enticingly around the room: Little Red Riding Hood, The Big Bad Wolf, The Three Bears, and Goldilocks.

As part of the plan, Mrs. Terrell was to line up the children at 11:30 AM to return inside for the next surprise. When the door opened, a blast of excited kids rushed into the room amid a chorus of "Oohs!" and "Ahhs!" Unable to contain themselves, they touched, fondled, and delighted in the beautiful costumes. Triumphantly, Mrs. Terrell announced, "Rainy days will now be fun, for the older children will act out plays for the younger ones, using these costumes. Now, there are some games for rainy days, also. Here are jacks, checkers, and cards."

Angel called above the excitement, "Now, who would like to have some lunch?" Every hand shot up, and a cacophony of yeses erupted. Sarah handed the plates around, while Angel dispersed the lemonade.

Remembering their manners, each child said, "Thank you!"

Angel finally knew what service projects were all about: blessing others always blessed the giver, too! She couldn't wait for the next holiday that would give her a chance to surprise the kids again!

Chapter Twenty-Nine

"Tonight's a perfect night," Ahab thought to himself as he guided the wagon to the rendezvous point at the marsh. Rain had been drenching the area all day, causing most folks to stay inside and not to venture too far out. Not a peep had been heard from the five slaves who were being transported to freedom. Canvas, the color of the bottom of the wagon, had been stretched over them. As camouflage, straw had been scattered on top of the canvas an inch deep to help create the illusion. The rendezvous point was off the beaten path at a coastal area inhabited by fiddler crabs and scavenging birds. No one lived or fished anywhere near this area.

Ahab had been careful to stick to the back roads, and for further safety a scout always preceded him by thirty minutes to reconnoiter the area for possible problems with fishermen or passersby. So far, eight successful Underground Railroad rides had gone off perfectly, bringing the total to forty slaves that had been smuggled to freedom.

Slowing down the team, he pulled on the reins to make a wide left turn onto the coastline path. Pausing, he gave the birdcall to announce their arrival. There was nothing but silence to greet Ahab. No clouds could be seen in the darkening overcast sky; even the moon had been obliterated by the mist. With only a mile or so to go, Ahab realized that he should soon be able to smell the saltwater.

Nearing the point, Ahab could make out the silhouettes of two of the men waiting to help them. Reaching the destination, he stopped the team and jumped down. Quickly, he began untying the knots he had used to secure the canvas. One Abolitionist waded out to the boat to pull up the anchor, while the other one came to help Ahab. Within a few seconds, the canvas was lifted, and the slaves, frightened to death, climbed warily out, trying to get their bearings.

"Pi-yow!" The first bullet hit one of the slaves in the back. Simultaneously, a volley of shots rang out before they could take cover. Another bullet caught Ahab with such surprise that he didn't even know he'd been hit until he felt the searing pain near his heart. Blood oozed out onto his shirt, and his fingers were covered when he touched the area. Slouching up against the wheel for support, he called, "Jim, Jim, are you okay? Get the shotgun from under the seat. I've been hit." Unfortunately for Ahab, Jim lay face down in the mud.

The slaves ran wildly in all directions, and Ahab could hear them screaming hysterically. Footsteps were approaching from behind him. Four men, Abolitionist haters, ran rapidly towards Ahab's wagon, while the fifth one waded out to the boat to make sure the captain was dead.

Holding the lantern high, the leader boomed, "Well, lookey here who we got! Why, it's Mr. Ahab McGee, traitor to the South!" With that, he threw the corpse of the scout toward Ahab. "And here's your Jezebel," he sneered. "But this time, Ahab, it's your head that's gonna roll." [16]

The steel sword blade swiftly found its destination, and Ahab's head was severed from his body in one swift stroke. Blood spurted three inches from the neck as the carotid arteries were severed. Ahab's head rolled awkwardly and then landed sideways in the mud.

"Let that be a message to you and your kind." He spat on Ahab's face in contempt. "Now get them horses and let's round up them slaves!" the leader barked. As he neared the water he yelled, "Jim, drop that anchor back down and then

---

[16]

burn that sucker so it won't never carry slaves to freedom again!"

Mounting quickly, each man rode off after one of the hysterical slaves trying desperately to flee for their lives.

"Trey, grab Ahab's head. We're gonna stick it on a stake in front of the hardware store as a warning -- No more traitors to the Southern cause."

Bang! Bang! Bang! The door shook on its hinges with the intensity of the knocking. "Who in the world could that be at 7:30 AM?" Setting down his coffee, Captain Rogers unbolted the door and jerked it open.

"Jed, you gotta come quick before anybody else sees it! Ahab's head is stuck on a pole in front of his store!"

Had it not been for his pale face and terror-stricken eyes, the Captain would have thought Bill Williker was drunk, but he saw quickly that the man was in shock.

"Let me grab my keys. I'll be right with you, Bill," he nodded to confirm the urgency. Locking the jailhouse door, he turned toward Water Street. Bill was already a few steps ahead of him. As he closed the gap, he called, "When did you find him?"

"Just a few minutes ago when I came to work. I hope no one else has seen it. It's horrible, Jed -- horrible beyond words!"

The Captain was not prepared for the sight that greeted his eyes when they arrived. Bile rose directly into his throat. The ground around the pole was spotted with dried blood, and fleshy particles clung to the post that supported what was left of Ahab's head. A swarm of flies feasted on his face, despite the putrid smell that was seeping from the exposed brains.

"Bill, see if you have some kind of a sack in your supply room I can use."

"Okay." Keys jangled and soon the door to the drugstore opened. Bill rushed to his stockroom. Spying a sack in the corner, he quickly emptied out the contents and ran back to the street. Shooing the flies away, Captain Rogers positioned the sack above the head and gently pulled it down. A couple of sharp pushes released the pole. Turning the bag down on the street, he eased the pole from the skull. After he threw the pole down the alley beside the hardware store, he closed off the sack so that the flies couldn't get to Ahab's face again.

Only then did the Captain notice the other travesty. The word "traitor" had been painted in large, red letters across the front of the hardware store window. "Bill, have you got a boy coming in to help this morning?"

"Yeah, Tommy's coming."

"Can you let him start right away on chipping this paint off the glass?"

"Sure."

"I just don't want his family to see this. If anyone tries to talk about it, don't say anything. I need to get to the family first."

Grabbing the sack carefully, he headed down the street, moving toward the coroner's office, wondering how in the world he would break this news to Ahab's family. No one answered his knock at the coroner's door so he walked around to the back. Silas was just turning the corner to come to work. Glancing down at the sack, Silas announced, "I guess I know what's in that sack – horrible business, just horrible. Poor Ahab's family. I heard about it at the livery stable when I came in."

The key jingled as Silas turned the lock and pushed the door open. The Captain stepped in behind him anxious to be rid of the sack. "Put it on the table, Jed," the coroner suggested over his shoulder as he hung up his coat and donned his apron. "Do you have the rest of the body?"

"No."

"Hmm. I heard a rumor that Negro churches had been smuggling slaves out by boat. You might wanna drift down the coast today and watch for circling buzzards. They'll lead you right to your man, unless the tide got him."

"Thanks, Silas. That's a good idea, but first I'm heading out to the McGee's home place."

"I don't envy you at all with that job. You know, part of the town's gonna brand him a traitor."

"I know. See ya."

News traveled fast that morning in Wilmington. By ten o'clock, the entire business population had heard of Ahab's beheading. In front of the hardware store, two men were in deep conversation.

"You know, the McGee's are a fine family. Been here a long time. His daddy was one of the finest men I ever knew. I don't agree with what Ahab did, but his stupidity can't change what the family represents," Mr. Konig announced, taking a long draw on his cigar. He took great delight in the giant rings of smoke that he produced in the air as he exhaled.

Mr. Townsend nodded. "Some people are saying Ahab has branded his family by being a traitor, but I say, let's just put it to rest. One mistake doesn't put a blight on the whole family; that's for sure. I'm going to continue to honor the family and support them in their sadness – no matter what." The church was packed to capacity with supporters for the

190

McGees in their hour of need. No one shunned the McGees because of what Ahab had done.

The minister read the appropriate Biblical verses, and the choir sang several beautiful hymns, all designed to bring comfort to the bereaved. The eulogy centered on the McGee family's history of contributions, illuminating Ahab's excellent management of the hardware store, his undisputed checker championship, and his true love of all of God's nature -- hunting, fishing and outdoor living. The minister was careful not to mention Ahab's political beliefs or the reason for his death, and the family was grateful.

Friends and neighbors came by after the funeral to offer support to the family, but by 9:00 PM they were all gone. As she shut the door on the last visitor, Mrs. McGee forced a smile on her face. "OK guys, let's figure out how we can run that hardware store next week."

Chapter Thirty

Days had turned into weeks, weeks into months, and months into a year. The night was dark, and the unit had been riding for hours in an effort to reinforce the Confederate frontline. Thorn's involuntary muscles continually jerked him back into awareness as he drifted into sleep sitting up. Slapping himself several times on both sides of his face, he attempted to bring himself into full focus. The last weeks had been a nightmare, and were it not for Lieutenant Gage's astute knowledge and intuitive analysis of the situation, the entire regiment could have had as many casualties as the other cavalry units had had. Irritating mosquitoes buzzed around his face searching for some spot not covered by sweat and stubble on which to feed. The army-issued horses were hearty enough when the cavalry had received them, but they, too, like their masters, were beginning to show the negative effects of the lack of food and rest.

How far away Angel seemed at this moment. "I wonder what she's doing tonight." Her beautiful face popped into his mind's eye; the sight of that beautiful, unruly reddish brown hair made him chuckle for a second, for she was always trying to tame that wild mane. Her penetrating eyes peered at him, sending messages of love and concern, and Thorn warmed at these thoughts of her.

The change in cadence quickly shook him from his longing into reality. The unit was slowing down. Immediately all neurotransmitters sent subliminal messages throughout Thorn's body. Caution. . .Caution. . .Caution. After a long year, Thorn knew that survival had nothing to do with weapons, but with the gut instinct. Lieutenant Gage lived by his instincts, and without an official blackboard lesson, each man in the unit had followed his role modeling of listening and welcoming the involuntary nervous system's subliminal messages. It was eerily quiet -- maybe too quiet -- the horses occasionally whinnied, and Thorn noted the heads bobbing, indicating their own apprehension.

Up ahead, Lieutenant Gage's silhouette was easily identifiable as he conferred with his sergeant. When Gage's hand shot up in the air, the entire unit stopped on a dime. Instead of being sleepy and tired, each man's senses had suddenly been heightened. Fear slowly crawled up Thorn's back and he swallowed hard. Gage turned his horse to the right and started down the right side. After that, everything happened in a split second. Two cannonballs were lobbed into their midst, creating chaos and disorder.

A strong, scorching smell simultaneously permeated Thorn's nostrils, while the red hot splinters tore through his right leg and into his horse's flesh. As the hot lead ripped into the tissue, the horse bucked and fell sideways. Thorn's leg was pinned under his horse as she vainly tried to right herself. Blood gushed everywhere as she struggled to get up. Swinging his good leg over her body, Thorn tried in vain to pull his right leg out from under her. In a matter of a minute, the unit was ordered into full retreat. Once more, Thorn pushed against his horse's backbone trying to free his leg. Suddenly, two strong hands grabbed under his arms, and with that impetus, his right leg was freed. Had it not been for Gage's drilled-in command of the responsibility of the man on your left, Thorn would have been trapped. "You must always know the whereabouts of the man on your left. Don't leave him behind." Latham's help had freed Thorn.

In a panic, Thorn accepted Latham's help as he hoisted him on his horse; and off they sped, leaving the carnage of half-blown-away horses and men behind. The middle of the unit had taken the direct hit, while the periphery of the unit was actively mobile, despite the sharp slices of the flying shrapnel.

Fast and furious they rode, with Thorn hanging desperately to his consciousness. Noting the forward slump of Thorn's body, Latham knew that he had to act fast. Quickly, he alerted the man to his right and pulled this reins tight. Dismounting, Latham pulled Thorn to the ground. There was blood all over his leg -- too much blood. Nathan also rushed to his side.

"We'll have to make a tourniquet. He's losing way too much blood." Slitting his pants leg with his knife, Latham gently pried the material loose, and goblets of flesh came off in long strips. There was no time to lose. Tying his leg quickly with the tourniquets, Nathan helped Latham sit Thorn once more on the back of his horse.

Within minutes, they caught back up with the unit that had stopped for damage assessment. Counting quickly, Gage announced, "We've lost some men, but they're not pursuing us, thank God. Let's rest here in these trees and dress the wounded so that we can see who's still mobile. Drink plenty of water and eat what little you have. Be sure to water and feed your horses. Our lives depend on them, and we'll leave before dawn."

"How bad is it?" Gage addressed Latham.

"He's lost a lot of blood, Sir."

"Cauterize the wounds and rig a splint to keep his leg straight. He won't be going on." With those succinct words, he moved to the next downed man to decide his fate. Disinfecting wounds and clearing shrapnel was as common a procedure as washing one's face to a soldier. This was the first time their unit had been directly hit, for the Sixty-fourth Regiment had always been the surprise attacker. The tables had been turned on this night, however.

"Damn!" Gage swore. "Those damn Yanks must have broken Sheridan's line. Thompson, there's a town within ten miles of here. Ride as fast as you can to get a wagon so we can move the wounded. I'm counting on you, Son."

"Yes Sir!" Thompson gave a salute and jumped into the saddle.

Sleep was fitful for the next few hours for most of the soldiers, as the throbbing shrapnel wounds diverted sleep into painful reality. At 4:00 AM, the bugles sounded, and they readied themselves to leave.

Thompson, after running the two horses as hard as he could, finally tore into camp with two volunteers from the nearby town riding on either side for protection. Each soldier jumped into action to help move the wounded into the wagon.

Nathan comforted Thorn as he helped move him. "You'll be fine and back to us soon." Unfortunately, Thorn was slipping in and out of consciousness, but he later remembered Latham's face leaning over him and Nathan's concern.

"Okay, Thompson, take them back and see that they get the medical attention they need. I'm headed for Shiloh. Catch up with us there." Bending in closer, Gage commanded, "Don't lose a single man, Son."

"Yes Sir!" Thompson saluted, but he couldn't help noticing a tear in Gage's eyes as he squeezed the hand of each wounded man.

"We'll see you guys as soon as you can rejoin us again." With that, he mounted quickly, and the much smaller regiment moved out. Clicking the reins, Thompson tore off toward the town.

Thompson swore to himself, "These men are gonna live. I vow that, and I'm gonna get them to safety." Unfortunately, one of the men was already too far gone.

For Thorn, the next days were a blur. Gage's silhouette, illuminated by the explosion, came riding toward him over and over again.

"Angel? Angel?" he called out in his delirious moments. Diligently, the farm owner's wife tended to his fever and to his wounds. While Thorn was blessedly in the throes of unconsciousness, the local doctor had surgically reset the bone sticking up out of the skin. Then he had sewn together, as best as he could, the gaping hole in his leg. Unfortunately, the five men that he was operating on used up his small morphine supply quickly, and whiskey was all they had left to dull the pain.

Sawyer died the first night, and Thorn teetered back and forth as his fever raged. Yet, God in his mercy gave Mrs. McCabe great energy so that she could tend to Thorn day and night, using the polstices and herbs as her grandmother had taught her. Heavily dispensing the homemade white salve, she warded off the rampant infection. Mrs. McCabe had a boy in service, and she hoped by helping Thorn that somewhere there would be another mother who would help her son if he needed it.

On the third day Thorn opened his eyes. A very tired Mrs. McCabe slept in the chair beside him.

"Where am I?" he mumbled.

Coming alive, Mrs. McCabe rolled into action, smiling at Thorn. "Oh, thank God, you're okay." Tears of gratitude welled up in her eyes. "You're safe, Son, here on my farm near Weldon, Virginia. You were wounded in a skirmish."

"And the others?" A sudden jolt of fear shot through Thorn.

"All doing fine. They're being tended to on other nearby farms. We'll reunite you in a few days," she reassured

196

him. She crossed her fingers as she told the lie, but she knew Thorn didn't need to know that one of his friends had died. He could be told that later.

"How about a little stew?" she offered.

"That sounds wonderful," he smiled back at her. Even moving those muscles to smile caused him pain. "And my leg?" he asked apprehensively, trying to feel if it was still there.

"Oh, you'll be fine. The doctor operated on you two days ago to reposition the bone, and he stitched the wounds in your leg up." Plumping up the pillow, she pulled Thorn higher. As she took a spoonful of broth from the bowl, she blew on it to make sure it wasn't too hot. Placing the spoon to his lips, she muttered, "Open wide."

Oh, but that did taste like heaven. The warmth was so soothing as it slipped down the esophageal passage. Eagerly, Thorn readied himself for another spoonful. "This is wonderful," he announced. "Please keep it coming. And, by the way, what's your name?"

"Mrs. McCabe." Chuckling to herself, Mrs. McCabe realized that Thorn must be like her own son. It would take quite a bit to fill him up.

Thorn was sorry when she pulled the bowl away.

"Now, that's enough for now. That rich taste may need to settle a bit since you've been without food so long." She clucked around like a fat, old hen, straightening sheets, pulling up the blanket, and lowering his head again by removing the extra pillow. "You sleep now, Thorn. You need your rest. I've put the pee jar on the table for you when you need it."

As he drifted off, Thorn noted the wisps of gray hair that had slipped out from under her bonnet and her genuine motherly smile. To Thorn she was the most beautiful sight in the world. As the fingers of sleep gently lulled him towards slumber, Thorn remembered Nathan. "Where was he?"

True to her word, Mrs. McCabe woke Thorn in four hours for more nourishment. Stew had never tasted so good. "You use the pee jar, Thorn, while I step outside, and I'll empty it for you when I return." She handed him the canning jar and walked to the door.

Leaning up to relieve himself brought a spasm of pain that punched him square in the stomach. Sweat popped out on his forehead, and he was chilled to his bone. Determined to see the damage, he peeled back the sheets and blanket. The left leg was fine, but the right leg was swathed in bandages. Blood had seeped through the bandage in places, but he counted ten toes. "I must have broken a rib or two," he mused, as he winced at the intense pain in the abdomen area.

After urinating, he placed the jar beside him and fell back onto the pillows. Controlling the urge to sob, he concentrated on being thankful that he was alive and still in one piece. "Thank you, God, for protecting me. Thank you, Latham, for saving my life. Please be with my unit and especially with Nathan and Lieutenant Gage. He's a good man."

In a few minutes, Mrs. McCabe returned. "Good boy!" she announced, finding the urine in the jar. "Now, you rest some more, and I'll have the doctor visit you this afternoon."

From the pillow all Thorn could see was miles and miles of gauze being unwound in a circular manner. The ancient doctor brought out of retirement had a few wisps of antique white hair on the top of his head.

"My God," the doctor announced, "I have unwound enough gauze for you to be a mummy." Near the last of the layers, the smell of the charred flesh filled the room, and a searing pain tore through Thorn as some of the newly-forming scabs came off with the gauze. Thorn thought that he might faint as his head swam with pain.

"Emma, you've done yourself proud! Not one bit of gangrene has set in." The doctor's eyes twinkled as he acknowledged her nursing skill.

"It's Momma's salve. I swear by it. I really lubricated him the first two days."

"Well, it worked! The surgical scars are beginning to heal very well." He peered over close to Thorn's leg through his spectacles, "Good job, if I do say so myself."

"Can I see?" Thorn inquired.

"Sure, sure," he assured Thorn. "Prop him up some more, Emma." Lifting Thorn's head gently, she pushed a pillow down under his back, elevating him. The sight that greeted Thorn was anything but great. A sob formed in his throat. Huge pockets of flesh were still missing up and down his leg, leaving gaping holes of puss and discoloration. Angry looking stitches in dark thread traversed the entire leg from the knee down. Swelling abounded despite the herbal treatment. "How in the hell anybody could call that sight great is beyond me," Thorn thought.

Snapping his bag shut, the doctor stood to put back on his jacket. Rolling his sleeves down, he slid his arms into his coat. "We're using the whiskey to dull the pain and sulfur to keep away the infection. I'm sorry, Son, that's all we have. We've used up the morphine." His kindly eyes held Thorn's for a minute. "I appreciate what your regiment has done to preserve our way of life."

"And the others, how are they?" Thorn questioned.

"Oh, fine, fine. Broken up like you, but on the mend." He perpetuated the lie about Reynolds's death. "Emma will take good care of you now." With a hug for Emma, he bounced out the door with a spring in his step.

"We'll let your wounds air out a bit before we reapply the salve, and then tonight, we'll re-bandage you." That was the routine -- eat, sleep, un-bandage, re-bandage -- for the next three days.

On the fifth day, Mrs. McCabe announced, "We're gonna go outside for breakfast and let you sit up on the porch. You've been cooped up inside long enough." Both fear and elation lodged simultaneously in his brain -- elation at being able to rejoin the world and fear at what it might cost him in pain.

"We'll leave the bandages on this morning until you come back inside." Deftly, Mrs. McCabe handed Thorn the pee jar while she rummaged around in the kitchen area. Returning, she announced, "You don't have any pants so I'm going to pin a sheet around you for modesty's sake, so you can stand." Taking the jar from Thorn, she sat it on the table. "Swing your legs to the floor, and I'll put my hands under them to guide them."

Stars flashed in Thorn's eyes as the hot lava pain flowed through his lower body. "Wait!" he mumbled, fearing that he may faint with the pain. Respectfully, Mrs. McCabe released the motion on the legs and allowed them to just suspend in mid-air, buoyed up by her hands.

After a minute or so, she lowered the legs to the floor. Pinning the sheet around his waist, she moved the covers away. "Now, I'll stand in front. Place your arms on my extended arms, and we'll pull you up. Remember to position the weight on your good leg. Ready?" She leaned down so Thorn could grasp her arms from his sitting position.

"I guess."

"Up we go," she announced as he slowly rose to a stance. Involuntarily, Thorn cried out, and Mrs. McCabe politely pretended not to hear him. "Now, let me support you, and we'll hobble to the door." Each hop sent a spasm of pain down the dangling right leg. Mercifully, a chair awaited him right outside the door, and Thorn slid into it with her support.

Quick as a wink, Mrs. McCabe slid a footstool under his wounded leg. As he willed the pain to go away by counting, Thorn placed his head against the back of the chair. After a few minutes, he slowly opened his eyes to see the beautiful cumulus clouds drifting against the azure sky. Further out he could see a fenced-in corral with a few pigs. The fields lay fallow around the house, resting and replenishing themselves for the next cotton crop. An old dog barked at some lurking animal, and Thorn noted with surprise at the expansiveness of the porch. Closing his eyes, he exhaustedly drifted off for a few minutes.

"Okay, Sleepyhead, time for breakfast." A pretty green napkin flopped in front of his face, and the lap tray was deposited across the arms of the chair. "I think you can feed yourself today." A huge mound of hominy grits was on one side of the plate with scrambled eggs on the other. Molasses covered two huge biscuits on a side dish, and a mug of steaming coffee completed the culinary delight.

Sitting up straighter, Thorn forgot his pain as he spooned his way into heaven. Mrs. McCabe pretended to be watering her plants, but she noted with great delight that his appetite was ravenous. The most skilled magician in the world couldn't have made that breakfast disappear any faster than Thorn was able to do.

The following week found Thorn still in pain, but hobbling on an old cane her late husband had once used and wearing her husband's old clothes.

"Let's go for a ride," Mrs. McCabe suddenly announced one morning after breakfast.

"A ride?" Thorn questioned.

"Yep, a ride. You'll see," she mysteriously answered with a twinkle in her eye. Shortly she returned with a smaller wagon used for hauling horse feed around the farm. "Sit down on the back and slide in." Thorn did as he was told, and she hooked the wagon's pull to the mule's harness. Off they clipped for an arranged surprise for the wounded.

Three miles down the road, Mrs. McCabe led the mule into the church picnic area. Three other wagons bearing Regiment Sixty-four soldiers were already there, and each soldier was in the process of being helped into a chair. When Thorn arrived, he was surprised at the emotions that bubbled up to the surface. He noted that they wept, too, at the sight of each other. Lieutenant Gage had made the Sixty-fourth Regiment into a tightly-woven family unit, and the men were like brothers.

Sliding to the end of the wagon, Thorn accepted Mrs. McCabe's help to stand. Using the cane, he hobbled the short distance to hug each surviving soldier. The pain didn't even register in his joy to see his buddies. A motley crew they were -- Summers had a bandaged head and left arm, Phillips appeared to have lost his left leg, Mullins was heavily bandaged in the chest area, and Thorn, of course, bandaged on the right leg. Yet to the caregivers, they were glorious beings who had sacrificed themselves for the cause. Their losses were temporarily forgotten in their joy of reunion and renewal of faith.

Finally, the hour of reckoning came. "But, where's Reynolds?" Phillips asked, knowing that he had been in the wagon with them.

The little doctor removed his straw hat and placed it across his heart. "He died the first night. We buried him here in our church cemetery." His right hand directed their attention to the new mound with the handmade cross. Raw emotions tore across their faces as they tried to choke back their anger, fear, and shock.

Each solider was happy when the minister announced, "Let's bow our heads for a word of prayer." That way, the tears couldn't be seen.

"Amen!" they all replied in unison, and each pretended not to see the others wiping their eyes with the back of their hands.

"On a happier note now," the minister continued, "the ladies of the church have prepared you a picnic lunch."

"Are you hungry?" the doctor asked.

Thorn, as usual, was famished. "Shall I bring some of everything, Thorn?" Mrs. McCabe cooed.

"Oh, yes! And two slices of that chocolate cake I see over there," he teased.

As they ate, the men relived that night and tried to piece together the snippets of information about the war that the caregivers had heard these last few weeks. At the conclusion of the meal, each soldier stood and thanked the town for their generosity and love. Thorn personally thanked the town, the doctor, and Mrs. McCabe for their roles in his healing.

"In conclusion," the doctor announced, "we have forwarded your names and conditions to the nearest hospital around here. Next week they'll decide if you are mobile enough to travel back to your unit, if you need to be checked into the hospital, or if you need to go home for some rest and recuperation."

203

Thorn felt that old lump in his throat return. Where would he be going? In each man's private world there was hope in going home; however, in their hearts, they knew that the regiment needed them. Worn out by his surging emotions, Thorn was truly happy when it was time to head back to Mrs. McCabe's comfortable home.

Chapter Thirty-One

Five sheets of paper had been balled up already, and the re-sharpened pencil was now a mere stub. Thorn knew that he needed to write Angel to tell her about his hospitalization. But for some reason, that life of romance, love, family unity, and passion lay somewhere outside the ring of reality of the world he lived in now, desolate and alone in a hospital.

The embers of the fireplace glowed brighter as a brush of air ripped by, scattering the cinders.

"Damn it! That's my life in a nutshell," Thorn thought. That tree branch was once so strong and straight like my leg until someone cut it down and reduced it to cinders.

"What do I tell Angel? Sorry, but I may not have a right leg when I come home? Sorry, I may not ever be able to farm my land again, but will you still marry me?" Thorn crumpled this paper in anger and threw it on the end of the bed. Everyone else in the ward was sleeping; he was the only one awake. The other men from the unit had been shipped back home. Thorn was the only one still here in the hospital in Weldon.

"I'm not happy with the way that the leg is responding," Dr. Rochelle had explained that morning. "The outside skin is healing well, but there's too much swelling still around the surgical areas. I'm gonna have to go in again to see what's wrong. If gangrene has set up in there, I'm sorry, but we'll have to amputate your leg from the knee down. But we can't, under any circumstances, let you leave this hospital now with that much infection in your leg." The doctor's pronouncement sounded ominous to Thorn.

205

As he was thinking of what to say to Angel, Thorn watched the fire cast shadows on the wall. While the flames danced and flitted, Thorn thought back to his carefree days as a child, lying in the meadows watching the big clouds drift by with not a care in the world. He thought to himself that being an adult just wasn't as much fun.

When tomorrow came, he would either face more hospitalization or face life without a right leg. Amazing it was that one small second, one small blast, could change the course of one's life forever. He reached for a piece of paper, and licking the stub of the pencil, he wrote:

My dear Angel,

> *You'll never know how much I have missed you. Just the memory of your beautiful smile has kept me going some days.*
> *Hopefully, in a few weeks I can come home for a visit. I have to have some surgery, and I plan to see you soon after I have recovered.*
> *I love you,*
> *Thorn*

"Shall I address this for you, Sir?" the pretty, young volunteer asked as she picked up the letter from the floor.

Thorn awoke and realized that he must have finally fallen asleep last night. "Yes, please." He dictated the name and address.

"I'll be right back, Sir," she smiled, giving him his privacy for the urinal that she had given him.

Thorn was so tired that morning that he had almost forgotten his scheduled surgery. Quietly he prayed, "Oh, God, I'm not a big church attender or a prayer person, but please take care of me today. I don't want to die or to have my leg cut off.

206

I promise I'll be a better person if you honor this request. Amen."

Sweat involuntarily popped out on Thorn's brow, and he felt his throat constrict in fear. "Oh, Dear God, please help me." Good now at holding back the tears, the only thing that betrayed him were his trembling lips.

"I'm going to give you this shot to make you woozy, Sir." She politely ignored his apprehension about the needle. "The orderlies will be coming for you soon."

"Coming for you soon, coming for you soon, coming...for...you... soon." The words blurred, and so did Thorn's grip on reality.

Two weeks later, the telegram that Tom Madison received didn't say much, simply:

"Thorn McAllister recovering from surgery, nicely. Will arrive on Wednesday, June 12, at 12 noon at the railroad station. Please have someone pick him up."

Dr. Rochelle
Weldon Hospital

Tom looked at his watch for the tenth time. The train was late. Angel paced beside him, anxious to see Thorn once again. The railroad station had always been busy, but since the war, trains had become much less reliable. The battles had inadvertently blown up sections of the track causing much delay in normally scheduled trips.

Simultaneously, Tom and Angel lifted their heads as they heard the train approaching long before the familiar "toot, toot, toot" finally sounded. Inside the train, Thorn had been awakened by the conductor, and he was hastily buttoning his coat and positioning his crutches. The hospital cook's sandwiches and cookies had long ago been consumed, and the bag lay crumpled in the corner of the compartment. A middle-aged lady sat across from Thorn gathering her things. They had exchanged polite conversation at the beginning of the trip, but Thorn had dozed off for most of the trip.

"Wife, girlfriend, or fiancé'?" she laughingly asked, noting Thorn trying to pat down his hair and straighten his tie.

"Fiancé," Thorn grinned. "And you?"

"Daughter."

Familiar territory loomed into view and Thorn's heart beat faster. "Oh, my God, it was good to be coming back home." Soon the train lurched and everything flew off the seats as the brakes were applied. Not wanting to miss one glimpse, Thorn was plastered against the window. There she was -- his sweet Angel! That unruly hair had been tied back in a ponytail, and a hat framed her beautiful face. She looked like a model from Paris in her outfit.

Tom and Angel were frantically trying to see all three compartment exit lines at once. Wisely, Thorn had realized that he needed to let the crowd die down a bit before maneuvering the tiny aisle with crutches.

As he reached the steps, a whirl of wonderfully smelling sweetness grabbed his chest, hanging on to him for dear life. Then standing on her tiptoes, she threw her arms around Thorn's neck and kissed him.

"You're a sight for sore eyes, Miss Angel! I missed you." Tearing his eyes away, Thorn acknowledged Tom with a handshake.

"Welcome home, Son! We've been so worried about you."

Angel thought that Thorn looked pale and tired, and no one had told her about his crutches.

Tom had been relieved when he saw Thorn's mobility. Privately he had been worried about Dr. Rochelle's earlier correspondence with a diagnosis of having to have another surgery.

"I'll go get the wagon and meet you in front of the station," Tom suggested.

"Okay, Dad!" Angel smiled brightly.

Tilting her head back, she looked up at Thorn. "I love you, Thorn McAllister, and I'm grateful that you have returned safely."

Thorn propped his weight on the crutches and drew her to him. "I love you, Angel. The thought of you helped me survive each day."

Pulling his arm, Angel announced, "Let's go, Honey! Sarah has a wonderful dinner for you."

Tom helped Thorn pull himself into the back of the wagon, and Angel climbed beside him, nestling in under his arm. Picking up the reins, Tom signaled the horses to move out. Soon the train station was behind them, and Tom headed toward home.

At supper that night, Thorn recounted his injury and told of the great kindnesses of Mrs. McCabe and the townspeople. Then he told of the volunteers and the nurses and Dr. Rochelle's skills at the Weldon Hospital.

Tom supplied what news he had of the war, but no one had heard anything about the Sixty-fourth Calvary.

"Run along, Angel, and get Thorn settled in the guesthouse. I put some shaving stuff and pajamas there for him," Sarah instructed.

"You know, Tom, do you think Angel ought to stay in the guest house tonight in case Thorn needs something? We wouldn't want him to sleepwalk or hurt himself; would we?"

"Oh, I think that's a good idea," Tom nodded, winking at Sarah.

Thorn and Angel were a little surprised at Sarah's blatant statement, but they made no objection. After a round of hugs, Thorn hobbled down the steps toward the guesthouse. "I would carry you over the threshold, my Angel, but crutches won't hold two, much less four legs," Thorn teased as Angel opened the door.

Fresh flowers adorned the sitting room table. Angel quickly lit the lantern and candles, and soon the room had a wonderfully romantic glow.

"I know you're tired, Honey. I'll just run get my toothbrush and my nightgown while you undress."

Thorn was glad for the pajama bottoms -- he wasn't ready yet for Angel to see his misshapen leg. He brushed his teeth and splashed his face before sinking gratefully in the fresh, starched sheets.

Angel was a little shy about undressing in front of him, so she pulled off her dress and hung it on the bedpost. She snuggled in beside him in her camisole and pantaloons.

Thorn smelled the sweet scent of her hair and felt the warmth of her body. "Sometimes we take the most ordinary things in life for granted and don't realize how wonderful they are until we don't have them," Thorn announced in the glow of the candles. Every sense of his was alive. He felt the

210

starchiness of the sheets; he smelled the hot wax of the candles, and he sniffed the heavy aroma of the lilies in the flower arrangements. "Oh, God! It was good to be back to normal again."

"Hold me tight, Thorn," Angel whispered. "I've been so worried about you."

As Angel curled up closer into him, Thorn felt pressure in his groin, and he smiled to himself. He had wondered if his body would be capable of performance. "Thank you, God!" he mumbled before kissing Angel passionately. Totally forgetting the look of his leg, Thorn cast the pajama bottoms aside, and within a few minutes the camisole and pantaloons soon dropped to the floor. Like riding a bicycle, neither one of them had forgotten how to perform the fine art of lovemaking. Long into the night, they held each other in the afterglow, afraid that they would be torn apart all too soon again.

"Shall I call them for breakfast?" Tom asked teasingly the next morning.

"Oh, I'm sure they were busy last night -- long into the night," Sarah laughed, as she sipped from the china cup.

"You look lovely, Sarah, all dressed up this morning!"

"Tom, could I go into Wilmington with you today to do some shopping and stay at the mansion for a few nights?"

"Of course, you can. I'd love for you to go, and I know Mrs. Bellamy would love to visit with you. She asks me all the time when you're coming again. We can take her out for dinner tonight. But why go today?"

"I want to give them time alone. I have fixed two days of meals, and I've written a note that we won't be back until Thursday night."

"Why, you scheming woman! I might sneak across the hall at the mansion tonight and climb into your bed."

"Oh, Mrs. Bellamy would die of a heart attack, Tom, if she thought you'd do such a thing!"

"I don't know -- she was young and in love once, too! Okay, let me grab my things from the office because I've got court today."

Two hours later, Angel found Sarah's note in the kitchen. She smiled, "Uh huh, things had gone just like the two of them had planned!"

Chapter Thirty-Two

A week after Thorn had returned home, Angel checked carefully to see that her dad was in his study; then she scampered softly to the kitchen looking for Sarah. Not finding her there, she ran toward her bedroom. She knocked on the door frame and called softly, "Sarah, are you in there?"

Yes. Come on in, Honey," she called rising from the kneeling position she had been in as she searched in her cedar chest. "I can't find that pink material anywhere!" she announced cheerfully as she turned to greet Angel.

Angel's pale countenance startled her. "Oh, my God, are you sick?"

"No," she muttered.

"Has something happened?" Sarah questioned, feeling a knot of dread welling up in her chest.

Suddenly, the dam spilled over, and Angel flew into her arms. Holding her tightly, Sarah wondered what in the world could have happened. With Thorn home, Angel should have been ecstatically happy.

"Now, now!" she comforted, as she patted her back. "When you're ready, tell me all about it and I'll try to help."

Angel pulled away from Sarah, wiping her eyes with her hands. "Sarah?" There was a long pause -- a very long pause. "Sarah, Thorn wants us to get married while he's home on leave." Angel paused and lifting her chin, she looked straight at Sarah. "And I told him, 'yes'. Dad has always told me to make decisions with my heart instead of my head. I almost lost him, Sarah. I want to be his wife, to share time with him, to try to conceive his child. I figure some time together as man and wife is better than no time. There are no guarantees that he'll come back next time." Angel's words had come out in spits and spurts, but Sarah knew that she had made her decision. There was no turning back.

In a few minutes, Angel spoke again, a little more softly this time. "But I always dreamed of the perfect wedding day and the perfect wedding gown and the perfect reception and a grand honeymoon. . ." her voice trailed into a whisper, and her lips trembled.

Putting on a forced smile, Sarah announced, "Well, Angel, I have a solution for your problem."

"What do you mean?" Angel was confused by Sarah's words.

"Just close your eyes and promise not to peek. Cross your heart and hope to die if you peek."

Moving her fingers across her breast, she mumbled. "Okay, I cross my heart and hope to die if I peek."

Sarah strode triumphantly to her closet and pulled out the carefully wrapped dress, bringing it to the center of the room. "Okay, you can look now," she called.

Angel opened her eyes and blinked the carefully-wrapped creation into view. "Come and read the card." Angel lifted the card --

For your special day!

I love you,
Sarah

Dumbfounded was the only word to describe Angel's reaction. Sarah gently undid the ribbon and peeled away the paper, revealing the exact wedding dress Angel had fallen in love with in the French magazine.

Sarah stated simply, "I made it for you while you were in Richmond visiting your college roommate."

"Oh, my God, it is beautiful!" Gently she extended her hand and touched the tiny seed pearls across the bust. As Sarah turned the dress around in a circle, Angel took in the long train and the beautifully tailored sheath.

"Oh, Sarah!" The tears started again.

"Be careful of the dress," Sarah cautioned, with a smile, as Angel grabbed her in a tight embrace.

"Thank you, thank you, thank you, Sarah! It's beautiful beyond my wildest dreams." She stood there like a little girl, staring at the fairy godmother creation.

"Now, help me wrap the paper back around it so we can put it away for now, and I'll show you the other things that I have made. There are some linens and a centerpiece for your reception."

Angel nodded, but her shaky fingers weren't much help to Sarah. Carefully tying the papers together with ribbon, Sarah placed the dress back in the closet. Closing the bedroom door, Sarah motioned Angel into the bedside chair and seated herself on the bed opposite her.

"The war has changed everything, Honey. Nothing is the same anymore." Sarah's tone held a tinge of sadness. "If you have the opportunity for happiness, then I say, go for it! You know, Angel, you could have a small wedding right here with just the people who really matter to you and Thorn. And then, when the war's over, you can have a big wedding at the church and wear your dress a second time. We could have the whole wedding ready in a week's time!"

"But, what about Dad? What will he say?" her voice quivered.

"Now, you go back out there to that guest house and make your plans with Thorn. Don't you worry about your dad. The only thing he has ever wanted is for you to be happy."

The smile suddenly returned to Angel's face, lighting her completely up. "Oh, Sarah!" She threw her arms around her, "You can fix anything."

"Not a word to your father yet," Sarah cautioned as she opened the door.

Angel gave her arm a final squeeze and bounded for the front door. Oblivious to all the emotional outbursts, Tom continued to read his book in his study.

"Oh, dear God, help me! Now how in the world will I present this information to Tom? And how can I pull off a wedding by the end of the week?"

Chapter Thirty-Three

"Tom?" Sarah called softly, careful not to startle him. The horn-rimmed spectacles perched on the end of his nose always tickled Sarah when she saw them, for they were so old fashioned looking.

With a smile warming his lips, Tom marked his place and laid the book aside. "What is it, Sarah?" he asked. Swinging his outside coat for him to view, Sarah stepped forward to entice him. "It's such a lovely day, Tom. Could we go for a walk?"

"Hmmm. There are other things I'd rather do with you this morning than go for a walk, but we have those lovebirds around, don't we?" Tom announced as he walked toward her.

Sarah held out his coat, and Tom slipped one arm in and reached with the opposite arm for the other sleeve.

"I'll hold you to that thought later," Sarah teased back lovingly at him. "I'll just grab my sweater and be right back."

By the time Tom made it into the kitchen to open the door, Sarah arrived in a blue flash of beauty. A worn path lay toward the periphery of trees that bordered the farm. Weather permitting, Sarah and Tom often took walks in the woods in the spring. The forest was especially lovely this time of year. Great shafts of sunlight illuminated certain areas of the trees that filled the forest. Pungent pine sap testified to spring's emergence from the icy slumber of solemnness. Little creatures scurried about, celebrating spring's rebirth upon the land long held in winter's domination, while bumble bees in their aerodynamic excellence visited the early wildflower

217

blossoms. Golden whirls they were, flitting from one tiny floral emergence to another. Overhead hawks circled, cascading tiny shadows through the sunbeams.

Hand-in-hand they walked for many minutes in respectful silence of the sanctity of the forest. Tom was the first to break the silence.

"Listen, Sarah." Bird calls resounded through the forest, some singing out invitations for mates, while others simply sang their joy of migrating home once again. Other little feathered creations were grabbing tiny stems and twigs to weave the wondrous nesting for the soon-to-be eggs.

Nearing the bend, they heard the stream before they saw it, bubbling along the north property line. A huge, flat rock, positioned just like a giant chair, ran along one part of the stream. "I'll beat you!" Tom announced, as he plopped down to unlace his shoes and flip off his socks. In an effort to compete, Sarah kicked off her walking shoes and rolled down her stockings. Her shapely legs did not escape Tom's notice. Reaching for her hand, he helped Sarah, who was trying to hold up her skirt and petticoat, step into the stream. Invigorating the water was, but cold, shockingly cold.

After playing in the water for a few minutes, Sarah was the first to emerge, seating herself upon the warm rock. She scooted back somewhat and swung her feet up to dry. Tom skimmed a few pebbles before joining her. Not quite sure how to begin, Sarah decided that honesty was the best policy.

"Tom, Thorn has asked Angel to marry him."

"Before he returns?" he repeated and sought Sarah's eyes for confirmation. Sarah nodded. "What did Angel say?" he asked. Sarah watched the skin tighten around his mouth as he prepared himself for the answer.

"She said 'yes'."

"But what about the wedding dress, the big day, the big party? Isn't that what she's talked about all her life?" Tom asked, quite puzzled by the whole idea. He plopped down beside Sarah.

"Tom, I have already made the wedding dress she wanted." Sarah placed her hand on Tom's arm, gently bringing him back to calmness. She watched Tom's face go from disbelief to concern and to acceptance.

"Well, they're certainly old enough to do what they want. Times are different now with this war. I think they should be married if that's what they want. God knows, Thorn almost didn't make it back this time, and there might not be a next time," Tom admitted softly under his breath. "So, what am I supposed to do?" Tom asked.

"Nothing. Pretend you don't know anything and wait for them to approach you for your approval."

"Well, where will the wedding be? At the church?" Tom had recovered from his shock now and was thinking a little more logically.

"I don't know, Tom. Maybe here at the house or at the church."

"Well, who's going to marry them?"

"I guess Reverend Watkins."

"Hmm" was Tom's only reply.

Sarah remained very quiet as Tom processed the whole idea. A large ant on the rock was carrying a dead spider twice his size. Sarah marveled at his ability to navigate the ridges in the rock. When she thought that Tom was ready to talk again she whispered, "A penny for your thoughts, my dear." She took his hand and held it tightly.

"You don't want to know my thoughts," he fired back with a short laugh.

"Yes, I do."

"I want to make love to you," he announced with a suggestive twitch of his eyebrow.

"Right here, right now?" Sarah asked, looking around nervously. Tom burst out laughing.

"There's not a person around here for miles, and you know it!"

Warming to the thought, Sarah smiled. "This rock would keep us from getting dirty, wouldn't it?"

"I've got a great idea!" Tom announced. "Stand in front of me."

Once she was in front of him, Tom unbuttoned each of the buttons on her blouse. Gently he stroked the cresting of her breast and smiled shyly at her. Taking his fingers, he freed her breasts from the protective stays of the corselet. Bending closer, he traced his tongue around the left nipple first and then taking it in his mouth, he suckled it. Ripples of pleasure surged through Sarah's body with each sucking sensation.

"Oh, Tom," she murmured under her breath. Gently he then moved to the right nipple. Was it the danger of some passerby discovering them, or the headiness of passion in spring Sarah wondered, but she had never been more aroused in her life. Tom knew that Sarah liked for her breasts to be gently sucked, and he also knew that it had always been a turn on for her. Sarah was sorry when he stopped awhile later.

He lay her gently back on the rock. Tom tugged off her pantaloons and pulled aside her skirt. Placing his hands on either side of her, he gently lowered himself into her. "Oh,

Tom," she laughed, "this is wonderful!" Dipping lower now, he pumped them both into an intense explosion. Tom leaned up to kiss her after the headiness was gone, and Sarah enjoyed the shivers that continued to run over her body.

They lay side by side, silently kissing and caressing. After a few minutes, Tom blurted, "My God, woman, it's just ten o'clock in the morning. What a way to start the day!"

"Tom, I haven't been that excited in a long time," she cooed as she kissed his lips.

An hour later, they emerged from the woods like any normal couple, hand-in hand, but with a slight smile on their faces and a spring in their step.

Chapter Thirty-Four

The winds were cool that evening as the five weary beyond measure men sat huddled around the crackling fire. Bo thoughtlessly shoved a long stick into the burning embers, and the others, sullen-faced, had drifted to memories of happier times and places to escape the reality of what had happened.

Nathan, sitting apart from the rest of the guys, marveled at the perfect campsite he had found. A narrow passage in the rock face had opened like Pandora's Box into a perfect, little canyon, secluded and shielded from the rest of the world. A quick scurrying into the contiguous vicinity had yielded a stack of branches to make a fire. Tim had volunteered to tether and water the horses, while Jason cleared a space for the fire near the back of the canyon wall. Tex had agreed to take the first watch and trudged back to the opening. Nearby, the horses whinnied uneasily carrying on their own conversation about the change of events.

Twelve hours earlier, disaster had struck the Sixty-fourth Calvary. . .

"All right, men," Lieutenant Gage had cautioned, "In about ten minutes, we'll reach the front line. General Brandywine has assembled cavalry, artillery, and foot soldiers for a surprise attack on the Yanks."

Yet, tragically, the tables had been turned; the Sixty-fourth Calvary rode straight into an ambush. The volley of bullets seemed to come from every direction – above, below, beside – and, as the men fell like dominos on all sides, only the men in the dead center of the regiment survived. Now, miles away from that slaughter, here they were with no leader, no knowledge of where they were, no maps, and no understanding of why they, of all the men, had been picked to survive. At this point, each man felt a little guilty that he had survived, but he was afraid to voice those sentiments. Glumly, they sat staring at the fire. War had always been reactionary to the Sixty-fourth Regiment. Ride here, ride there, charge here, charge there, whatever Gage had told them to do they had done. But now, Gage's cavalry hat rested on a crude wooden cross several yards away.

Nathan felt pangs of guilt about his decision to bring Lieutenant Gage on the retreat. Buddy check had revealed that only the five of them had survived, but when Nathan came across Gage, still breathing, he made a decision to carry him with them. Seeing Nathan's movement, Tex had dismounted and helped hoist Gage across the horse's flank. Blood splattered on both of them upon impact, but each remounted hastily and tore off in fast retreat with Gage in tow.

A few involuntary moans had come from Gage as the horses galloped westward. Incessant droplets of blood continued to mark the path of their rapid flight. Mercifully though, Gage never regained consciousness. When they broke to rest, Gage was already dead.

Earlier that afternoon, they had dug a makeshift grave with large rocks, and respectfully laid him to rest. Not knowing what to do, each man dropped a handful of dirt on his chest as a farewell gesture. In unison they recited the Lord's Prayer as best they could despite the wave of emotions that overtook them. Here was a greatly loved and respected man, a father to most of them, yet he had been cut down like an animal in a volley of bullets.

Each man then bent to his task of pushing the dirt with the large rocks so that the body could completely be covered.

As an afterthought, Nathan remarked, "Let's cover the grave with some rocks so that the wild critters won't be able to get to him."

"Great idea!" Jason called.

Happy to have a project to divert their sense of loss, each man quickly scoured the nearby land collecting large stones. Within twenty minutes the job was complete. Drawing a paper from his pocket, Nathan then sketched the landmarks because he planned to return after the war to retrieve Gage's body so that he could be given a proper burial.

As Nathan was the oldest survivor, he realized that the leadership had now been placed upon his shoulders. The lives of these four men depended on him. Tipping his cap toward Gage's grave, Nathan promised, "I'll do my best to get them home, Gage." Depositing the papers safely back in his pocket, Nathan then announced that Tex had volunteered for the first watch.

What tomorrow would bring was their greatest fear. Had they been tracked? Did the enemy know of their whereabouts? Where in the world was a Southern line that they could join? Too tired to sleep, each man simply sat mesmerized by the flickering of the fire.

Nathan bellowed, "Okay, guys, listen up. I've drawn a crude map here in the dirt of our probable location as related to Lee's known location two days ago. Our best bet is going to be to ride back toward the front line, and, of course, we will have to travel under the cover of darkness and rest by day. Holt, what do you think?"

"Oh, I don't have a plan, Nathan. Sounds good to me."

"What about you, Bo?" Nathan fired back.

"Anything to get me home."

224

"Okay," Nathan affirmed, "tomorrow we'll scout the area for water and possible grazing for the horses. We might even find a rabbit or a turkey," he added, with a forced smile. "Okay by you, Tom?"

"Yep, "he nodded in agreement.

"Okay, I'll go inform Tex of our plan. See you in the morning."

At the sound of footsteps, Tex whirled quickly with the musket.

"It's just me, Tex," Nathan called. "Sorry I startled you."

Lowering the musket, Tex relaxed and picked up the cigarette he had quickly discarded a few seconds earlier. Nathan told Tex of the plan.

"Sounds good to me," he mumbled.

"Hey, Tex, what's the biggest thing you ever shot?"

"Why, Nathan, I killed a bear once."

"A bear? You are kidding!"

Nathan was all ears as Tex began his narrative. He hoped that Tex had a lot of stories to tell because he wasn't sleepy at all.

A few days later, the five of them joined up with Lieutenant Jamison's unit. Jamison had had little experience in leading men, and Nathan quickly realized his chances were better if he commanded his own regiment.

At that point, Nathan volunteered to set up a make shift camp to train and transition the new constriptees and the new

225

joiners. During the next few weeks of training time, he culled a battalion for himself. Remembering all that Gage had taught him, he emulated every commanding skill that Gage had ever exhibited with his new men. Today, he and his men were headed toward the Virginia line with the horses they had stolen from the Yankee supply train.

Chapter Thirty-Five

As if by magic, the garden had yielded tremendous bounty the week of Thorn and Angel's wedding. Huge bouquets of camellias adorned the entry hall table and the dining room credenza. All week Sarah had polished the silver serving pieces and cooked and cooked and cooked. No one would ever be able to say that Angel's reception had not been top notch.

Tom had stayed in Wilmington as usual for his normal courtroom cases, giving Sarah the house to herself so that everything would be just like she wanted it for Angel and Thorn's big day. By Thursday, the house gleamed under numerous waxings and polishings. Even Tom was impressed when he returned Thursday night.

"My God, Sarah! This looks like a European inn. It's so sparkling and lovely." Sarah was happy that Tom approved of all the special touches that she had done.

"Thank you, Tom." As she leaned over to give him a kiss, he wrapped her in his massive arms.

"I've missed you, my Dear." He raised his eyebrows and looked from left to right. "Are we alone?"

Sarah let out a laugh. "Well, not exactly. Angel and Thorn will be over for supper."

"Have you seen much of them?"

"No! On Monday, I told them I didn't want to see them again until Thursday night's supper. On Tuesday, they rode

227

out to Thorn's place to spend a couple nights, and they returned here last night. Angel would burst in every once in awhile offering to help, but I shooed her out to be with Thorn."

"Oh, Lord, what a time they must have had these last few days -- unchaperoned!" He pretended to be shocked and then he broke into laughter. "I hope there will be some time for us tonight!"

"You can count on that, Tom!" Sarah threw her arms around his neck and sealed the bargain with a kiss. "Go wash up and I'll let you help me set the table."

"Yes, Ma'am!" Tom gave a mock salute and turned to go. "Sarah," he called from the hall, "thank you for being so wonderful to my Angel."

"You're welcome," Sarah called as she bent over to place the sweet potatoes on the stove. Picking up her glass of wine, she toasted, "To tonight." A big smile spread across her face.

Saturday morning had come all too soon. Sarah had had a stern talk with herself all week about not crying and remaining calm on Angel's wedding day. Yet, when she snapped the train on Angel's slim waist and stepped back to see her handiwork, tears flooded her eyes. "Oh, my God, Angel, you are beautiful!"

Angel turned to the long, free-standing mirror in Sarah's bedroom. "Oh, Sarah, this dress is so gorgeous! Hanging on the hanger just doesn't do justice to its beauty. I'm amazed at all the intricate work you've done." Both of them stood there surveying the white pearled loveliness.

"Let's see about the veil now," Sarah announced. Reaching over on the bed, she grabbed the pearl encrusted tiara with its scoop netting. Angel stooped down a little, and Sarah secured it with hairpins. Once more, Angel peered into the mirror, and two huge tears formed in her eyes.

"Thank you, Sarah. That is just beautiful."

"Now Angel, I know your mother is watching from heaven today, proud as she can be," Sarah announced. "Don't think for a moment she's not here."

"Sarah, in all the confusion I forgot to tell you that while I was staying out at Thorn's farm, Mother visited me in a dream. She hasn't done that in a long time!"

"She was just letting you know that she was aware of the wedding." Sarah smiled and hugged Angel. "Now, can we call your dad?"

"Yes!" she beamed.

Sarah stepped to the door and opened it. "Tom, we're ready!"

Tom, resplendent himself in his formal wear, appeared at the door. At the sight of Angel, Tom's emotions got the best of him. His voice broke as he took her hand. "Angel, Honey, you are truly beautiful, a sight to behold. Turn around and let me see the back." Angel turned slightly to the right. Nodding agreement, Tom looked over at Sarah. "You have outdone yourself, Sarah. This is the most beautiful wedding gown I have ever seen."

"Why, thank you, Tom!" The three of them stood there immersed in their safe cocoon of love and admiration that they had woven over the years. It was a memorable moment in the celebration of life and one that Tom would use to comfort himself in the years to come.

"Tom, you two go ahead to the church. I'm going to quickly change, and I'll ride in the carriage with Thorn." With that, she shooed them from her room.

Early that morning, Sarah had fixed her hair and applied her makeup. She threw off her blouse and skirt and pulled the designer dress over her head. "Well, well, well," she thought. "It's still the loveliest dress in the world." Two years ago while they were vacationing in Paris, Tom had treated both Angel and Sarah to a designer ensemble. Sarah had never worn hers, and she laughed that two years later the sleek design had still not yet become fashionable in the United States.

Soft blue taffeta the dress was with a bustle in the back. The tight fitting lapels of the bolero jacket were piped in the faintest hint of purple, but the crème de la crème of fashion was the matching parasol, also faintly trimmed in purple. Sarah's complexion perfectly accented the silky blue. After putting a little more rouge on her cheeks, she filled her lips with a soft pink. Angel and Tom had not yet seen Sarah's dress, and she hoped that they would be pleased.

Hearing the carriage approach in the driveway, she stepped quickly to the front door. A wolf whistle greeted her ears. Thorn, waiting on the porch, extended his arm. "May I escort the Mother of the Bride to her carriage? My God, Sarah, you are breathtaking in that dress! I've never seen anything like it!"

"Wait till you see Angel's dress," Sarah responded stepping lightly on the block step the driver had provided. With a swish and a swirl, she sat the best she could. "Wow, the price we pay for top-grade fashion," she thought. "This bustle's uncomfortable!" Thank God she had the parasol to balance her weight on the ride.

Once they reached the church, Tom had deposited Angel in the choir room so that no one at church could see her, knowing that Sarah would join her there when she arrived. Tom checked the church. No invitees yet. Mr. Watkins, the minister, greeted Tom warmly.

"Quite a handsome figure you cut, Tom."

"Well, thank you, Reverend. You look nice yourself, all decked out in your marrying robe."

"Where's Angel?"

"In the choir room," Tom answered, looking for Max.

"I'll check on her."

When Max Needham arrived, he quickly removed his hat, hanging it on the nearby peg. "I came a little early, Tom, in case there were some last minute instructions. Boy, Tom, you look handsome!"

"Thanks Max. Now here's the list of the seating in the family rows: Mrs. Bellamy, my silver-haired friend from Wilmington, will be seated in our family row, and Miss Lizzie from the orphanage, and Mrs. Terrell from the school. I guess the only one you won't know by face is Mrs. Bellamy.

On Thorn's side, I want you to seat Mrs. Bernadette Walsh and her husband in the front row -- she's going to be the substitute mother for Thorn -- Mr. and Mrs. Lancaster from Wilmington in the second row, Natalie, John's wife, and the McGee's. The parishioners can seat themselves behind the white bows."

"I won't let you down, Tom. You've been too good to our church." Max squeezed his arm. "Now go tend to your daughter!"

At that moment, Sarah entered the church door, and Max's jaw dropped. "Why, Miss Sarah, you look gorgeous!" The open parasol silhouetted the loveliness of Sarah's face as it rested gently across her shoulder.

231

"Why, thanks, Max," she smiled back. Tom was speechless. He knew that Sarah was beautiful, but today she was absolutely gorgeous.

"Wow, Sarah, you look outstanding! Where in the world did you get that dress?"

With a happy smile, she whispered, "In Paris, you silly man. You bought it! Now, how's my Angel holding up?"

"I was just going there." Tom offered his arm and after Sarah snapped the parasol shut, she took it. Together they marched toward the choir room, cutting quite a figure.

Angel was standing in the center of the room, adjusting her veil. Seeing Sarah in the mirror, she turned, "Oh, Sarah, you look beautiful! Is that the dress we bought in Paris?"

"Yes," she laughed.

"I had forgotten all about it. You look so lovely." Angel's eyes beamed the love and admiration that she held for this wonderful woman.

"I have something for you, Angel," Tom announced. "I gave this to your mother on our wedding day, and I've saved it for you all these years."

A slip of the ribbon and a tearing of paper revealed a jewelry box. Opening the hinged box, Angel gasped, "Oh, Dad, it's beautiful!" Gingerly, she lifted the diamond and pearl bracelet out. Giant sparkles leaped out from the diamonds and danced across the walls.

"So this was Mom's. Oh, Dad, thank you, thank you!" Looking up, she smiled, "So in a way, Mom, you are here, too."

Tom fastened the bracelet over her wrist and kissed her hand. "May this day be one of the happiest in our lives." Angel reached for Sarah's hand, and Tom completed the circle. Hand-in-hand they stood, basking in the love they shared.

Finally, Sarah announced, "Tom, you look handsome."

"You do look great, Dad," Angel chimed in. "When is the photographer coming?"

A knock sounded on the door, and all three laughed simultaneously.

"Right now, I think."

Behind a hooded camera a man stood, as Tom opened the door. "Mr. Peterson, I presume?"

"Oh, yes." Setting down his paraphernalia, Mr. Peterson turned around to conduct his business, but when he saw Angel and Sarah, he broke into a beaming smile. Rubbing his hands in glee, he laughed. "There'll be no one breaking the camera today! You are two beautiful women, and I mean TWO beautiful women."

Stepping into his professional manner, he then placed Angel at complete ease as he helped her arrange her dress. He turned her this way and that way to give justice to her beauty and to the beauty of the gown. Tom and Sarah posed together, and then Sarah and Angel posed. Finally, the three of them posed together.

All of the guests had arrived by the time Tom went to check again, and he was thankful that Mrs. Bellamy had made it from Wilmington. Within a few minutes, Sarah was seated at the front of the church, and Tom took Angel's hand. "I know with all my heart that your mom is here to see you."

"I believe that too, Dad!"   She kissed Tom on the cheek.

The strains of "Pomp and Circumstance" peeled forth to announce the bride.   There was an audible gasp as Angel emerged – minus the traditional hoop skirt -- in her beautiful French creation.   Thorn's eyes brimmed with tears when he saw her, and he smiled at her with genuine joy. "My God, she is radiantly beautiful!"   He took in every inch of her countenance from head to toe. The parishioners were amazed by the high fashion of the straight dress and the long train. Southport had never seen such high design; but each person was genuinely happy for Tom's family, for he was greatly respected.

Two of the congregational members, Mrs. Thompson and Mrs. Johnson, had volunteered to skip the wedding and to have everything in place back at Tom's home for the wonderful reception.   Just as the last silver trays were placed on the wedding table, the carriages started arriving. Ice clinked in the finely etched crystal glasses, beautiful chamber music flowed from the porch, and the delectable aromas arose from the chaffing dishes.   The finest chefs in Europe could not have done as well as Sarah had done to make this a perfect day for Angel and Thorn.

Two years earlier, while they were vacationing in France, Sarah had observed the fine dining linens in Europe and had duplicated every detail that she had memorized. It had taken her two days to create these beautiful linens.   As a centerpiece, Sarah had created two lovebirds that faced each other out of the same detailing as the wedding gown.   The birds, attached from the ceiling, seemed to fly over the table. A ribbon bedecked with the tiniest fresh flowers was gracefully hung between the two beaks and played down toward the table. A satin tablecloth had been made with seed pearls interwoven in rectangular outlines. In true European design, Sarah had box pleated the edges of the tablecloth, and secured them by a miniature replica of the larger lovebirds.

"You have done Tom proud. My compliments to you, Sarah. The centerpiece is unbelievable," Mrs. Bellamy cooed. "Everything has been done to perfection."

"That's a real compliment, Mrs. Bellamy! I have been to your parties, and they were magnificent!"

"Yes, but they were catered. This one has been done with love. Oh, there's the groom! I must speak to him about the key." Mrs. Bellamy had given the newlyweds her Wilmington home for their honeymoon week while she would be visiting her sister. To maintain their privacy, her staff would only come to serve at the evening meal. Thorn and Angel were thrilled, for Wilmington had much to offer and would give them a wonderful time together.

At 7:00 PM, Tom and Sarah were entertaining the last of the guests when Mrs. Thompson caught Sarah's eye. Excusing herself, Sarah came over to her. "It's all washed up, cleaned up, and put up," she said triumphantly. "Sarah, you have created a wonderful day for this family. You are just as beautiful inside as you are outside. I'll see you at church this week." She squeezed Sarah's hand and slipped out the back door.

"Thank you, thank you, thank you," Sarah called as she blew a kiss to her. In the privacy of the kitchen, she massaged her back. "This bustle is a pain!" Regaining her hostess posture, she moved toward the library. By nine o'clock, the guests were gone, the fancy clothes were off, and Sarah and Tom were enjoying an after-dinner drink by the fire.

"Tom, it was a magical day; wasn't it?" She breathed in a whiff of the delectable aroma of the magnolias and appreciated the silk of her robe, rather than the restrictions of the bustle on her dress.

"But there's one more piece of magic before the day is over."

"What do you mean, Tom?"

"I think the mother of the bride should also receive a gift."

Reaching into his robe pocket, he pulled out a beautifully wrapped rectangular box. Sarah's eyes danced with excitement. "Oh, Tom, you shouldn't have!"

"Oh, yes, I should! You, my dear, created this day for Angel, so I asked the jeweler to create something for you to have to remember this special day. Open it."

Sarah tugged gently on the white satin ribbon and deftly slid her fingernail down the paper. With caution, she held the box and pried it open. Inside lay a diamond and pearl encrusted locket.

"Turn it over." Engraved on the back were the words:

Love, Tom and Angel.

"Oh, Tom, it is beautiful! You shouldn't spend this kind of money on me!"

"Money is to be shared, Sarah, and no one deserves lovely things anymore than you."

She leaned over then and gave him a huge hug. "Thank you, Tom. Sometimes you overwhelm me with your generosity."

For a long time they sat by the fire, with Sarah's head comfortably resting on Tom's shoulder. From time to time, Tom patted her lovingly, comfortable in the love that they shared.

Chapter Thirty-Six

Tom watched from the window as Thorn tried over and over again to mount his horse. He was able to secure his left leg in the stirrup, but he just did not seem to have the body strength to throw the right leg over. From the pain on Thorn's face, Tom knew that the experience was torturous, and he wasn't sure that two more weeks of furlough would make any difference.

Tom knew what he had to do, and he prayed to God that he was making the right decision. Picking up a piece of paper, he composed the telegram that he would send the next morning:

September 13, 1862

Attention: John Thompson
Jefferson Davis Headquarters
Richmond, Virginia

Thorn McAllister's right leg wound will not allow him to return to the front line. If you have an office job in Richmond, please invoke his assistance as soon as possible. The telegram can be delivered to my law office in Wilmington, 302 Orange Street. He is recuperating with us.

With warmest regards,
Tom Madison

A few days later, the office bell jingled, and Tom looked up from his brief. A young lad announced, "This telegram came for your office, Sir!" Tom walked over to the counter and fishing in his pocket, he found a small coin to give to the young man.

"Thank you, Sir!" the young boy excitedly yelled and charged out the door.

"Just in time! Just in time!" Tom smiled to himself as he pocketed the telegram. Clearing his desk, he put the "closed" sign in the window and headed for the livery stable. "Thorn would get his telegram tonight!"

In his expectant mood, the ride to Southport didn't seem so long.

"Where are Thorn and Angel?" Tom asked, after Sarah had greeted him with a kiss.

"They'll be here for supper in a few minutes."

"Okay, I'll just wash up."

A few minutes later, Angel charged through the door with Thorn and his cane close behind. "Hi, Dad!" Angel called, giving him a peck on the cheek.

"Hi, Tom. Glad to see you're back, Sir!" Thorn shook his hand warmly.

"A telegram came for you today." Pulling the telegram from his coat pocket, he handed it to Thorn. Angel moved closer, and Tom excused himself and headed for the kitchen.

"How was your week in Wilmington?" Sarah asked, as she sliced the meat.

"Oh, just fine," he mumbled, trying to overhear any conversation between Thorn and Angel. Sneaking one of the deviled eggs, he grimaced when Sarah caught him red-handed.

"Why, Tom, you're too old to behave like that!" she reproved, and then burst into laughter. "Will you help me carry these dishes into the dining room?"

"Sure."

A few minutes later, Sarah called the lovebirds to the table. Supper was a lively affair, with a feast of ham, potato salad, field peas, creamed corn, sliced tomatoes, and deviled eggs. When the men retired to the library after supper, Thorn began, "Tom, do you remember my friend, John Thompson?"

"Yes. Very promising young lawyer."

"Tom, that telegram was from him. He's working in Richmond for Mr. Davis, and he has offered me a job at Headquarters. He thinks a man who has been on the front line can help him with supplies, hospital refurbishments, distributions, and equipment."

"How do you feel about that job?" Tom inquired.

"It's an answer to a prayer! I'm no good to my unit now, Tom. I can't even mount a horse, much less ride one in a cavalry charge. I didn't want to desert the army, and, Tom, this will allow me to keep helping the Cause."

"You'll be more help than you can imagine! John has no idea what medicines are needed or what articles of clothing are in short supply. There are very few men with a college education, Son, at any headquarters. You will be more than an asset."

"Thanks, Tom!" Thorn squeezed Tom's arm. "Now, can we have some of that European brandy? I went a year with nothing to taste but homebrewed stump hole whiskey when we could confiscate it."

239

"Here you are, my son." Tipping his brandy sniffer to Thorn's, he announced, "Congratulations on your new job!" To himself he said, "Thank you, God, for answering my prayer!"

The next two weeks flew by, and all too soon Thorn's day of departure arrived. Tom shook Thorn's hand and then excused himself. Angel and Thorn kissed passionately, oblivious to the hustle and bustle of the train platform.

"I'll try to write you as often as I can, Angel. The first week will probably be the busiest, but after that, maybe things will calm down."

"Could you telegram me that you made it okay?"

"Yes, I'm sure John's office has a machine."

Toot! Toot! Thorn grabbed his cane, gave Angel one final kiss, and hobbled aboard. Finding his compartment, he sat at the window so he could memorize Angel's face one last time. Throwing her a kiss, he watched her until she faded from sight.

Clickety, clack, clickety clack, clickety clack. The train's iron wheels measured its forward momentum as each eighteen-foot span of railing was marked by the clicking sound. For some passengers, the monotony of the sound was the subliminal messaging of relaxation that ultimately produced sleep. For others, the clicking was a background noise that eventually faded into oblivion as they immersed themselves in the process of reading or writing.

Thorn, however, did neither of these. His thoughts were happy thoughts of seeing his friend John again.

Almost two years had gone by since the four friends had stood in McGilly's Tavern to say their goodbyes. The war had destroyed many things, but Thorn knew that it had not destroyed their friendships. As truly sad as he was to leave Angel, there was a mounting expectancy within him as Richmond came closer and closer.

When the conductor walked through announcing the Richmond arrival, Thorn pressed his face against the window. There he was, hat in hand, that strawberry blonde hair shining in the sun. John had not changed one bit Thorn realized.

With excitement, Thorn grabbed his suitcase and steadied himself with his cane. When the confusion died down, Thorn made his way to the exit door.

"Well, well, well, marriage becomes you, Thorn!" John announced before enveloping him in a big bear hug. "Give me your suitcase," John demanded as he reached for the handle. Steering Thorn to the right, he continued on, "I have a carriage waiting for us, and I took the liberty of securing a room for you in the boarding house I stay in. Oh, God! It's good to see you, Thorn!"

Some things don't change, and John's taking charge like he always did humored Thorn. He had really missed John, and he hoped John might have some news about Nathan. Neither mentioned Ahab's death, for the sadness was still too overwhelming. They wanted tonight to be a night of joyful reunion.

During dinner that night, Thorn caught John up on the Wilmington news and gave him the home cooked food Natalie had sent by him. Then John explained the job that he wanted Thorn to do. "I need someone to be in charge of shipping – nothing else. The front lines never seem to have enough guns or bullets or cannons. The regiment leaders constantly complain about not enough food or medicines."

"It's true," Thorn interrupted. "We were in very short supply with medicine all the time. Rations were such a joke that we would ransack the dead Union soldiers, grabbing their guns and food sacks. The other way we got food was from the Southern families whose land we camped on. Otherwise, we would have starved to death!"

"You are an answer to a prayer, Thorn. You have battlefield experience so you will know exactly what needs to be shipped, whether they ask for it or not!" Slapping him on the shoulder, John extended his hand, "Welcome aboard."

Long into the night they talked, enjoying being together again brother-to-brother.

Thorn reported for duty the very next day. A small office with a filing cabinet and a desk had already been set up for him. On the desk lay a huge stack of supply requests. "Corporal Edmondson will show you around the building and show you how we have been filling supply requests. Sorry, I have a meeting, but I'll meet you here for supper at 5:30 PM Okay?" John announced, and then he disappeared.

Thorn had no idea how demanding this job would be until he experienced it for himself that first week. He knew what it was like to be cold, wet, hungry, tired – and he was going to help those enlisted guys the best he could, which meant that most nights he worked past the supper hour – way past the supper hour.

Thorn hadn't been on the job but a month when President Davis, himself, stopped by his office. "I'm mighty grateful to you, Son! The lieutenants have all thanked me that supplies and medicines are more available!"

Pushing himself up from his chair, Thorn hobbled around to shake his hand. "You're welcome, Sir! I'm happy to be able to serve the Confederate Army!"

With the compliment paid, President Davis turned on his heel to attend to the next order of business.

With a smile, John chimed in, "He's right, Thorn! You are the best. I know that it's a difficult job keeping up with all that paperwork. I don't know what we would have done without you."

Leaning against the desk for support, Thorn exclaimed, "You know, John, I really have to thank you for offering me this job. I wasn't physically able to go back to my unit with the bum leg, and you gave me the opportunity to feel useful again."

"Useful? Good Lord, you're irreplaceable!" John fired back. "Hmmm! Maybe we'd better go to lunch now before your head swells so big you can't get through the door!"

With a laugh, Thorn grabbed his cane and hobbled out into the hall where John was waiting. He had an idea. "John, is there any way that we could track down where Nathan is?"

"Hmm! I'm not sure, but I know someone we can ask!" After lunch John inquired with a smile, "Did you finish with the medical supply inventory?"

Thorn held up a stack of papers. "I am working on that report right now. I should have it ready within the hour."

"Good man! Good man!" John answered, returning to his own office.

In a strange way, Thorn's wounding had given him a greater way to help the Cause. As a Cavalry member, he had served one cavalry unit, but now he was serving hundreds of units. "God sure does work in mysterious ways," Thorn mused to himself.

It took awhile for the chain of command to answer, but several weeks later, John came rushing into Thorn's office. "He's alive, Thorn, he's alive!" Giant tears hung in the corners of his eyes, and John couldn't control the silly grin that covered his face.

Thorn jumped up from his desk. "What does the report say?"

John pointed to the handwritten paragraph.

> *"The Sixty-fourth Regiment under Lieutenant Gage doesn't exist anymore. Nathan and four others were the only ones to survive the ambush. They made it back to the front and were absorbed into another unit."*

John looked up from the paper, and he was shocked that Thorn was crying openly. "What's wrong, Thorn? I thought that you'd be happy that we have found Nathan."

Trying to overcome his rush of emotions, Thorn cleared his throat. "John, Lieutenant Gage was like my father, and the men were my brothers. I feel like my family has been taken from me, all over again, but I am happy – deeply happy – about Nathan." Thorn managed a wobbly smile.

Before John could respond, Thorn teared up again. "I never thought Lieutenant Gage would be killed. He was one fine man."

John spoke in seriousness, "As long as you love and revere a man, he's still alive." John patted Thorn on the arm.

"Why don't you take a break? We can finish this report later today. I'll come back later."

Thorn hobbled back to his desk and plopped down heavily. Picking up his pen, he tried to come back to reality. The figures blurred in front of his eyes as the tears came again. "Lieutenant Gage, may your soul rest in peace," he prayed. Knowing that concentration was impossible, Thorn gathered his coat and cane. "A walk will do me good," he muttered to himself. So bittersweet the news was.

Outside, he glanced up at the sky. "Give me a sign, Lord. Give me a sign that Nathan is still okay!" [17] The buildings were not much help in shielding the billowy wind. As Thorn trudged along, he offered a final prayer. "Thank you, God, for watching over Nathan. Please bring him home safely."

At that moment, a beautiful plump cardinal lit in the tree in front of him. "Wow, God, it's hard to not see that sign!"

Lightened in his mood, Thorn turned back toward the headquarters. "Somehow, some way, I'm going to honor you, Gage!" he silently vowed. "It's the least I can do."

January 1, 1863, however, brought another tremendous blow to the Southern Cause. Lincoln's Emancipation Proclamation freed all the slaves; suddenly there were no slaves to work on the damaged railroads. Thorn's job became much more difficult.

Supply wagons became the new transportation. Having to travel under the cover of darkness, greatly hampered supply efforts. Slowly, but surely, the tide was turning in the war and it wasn't in the South's favor.

---

[17]

Chapter Thirty-Seven

Rarely did Nathan have to enforce the confiscation law, but to feed his men and to keep them mobile, he occasionally had to ask for food from the Southern families as they traveled along.

Nearing a Virginia plantation, he slowed the battalion to a halt. "Jansen, you and Smith come with me. The rest of you can rest beneath these pecan trees."

Nathan's heart hurt as he watched his weary battalion dismount. Their uniforms were tattered and torn in places, and a few had boots with so many holes the water seeped right through. Bone weary the horses were, and hungry, just like their owners. However, everywhere they stopped Southern families welcomed them and shared what food they had in an effort to honor the men.

Confident that his men were settled beneath the trees, the trio set out to investigate what the plantation might have that could help them.

Pushing back a few stray blond tendrils, Melinda rested the ax. Chopping wood had always been a man's work on the plantation, but with no men the task had fallen to her. Her once expensively tailored dress was now just everyday wear, complete with boots for avoiding mud and aprons for avoiding grime. When she should have been making her debut, she was out chopping wood. Times had definitely changed.

There was no way that Melinda could know, however, that she was both grace and beauty in motion, for there was no one to observe her beauty except a few chickens and one lone old milk cow. Her once beautifully manicured hands were callused from farm work, yet, oddly enough, her face was even more radiant from the fresh air and the slight tan from the outside work.

Melinda's mother labored long and hard beside her. Thankfully, her dad's mother and father had moved in with them on the plantation at the beginning of the war to help out. A few old house servants remained behind to help them, but two years earlier her father had taken the slaves when they were conscripted by the government to work on repairing the railroad.

When she heard horses approaching, Melinda ran toward the barn calling for her grandfather. "Grandfather, Grandfather, soldiers are coming!"

Grandfather Sawyer jumped into action. Pushing the camouflage straw aside, he flung open the strong box and lifted out two pistols. Scooping out several bullets, he pumped them into the chamber. Pocketing one, he passed the other to Melinda. The gun disappeared into her apron pocket.

The two of them were placidly pitching hay when Nathan dismounted in front of the barn. "Hello in there!"

Melinda's grandfather strolled out, relieved to see the Confederate uniform. "Hello, to you, Sir. Who are you with?"

"We're from the North Carolina Regiment, Sir." Nathan saluted the old man.

"I'm afraid we don't have much to offer but some sweet potatoes and some brown potatoes. The muscadines are yours for the picking, though. How many do you have?"

"There are twelve of us," Nathan replied.

"Melinda, tell your momma to rustle up some dinner for these hungry men." As Melinda came out of the barn, Nathan turned to tip his hat, and his heart fell to his feet. There stood the most beautiful girl he had ever seen.

"We'll be glad to share with you all," Melinda responded and smiled genuinely as she turned toward the house.

"And I'll be glad to learn something about the war. We don't get much news here."

Nathan replied, "There's not much to tell, Sir. The South was badly beaten at Gettysburg, and we have been trying to reorganize."

"My unit has been reassigned to Virginia, and we're on the way there now."

"Well, bring the rest of the men on up. They can feed the horses with our oats and water them. Then, they can bathe down in the pond if they want to! There's plenty of cleared land to pitch tents for the night, and I'll be glad for some male conversation!"

"Thank you, Sir! We'll be back."

Nathan wasn't sure whether his announcement about the bath or the food made his men happier, but back on the horses they were in just a few seconds.

Once the horses had been watered, fed, and led to the green pasture, his men quickly found the pond, and in various stages of undress, they enjoyed the invigorating water.

Spreading out various garments to dry, most of the men lay down, enjoying the kiss of the afternoon sun and drifted off into a much needed rest. Others played cards, and a few wrote letters back home. Nathan, however, ambled toward the house.

Knocking politely, he introduced himself to Melinda's mother and grandmother and offered his assistance.

Noting how handsome Nathan was, Mrs. Sawyer quickly suggested, "Melinda, why don't you and Lieutenant Summerville go out to grab some of the muscadines."

Without any rebuttal, Melinda beckoned Nathan outside where she grabbed a rolling cart that was used to feed horses. "Let me push that for you!" Nathan retrieved the cart from her, remembering his manners.

"Oh, tell me how things are going with the war. My dad and my two brothers are all serving, but we haven't seen them in a year. They sent word that they were okay, but that was six months ago," she commented, as she fell into step beside him.

"To tell you the truth, I'm just back into the front line work. I have been training new recruits for the last eight weeks." Nathan set the cart down, and they began robbing the grapevine. As they worked, they talked easily back and forth about Melinda's life since the war had started and how things had changed for her family. Once the cart was full, Nathan pushed it back to the house.

"We'll need to wash them off in this big pot," Melinda directed. Spreading a blanket, she announced, "The clean clusters can go on this blanket." Soon the muscadines were drying in the sun. Enjoying Nathan's company, Melinda suggested they rob the hen house. An egg basket was soon filled, and the two turned back to the cook house.

"I've fixed some sweet tea," her mother called. "Why don't you two rest on the front porch?" Both were only too happy to comply.

The afternoon wore on, and Nathan's banter easily fell into his bachelor days of charming and pleasing. Melinda, happy to have a handsome man around and to have someone her age to talk to, suddenly blossomed into the ability to flirt and to be coy – quite to her surprise. The war had taken Melinda's debut away, but Nathan afforded the opportunity to practice her pent up wiles.

Each was sorry when the call to dinner came. Nathan easily transformed himself from suitor back to commander, while Melinda reported to the kitchen.

After dinner, with their bellies full of home baked biscuits and strawberry preserves, sweet potato pie, and mashed potatoes, the soldiers repaid the hospitality with harmonica playing and singing. Nathan beamed like a proud parent as his men reciprocated the kindness.

"Would you like to go for a walk?" Nathan suggested, as dusk descended.

"Oh, yes!" Melinda replied, with a smile.

It was like any other summer night, but for the two of them, indelible impressions were made. For Nathan, the moonlight illuminating Melinda's beautiful face and the interesting way she had of screwing up her nose when she asked a question would be remembered by him for a long time. For Melinda, the handsome man in the uniform fulfilled her romantic notions of war. Nathan's expressive eyes and face more than fulfilled her dreams of a great man to marry. Hungry for the opposite sex, they strolled along talking long into the night and finally settled on the veranda once more.

Nathan's men noticed the absence of their commander and smiled to themselves. Nathan was the only man in the whole regiment without a girl or a wife back home. The attraction between the two of them had not been missed by Melinda's mother and grandparents either, and they smiled knowingly, being happy for her.

At midnight, Nathan said, "I guess I'd better join my men." He rose from the chair, and Melinda stood to acknowledge his leaving. Nathan felt the all too familiar stirring in his groin, dormant for so many months. Placing his hands on Melinda's waist, he managed to mumble, "Thank you, Melinda, for a lovely evening." Bending his head down, he gently touched her lips with his. The shock that ran through both of them was electrifying. Even the seasoned bachelor was caught off guard. Hungrily then, he crushed her to him in a passionate kiss, and she responded in like manner.

"I'll see you in the morning. Sleep tight." He squeezed her hand, and darkness claimed him as he stepped from the porch. Most of the men were asleep when he returned, but a few chuckled quietly to themselves at the lateness of the hour.

The smell of fresh baked biscuits greeted the sleepy men the next morning. Quickly, they scrubbed up -- Nathan included -- and were lured by the savory smells to the main house. Melinda, resplendent in a new green dress, glowed with last night's excitement, and she made small talk with the men as she poured their coffee.

"Good morning, Melinda. You are looking beautiful today." Nathan was amazed at how easily social conversation had come back to him after these long months of war. Melinda blushed and handed Nathan a cup. As their hands touched, the same shockwave resurfaced, but both pretended they had not noticed it. Melt-in-your-mouth biscuits and sweet tasting corn chowder gave a wonderful breakfast change from the soldier's staple diet of hard tack. The men looked longingly at Melinda's family, anxious to see their own families again.

Nathan surprised even himself as he blurted out, "Men, we're ahead of schedule on our trek. Let's help this family do some things around the farm today and enjoy a day off from the war." Genuine joy showed in their faces as they anticipated the feel of farm life again.

"Mrs. Sawyer, will you exchange another wonderful dinner for some extra hands to help you today?" Nathan asked, turning toward her.

"Oh, yes! You men are a blessing to my family! Thank you, thank you, thank you!" Tears of joy filled her eyes. The men knew that Nathan wanted more time to court Melinda, but they were happy to have some downtime, too.

"We'll work in shifts of four so that most of the day can be yours. Get up the work roster, Gibbon."

"Yes, Sir!" The young man saluted, happy to have a nice summer day off.

In actuality, Nathan had started their journey ahead of time in case of bad weather, so the battalion could easily reach their destination on time, even with the day off.

"Now, what kind of things do you need help with, Mrs. Sawyer?" Nathan inquired.

"We need to pick the beans, weed the garden, till some new land for planting, hunt some rabbit for stew, prune the grapevine, and mend the wheel on the wagon." On and on she went with a thousand items.

"We'll do as much as we can today. What are the most pressing problems?"

"Ah, fixing the wagon, for sure. Then, um, tilling the ground, and weeding the garden."

"Okay. The first four up will do that. Gibbons, see which four men have had experience in that, and they'll do first duty."

"Yes, Sir!"

Mrs. Sawyer liked Nathan's take-charge, seize the moment manner, but she wasn't fooled for one minute about Nathan's intentions. She chuckled to herself, "A beautiful daughter is certainly an asset."

As the day wore on, Nathan and Melinda worked together on many of the projects, laughing and talking excitedly. By a miracle, McClellan shot two rabbits, enabling the cooks to produce rabbit stew for supper, along with potatoes, cucumbers, and string beans. Mrs. Sawyer was glad that she had a large stock of jellies and jams for the eight dozen biscuits that she and the cook had planned to make.

Nathan made sure that he spent a large portion of the day chopping wood and kindling, and he kept a constant rotation of men on the tasks. "Think of me when you use this wood you don't have to chop," he teased. By late afternoon, the stock of neatly-placed stove size chunks was impressive.

After dinner, the two set off again for a moonlight walk. After much conversation, Nathan selected a tree near the house, and he carved their initials inside a heart. "If I don't come back," he said, turning to look at her, "just know there's one man who carried you in his heart for the duration of the war."

Tears touched Melinda's eyelashes. "You must come back, Nathan."

Nathan took her in his arms in a passionate kiss, memorizing the feel of her breasts against him, and the sweetness of her scented curly blonde hair. They clung together salvaging the only thing that war had not taken from the South – love and longing for companionship. Nathan pulled them down against the tree trunk. Placing his hand on her cheek, he kissed her softly. Following her body contours, he kissed her neck and then her chest, arousing her not yet discovered passions. With nimble fingers, he unbuttoned the top of her dress to reveal the cresting of her breast. Gently he traced his fingers slowly back and forth from one mound to the other. "You are so beautiful, Melinda." It wasn't a ploy; Nathan meant it from the bottom of his heart. He had found the girl he wanted to marry. Gently, he leaned to kiss the tops of her breasts and then traveled his kisses up against her neck.

Melinda was shocked at the rising desires of her body to be touched and loved, and she offered no resistance as Nathan gently edged his fingers into her corselet. Melinda felt her groin tighten, and her nipples crested with delight at Nathan's touch. "May I touch you?" he whispered.

"Oh yes, Nathan. Oh, yes."

Fingers of pleasure surged through her body as Nathan slowly unbuttoned her dress all the way down to the waist and pulled her arms from the dress. Folding the corselet down, her upper body was now free. Pulling her down beside him, again and again he lovingly traced around her breast and suckled them, delighting in his and her arousal. They lay there together talking and touching for several hours.

"Will you wait for me, Melinda?" Nathan finally worked up enough courage to say.

"For the rest of my life," she answered in truth.

"I'll come back for you after the war. I promise."

"And I promise to wait."

Bitter sweet it was to leave, but Nathan did not want to dishonor Mrs. Sawyer's trust in any way. He had had no intention of taking Melinda's virginity. He was happy to wait until they were married.

At 5:00 AM the unit pulled out, and Melinda watched sadly from the upstairs window, praying for his safety.

Like clockwork, Melinda journeyed each day to touch their initials on the tree to awaken the memories of their night of love. Many prayers were uttered for his safe return each day. Hope remained steadfast in her heart that the man she loved would return to marry her.

Chapter Thirty-Eight

Sarah had not paid that much attention the first time she heard the horse whinny, but when the noise happened again, she jumped up. All the horses were whinnying now, and that meant one thing – danger. Grabbing the gun from her bedside table, she opened the vault, popping in the necessary bullets. Running around the barn to the corral, she saw the problem. Three slaves were grabbing at the horses trying to attach lead ropes to their halters. Her mare, Winnie, had already been connected. Hoisting the gun, she pointed it in dead aim at the closest man's head. "Stop right where you are! Those horses are NOT going with you!" Surprised, the men turned toward the voice only to find a tall, beautiful woman with a gun aimed at their heads.

"You can't stop us! They's three of us!" the leader sneered. "Ain't none of you white people gonna ever stop us again!" The other two were frozen in place. Angrily, he charged toward her, and the first bullet hit him in the shoulder. Blood seeped quickly onto the cotton shirt, and he involuntarily grabbed his shoulder, stopping dead in his tracks.

"The next one comes to your heart, Mister. Now move on off this property!"

Sarah never heard the man behind her. A massive black arm seized her around the neck and snapped it in two before she could even let out a cry. Her gun dropped from her fingers with a thud, and he threw her down. Forward she fell into the dirt.

"Now git them other horses out of the barn, and let's git going!" he ordered. Coming out of their stupor, the slaves bolted into the barn. Within minutes, they were saddled up, and they headed west. The dust they kicked up hovered in the air for just a minute and then scattered in the breeze like Sarah's life force.

Jeff was the first to find her at noon as he returned from the fields. "Miss Sarah!" he cried and jumped from his horse. Gently, he turned her over and watched in horror as her neck remained in the opposite position. He felt her pulse and panicked when there was none. Huge tears welled up in his eyes, and he picked her up being careful to support her head. Tenderly, he carried her inside and placed her on her bed. As an afterthought, he closed her eyelids.

"God have mercy on your soul, Miss Sarah."

Jumping on his horse, he tore home. "Rebecca, Rebecca! It's Miss Sarah!"

"What's wrong, Jeff? What's wrong?" She ran outside in a panic.

"Sarah's dead! Her neck's broke! What are we gonna do?"

Rebecca recovered first. "You go get Mr. Tom, and I'll go see if there's any life left in her." Rebecca ran up the dirt road, lifting her petticoats high, but she already knew in her heart there would be nothing she could do.

"Why Miss Sarah looks peaceful," she thought. She noted that Jeff had lovingly placed her head directly in alignment with her body so that she almost looked like she was just sleeping.

Jeff was riding as fast as his horse could go into Southport to get Mr. Tom. "Oh, my God, what am I going to say?" He slapped his reins again and again on the horse, urging her to make better time. Shirttail flying, he made the trip in record time. In the meantime, Rebecca had washed Sarah's face, hands, and feet. Gently, she brushed the dirt from her clothes and placed her Bible beside her. Reverently, she lit a candle and positioned her chair beside the bed so that Sarah wouldn't be alone.

A half hour later, Tom found them this way. "May I have a private moment, Rebecca?" Tom whispered, close to tears.

Jumping up, she stammered, "Yes, Mr. Tom. I'm so sorry." She left the room quickly, being careful to shut the door behind her.

Tom crossed to the bed and sat beside her. Even death could not mar her beauty... He stroked her face lovingly. Taking her hand, he spoke to her softly. "No one can ever really take you from me, Sarah. I have your beautiful face indelibly printed on my mind, and our wonderful love imprinted on my heart. I'll always cherish you, and I look forward to the reunion that we will have one day in heaven."

His lip quivered though with the next words. "But, Sarah, what will I say to Angel?" With that, he buried his face in her chest and cried like a baby. A few minutes later, he crawled in bed beside her and put his arms around her, sheltering her, not wanting to leave. After an hour or so, he got up from the bed and stood by the side looking at her. With great sadness, he opened the bedroom door and walked back into reality. Rebecca and Jeff had put together some sandwiches and made some hot tea.

"Ride into town and get the coroner, Jeff, please. Thanks, Rebecca, for staying with her. That meant a lot to me."

"I'm so sorry, Mr. Tom."
"We all are, Rebecca. Now, run along home to your own family. I've got work to do." Tom labored and labored

over the wording on the telegram:

Angel McAllister
c/o Thorn McAllister
Jefferson Davis Headquarters
Richmond, Virginia

*   Angel, catch the first train home. Sarah has been in*
a fatal accident.

Love,
Dad

Tom knew it wasn't an accident. It was cold-blooded murder, but it sounded better than Sarah was killed or Sarah died. The word "fatal", however, would not leave any false hope.

Two hours later, Tom accompanied Sarah on the last part of their journey together. He rode in the back of the coroner's wagon, sheltering her from the darkness. Blame had already gained a foothold in Tom's thoughts. "I should have hired someone to be there when I was gone. I should have bought a dog. I should have stayed home more often." But all the "shoulds" in the world would never bring Sarah back.

"Giddy up," Mr. Gardner called to his two horses as the wagon bumped along, with Tom's horse tied behind. His heart was sad, ever so sad, for Tom's loss. He knew enough about grief to leave Tom alone with the woman he loved.

Once at the funeral home, Mrs. Gardner came to the wagon. "I'm so sorry, Tom." She squeezed his arm and left it at that. She had placed candles all around the holding room, and an arrangement of magnolias stood beside the coffin in which Sarah would rest for the night.

"I'll stay with her tonight, Tom," she whispered. "You go on over to the sheriff's office, and Sam will go to Wilmington first thing tomorrow to get a proper coffin for Miss

Sarah. We'll leave you alone with her now, but we'll be right outside. Sam will send the telegram for you now."

A slight scraping of wood indicated the door had been closed. Alone in the room, Tom touched Sarah's hand. "I know why God would want you up there with Him, Sarah, but what will Angel and I do without you?" Huge, wracking sobs overtook Tom. He didn't even try to stop them. After a few minutes, he blew his nose a few times and put away the handkerchief. Grabbing her hand, Tom managed to utter, "Find a way to let me know that you are okay. Please come back to me in some special way. That's all I ask. [18] Good night, Sarah. I'll be back tomorrow."

As he opened the door, he put his arm around Mrs. Gardner. "Thank you for taking care of her tonight," Tom managed to say.

"One of us will be with her all night, Tom. You and Angel will need to decide on what dress she'll wear."

"Okay." Afraid of his emotions, Tom hurriedly opened the door and stepped out into the night. Grabbing the reins, he hoisted himself upward and headed for the sheriff's office. Two shot glasses and a bottle of whiskey lay in waiting on the sheriff's desk.

"I figured you'd need a drink."

"Thanks, Bob." Tom practically fell into the chair opposite his desk and raised his hand to take the offered drink.

"I've walked the grounds, Tom. There's lots of scuffling footprints in the corral, but no horses. We've either got some rustlers or some runaway slaves. I guess Sarah went out to stop them. I've searched everywhere for a gun, but I

---

[18]

260

didn't turn one up. I followed the trail awhile, but that trail was cold."

"She had a gun," Tom offered mutely.

"Well, there wasn't a gun left outside. I didn't go in the house though, so I'll need for you to see if anything was stolen from the house – silver, guns, money – anything of value. My guess though, Tom, is that she ran outside when she heard the horses, and someone got her from behind. I'm so sorry, Tom. Miss Sarah was one hell of a woman. You go on home now and get some rest, and I'll ride out in the morning to see if you found anything missing."

Sheriff Watson filled Tom's shot glass a second time. Tom tossed the whiskey down and rose from the chair. "Thanks, Bob. I appreciate it, and I'll see you in the morning."

Tom's horse bobbed her head up and down snorting her impatience. She wasn't used to being ridden at night, and her supper was way late. "Come on, girl," Tom called. "Let's go home." But Tom knew it wouldn't be much of a home anymore without Sarah. He tried not to be angry at God for losing Sarah, but he saw no reason for Sarah to die. She had never harmed a soul. It saddened Tom that his belief in the divine plan failed him now, for he was beside himself with grief.

Chapter Thirty-Nine

Southerners have always been known for their hospitality, but Tom had never seen anything like what happened after Sarah's death. Mrs. Jefferson, one of the local ladies from Tom's church, appeared the next morning. "Good morning, Mrs. Jefferson," a bleary-eyed Tom announced. "Won't you please come in?"

"First of all, Tom, I'm so sorry about what happened to Sarah. Life is hard to figure out sometimes; isn't it? Anyway, I've come to volunteer to handle all of the answering of the door and to organize the food for the next three days so that you and Angel can be free. Mrs. Thompson volunteered to assist me with this."

Tom was embarrassed that he was still in his pajamas at 9:00 AM. He had walked the floor most of the night, and he figured that he must have fallen asleep on the couch in the wee hours of the morning. Finally, he was able to respond politely, "Why, thank you, Mrs. Jefferson, that's very kind of you. The kitchen is right this way." Not knowing what else to do, he led her into the kitchen.

"Tom, now as a man, you have no idea what will happen over the next few days. You're going to need to make a thousand decisions, and you need to know the home base is covered. Trust me on this." She patted Tom on his shoulder as if he were a small boy needing comforting.

"I...um...I'll just go and get dressed," he muttered.

"I'll have some breakfast for you in a bit." Spying Sarah's apron hanging on a peg, she pulled it over her head and started looking for the eggs. Tom had barely finished his breakfast before the minister came, followed by Mrs.Anderson. Soon after, four ladies arrived with huge baskets of food. True to her word, Mrs. Jefferson met them all at the door and had them sign the register that Mrs. Anderson had brought. She tagged the dishes with names in careful script so that they could be returned and so that Angel could easily read it later. She recorded each lady's name and the gift of food items that she had contributed.

"All the dishes will be returned to church next Sunday," she was careful to tell each and every lady. Mrs. Thompson arrived at noon, and a grateful Mrs. Jefferson asked her to take over the registry. The sideboard was already overflowing with food – fried chicken, melt-in-your-mouth biscuits, sweet potatoes, green beans, cabbage, succotash, and potato salad. On the dessert table were four pies and a seven-layer cake. In the South, it was customary for everyone who came to call to be offered food while they were paying their condolences.

When Jake brought the buggy around, Tom could not believe it was already two o'clock and time to pick up Angel. Tom's stomach was in knots. "What would he say to Angel?" She would be devastated, and his emotions were barely in check. He hoped that not many of the people he knew would be at the train station.

"Hope the train's on time, Tom." Because Wilmington was the major port, the railroad tracks were repaired often. You never knew though, how reliable the train would be. Jake called as Tom climbed down from the carriage. "I'll wait for you over there."

"Okay."

Neither looking left nor right, Tom strode out to the platform that was all but deserted. "Please help me, God, to say the right words. Please help me to be strong for Angel." Huge tears welled up in his eyes, and he fought for control of his emotions. Mercifully, the train was on time.

Angel thought that she was all cried out, but when she saw her father standing there, so alone with his hat in hand, she broke down again. Grabbing her suitcase, she stumbled toward the door. Angel literally flung herself into her father's arms as she wept uncontrollably. Her suitcase lay fallen on its side, forgotten in the dust. Tom stroked her hair and patted her on the back, allowing her grief to subside.

With an attempt at a smile, Tom announced, "Jake's waiting for us, and I'll tell you all about it on the ride home."

Wisely, Jake just tipped his hat to Angel, not trying to engage her in conversation. Throwing her bag up top, he jumped into the seat, and within minutes had them safely headed to the funeral home.

"Some freed slaves came by the house and tried to steal the horses. We assume that Sarah came outside to stop them."

"How did she die, Dad?" Angel looked Tom in the eye with defiance in her voice.

"Her neck was broken."

"Did they harm her in any other way?"

"No. Jake found her lying on the ground when he came back to the barn, and he came straight to get me at the office."

"Have they found the men yet?"

"Not that I know of, Honey."

"Why Sarah, Dad? She never did anything but love people. Why did *she* have to die?"
"Maybe she had completed what she came here to do." Tom wasn't sure where those words came from. They just

popped out of his mouth. He wasn't even aware that he held that thought in his consciousness.

Angel's eyes registered shock and then acceptance. "Well, that's a nice way to look at it, Dad. She had completed what she came here to do." With that, she nestled down under his arm, and Tom held her like a small child, comforting her all the way toward Southport.

"When can I see her, Dad?" she mumbled.

"I thought we'd stop at the funeral home on the way home."

"Okay," she muttered weakly. She wasn't even sure she wanted to see Sarah. She still felt in a way that the whole episode was just a bad dream, but she knew that once she saw Sarah, the nightmare would begin. "Have you seen her, Dad?" she asked with her voice trembling.

"Not since I brought her to Mr. Gardner's last night." So far Tom had been able to hold his emotions in check, but he was dreading the finality of seeing her in the coffin.

By their grim faces, Mr. Gardner knew better than to engage them in trivial conversation. "Hi, Tom. Hi, Angel. Come right this way." He beckoned them into another room. "I've just finished all the preparations. When you're ready, just open that door, and I'll wait out here for you." Mr. Gardner had bought the finest coffin that Wilmington had to offer for Sarah that morning, and he and his wife had dressed her in the blue silk dress Tom had sent back by the sheriff.

Mrs. Gardner had expertly applied a little makeup to Sarah's beautiful skin and arranged her hair just like she wore it on Sundays. This was their way of giving back to Sarah for her many kindnesses. She had also lovingly arranged two bouquets of flowers which she had placed on either side of the casket, and true to her word, she had kept the candle burning the whole time. Sarah's Bible had been placed in her right hand.

The heavy perfume of the lilies hit Angel's senses first. Once her eyes adjusted to the somewhat darkened room, she saw the white satin of the casket. A huge wracking sob escaped from her, and she grabbed for her father's hand, afraid to venture forward. Tom blinked back his tears, grateful to have Angel beside him. In silence they walked the longest five steps of their lives. They stood there mutely until Angel broke the silence.

"Why, she looks just like she's sleeping; doesn't she, Dad?"

"Even death can't take away her beauty, Angel; can it?"

Tom reached over lovingly to touch her hand, but recoiled inside at the coldness and stiffness of her skin. Angel brushed her face lightly with her fingers and leaned over to kiss her on her cheek. Hot tears lobbed against her eyelids.

"Why, there's her Bible," she noted with a smile. Seeing the flowers, she registered confusion. "Are you going to let her stay here for the wake?"

"Oh, Honey, no. She'll come home to us this afternoon before all the visitors arrive."

"Okay," Angel managed to mutter.

Tom put his arm around his daughter and held her closely, like he used to do to a much smaller Angel. They stood reverently for a long time just looking at her.

"I guess we'd better go. Reverend Watkins will be out this afternoon to discuss the funeral. I didn't want to plan too much without you."

266

"Bye, Sarah. I'll see you this afternoon," she called softly, "when you come home."

The sunlight was welcoming when they crossed into the outer room. "Thank you, Sam. She looks beautiful. And thank you, Mrs. Gardner, too." Tom remembered his manners, but the words were delivered in an emotional tone.

"Will 5:00 be okay, Tom?"

"Yes, we'll see you then." Tom nodded his agreement.

"Mrs. Gardner will stay with her until then, Angel."

The thought that Sarah wouldn't be alone comforted them both. Jake jumped down to open the door, nodding a greeting as they climbed wearily into the carriage. Angel scooted beside Tom, and he placed his arm protectively around her.

"I guess we'll place her in the library. What do you think?" he added.

"Oh, she'd like it better in the kitchen, Dad." They both laughed a little, knowing that what Angel had spoken was the truth.

Tom had originally worried about trying to notify any living relatives in New Orleans, but Sarah had told him that they had all died out. She hadn't even visited New Orleans in the last five years. A thousand thoughts had ricocheted through his brain in the last day. He was glad Angel was home now to help him do everything just right for Sarah.

"Angel, please check with Mrs. Thompson and Mrs. Jefferson when we get home. I don't know much about this ladies stuff with food and flowers." As they turned on their road toward the house, Tom and Angel were amazed.

"There must be fifteen wagons at the house, Dad."

"Oh, my Lord!"

Calico dressed ladies marched to and fro, some bringing baskets of food, others returning the baskets to the wagons. Groups of men congregated in the yard under the trees, patiently waiting for Tom to return. "Brace yourself, Honey. We're going to be on call." Tom appreciated his friends and neighbors' kind gestures, but he was overwhelmed.

Angel smiled. "They're showing their love for Sarah, Dad, and we will receive it in her honor."

Tom looked with new appreciation at Angel. "What a lovely way to look at the situation."

Seeing Tom's carriage arrive, the men began sauntering toward the house. Tom greeted them warmly, while Angel extended her hands to the ladies. Once inside, Angel hugged Mrs. Thompson and Mrs. Jefferson and thanked them.

"Dad tells me you've been wonderful, and I thank you for freeing us up."

"There have been forty-five people here already today," Mrs. Thompson whispered conspiratorially. "Your Sarah was greatly loved and respected. Do you want something to eat, Angel? I can make you a plate. God knows there's plenty of food."

"Actually, I am hungry," Angel realized. "And could you fix Dad one too?"
Tom finally broke away from the men to check on Angel.

"Here, Dad. Let's eat something quick while the coast is clear."

Mrs. Thompson poured two glasses of sweetened tea and plopped them down on the kitchen table. Motioning to Mrs. Jefferson, she suggested, "Let's give them some privacy."

Angel had never seen so much food in her life. It was stacked everywhere, but she had no idea at that time how much food would actually be consumed during the visitation days.

In a few minutes, Mrs. Jefferson returned with a smile. "Here's some dessert."

Tom and Angel had both eaten a little food, but not with any enjoyment. Even desserts did not tempt Tom despite his sweet tooth.

Mrs. Thompson announced a few minutes later, "Reverend Watkins is here. I took him into the study."

"Thanks," Tom muttered. He reached across the table to grab Angel's hand. "Are you ready?"

"Yes, Dad. We'll make Sarah's funeral a wonderful one – just what she would have wanted." The forced confidence did not match the feeling of devastation and emptiness she was experiencing. Everywhere her gaze went in the kitchen there was a memory of Sarah. Angel wasn't sure that she would be able to do this.

"Thank you for coming, Reverend," Tom offered, extending his hand as they entered the study.

"May I offer you my sympathy, Miss Angel?" The kind old man kissed Angel on the cheek and gave her a hug.
"Sit down, Reverend. Can we get you something to drink or eat?"

"I'll do that later. Now what have you two decided, Tom, as far as the service?"

The three exchanged ideas for well over two hours. In the end, all three were satisfied with the tribute. The Reverend stood first.

"I heard Miss Chitwood sent shoofly pie over here, and I want to get a piece before it's gone. I'll shut the door behind me so you can talk privately, and I'll be back in a few minutes." Neither Tom nor Angel could think of another thing, and they sank gratefully into the comfort of the leather chairs, happy to have a reprieve.

Chapter Forty

The wake was exhausting. Hundreds of people came to pay their respects. Angel had her special set of friends from school; Tom had his set of friends from Wilmington; and Sarah had a huge group of friends from the Women's Auxiliary groups at church. The entire community of Southport in general paid their respects. Angel didn't know what she would have done without the organizational skills of Mrs. Thompson and Mrs. Jefferson. Rotating groups of women from the church served the food, replenished the food, washed the dishes, and bundled up the trash. Jake kept the carriages parked in various areas of the farm so that the wagons could move systematically with no traffic jam. The other tenant farmers volunteered their time to feed and water the horses and to provide food for the drivers who had accompanied the Wilmington visitors.

The night before the funeral Angel fell into bed totally wiped out, but at 5:00 AM she awakened and began her final tribute to Sarah.

My dear Sarah,

The two of us have always discussed our belief that there is another existence after death, and I trust and believe that you are in a safe place now. How happy God must be to have you back with Him to bring beauty, laughter and joy to His heart as you did to mine.

You were not my biological mother who gave me the gift of life, but you were my chosen mother who gave me the gift of love. No genetic bonding is any more strong than our soul bonding, and I thank you for our journey together. You were there for me when I skinned my knees, learned to ride horses, tried to cook, endeavored to sew, talked about God, and you were especially there for me when I met the man I would marry. What more could anyone ask from someone?

My only regret is that you will not be here to help me raise my children. But you have taught me well, and I promise that I will role model your style of motherhood.

I know that you are enjoying your reunion with those in your family who have gone on before you, especially with your own mother, and I am happy for that.

I am deeply troubled that we did not have a chance to say goodbye, Sarah, but I am secure in the fact that you know how much I love you. I am also confident that you will find a way to return to me, to let me know that you are okay, and I'll await your return.

> *With as much as love as I have,*
> *Angel*

Satisfied that she had done something special for Sarah, Angel tiptoed down to the library. She and her dad had taken turns staying at night with Sarah, and she gently opened the door so that she wouldn't awaken her father who was sleeping peacefully on the library couch. Gently, she slid the letter into Sarah's Bible and left the room.

That afternoon the church was filled to capacity for Sarah's funeral service. Attendees even stood outside when the seats were filled. Afterward, Sarah was buried in the church graveyard. Angel and Tom held hands at the graveside service and were comforted in the knowledge that Sarah's shell was being buried, but that her spirit would live on forever with them in their hearts. Only the closest friends came back to the

272

house after the funeral, and the family enjoyed their company tremendously, now that the pressure was off.

As they were trudging upstairs that night to go to bed, Angel's eyes welled up with tears, "What will we do now, Dad?"

"We'll honor the way she taught us to live." Tom kissed her on the cheek, "Goodnight, my love."

"Goodnight, Dad."

Once inside her room, she leaned back against the closed door and prayed, "Don't forget! Come and let me know that you are okay." Without even undressing, she fell across the bed and was out like a light.

Chapter Forty-One

"Dad, when Sarah redid my room after I went off to school, do you know what she did with my childhood books and toys?" Angel asked as they were eating dinner one night. "I want to use them in the nursery."

"Hmm. If I had to guess, I'd say that she probably put them in the attic. Do you want me to look up there after supper?" he offered.

"No thanks, Dad. I've got to get that speech ready for the printer. I'll get to it tomorrow."

"By the way, Angel, this chicken and dumplings is very, very good."

"It's Sarah's recipe," she proudly announced. "After Thorn went to Richmond, I asked Sarah if she would write down what she was doing as she was cooking, and she was happy to help me."

"I miss her terribly, Angel," Tom replied with a sigh.

"It just doesn't seem fair; does it, Dad? We didn't even get to say goodbye." Angel's eyes brimmed over with tears, and she tried to compose herself. "And she won't be here to help me with my baby."

"Even so, we were lucky to have her in our lives, Angel." He reached over and squeezed her hand. "Very lucky."

"I know, Dad, but I miss her so much." Both were silent for a few minutes, lost in their remembrances.

After breakfast, the next morning, Tom went into his study, and Angel decided she would check the attic for the books she was looking for. As she climbed the extra set of steps to the attic, she couldn't remember the last time she had been up there. Pushing open the door, she realized that she would need more light to see in this dimly lit room. Down to the kitchen she went where they kept the kerosene lanterns. Fumbling in the drawer, she found a match, primed the wick, and lit the lantern. Once contact was made, she replaced the globe.

Back up the steps she trekked. Holding the lantern aloft, she muttered, "Now, let's see what's in this dark tomb." Not too far from the door, she spied Sarah's familiar handwriting. She had taped a sheet of paper on top of a trunk, "Angel's Childhood Books and Toys". Inside, neatly stacked were her four little books and several types of toys. A rush of memories came flooding back from years long ago in her childhood. Taking the books and a couple of the toys, she stood up. Careful to close the lid securely, Angel thought, "Wonder what else is up here?" and she held the lantern up high.

To her left were big old bulky things with sheets over them, "Probably furniture," she mused, but over to the right, Angel could make out a table and an easel with a chair in front of it. "Well, that's odd," she thought. "No one in our family paints." Realizing that there was a shutter on that side of the room, she eased her way over and pushed the shutter open, letting in a burst of sunlight. As her eyes were adjusting, she first saw the canvases lined up like little soldiers across the walls. Beautiful jewels they were, sparkling in the sun and illuminating the room. Peering at the canvases, Angel recognized a house, a park scene, a church, minstrels, and a school house. "Oh, my God! These must be scenes of Sarah's New Orleans home!" As she stepped closer, a breath caught in her throat. Sure enough, there were Sarah's three initials, "S",

"A", "R", just like her monograms. "Oh, my God!" Excitedly, she turned to run to get her dad, but she was stopped dead in her tracks. Her heart was beating so fast she thought that she would die. There was Sarah right in front of her, resurrected from the dead. For a second, she thought she might literally faint, the portrait was so real. "We haven't lost you, Sarah! We haven't lost you!" she sobbed. Gently, she touched the face on the canvas. "Oh, Sarah, I miss you so."

Stumbling now, she rushed down the steps, screaming at the top of her lungs, "Dad! Dad!"

Terrified, Tom jumped up and ran in the hall, "Where are you, Angel?"

"Here on the stairs!"

He called as he ran to her, "What's wrong? What is it?"

"You've got to come! You've got to come!" She grabbed his hand and pulled him literally back up the stairs.

"Where are we going?"

"To the attic," she announced, over her shoulder, never once breaking her stride. Tom was winded by the time they made it to the attic, but Angel kept pulling him on to the other side. "Sarah's here, Dad! Look!" Angel pointed to Sarah's portrait of her mother. Tom stood in total shock. Involuntarily, tears rolled down his cheeks as he drank in the beautiful face and felt her eyes peer into his soul.

"Oh, my God, Sarah, you *have* returned to me!" Great wracking sobs overtook Tom, and he grabbed Angel tightly in a hug. "You *did* find a way to come back. You did."

As Angel peered over his shoulder, she gasped out loud. Tom thought that he had hugged her too hard, and he started apologizing. Transfixed, Angel simply stared into space.

"What *is* it?" Tom asked, seeing the strange look on her face. She pointed in the opposite direction. Tom turned and then he saw what Angel had seen – her portrait was on the easel. Both of them advanced for a closer look. Tom was utterly amazed at Angel's likeness, at the precision work, and at the capturing of her inner beauty. "Only someone who loved you very much could have created this." Tom pulled Angel closer and they stood there together stupefied, in total mesmerization.

"Oh, let's take them downstairs," Tom suggested and he reached for Angel's portrait. Then, simultaneously, they both saw it lying there on the desk. Placing Angel back on the easel, Tom walked forward. There was *his* portrait. They exchanged a look of reverence and awe. Perfectly detailed was his portrayal, even down to his Bible. Words could not express what they felt at this moment. Sarah had not left them. She was back -- touching their hearts -- even now.

"You know, Angel, we didn't have a chance to say goodbye to Sarah, but *she* found a way to cross the barriers of time and space to show her love for us," Tom whispered. Tom couldn't stop the big smile that was spreading across his face. His Sarah was back! After the shock wore off, Tom and Angel proudly hung all three portraits in the entry hall. Her beautiful New Orleans oils were dispersed throughout the house for all to enjoy.

Each day they stood in the hall, rejoicing that Sarah was back. Never once did it dawn on them that Sarah had actually painted her mother's portrait instead of her own.

Chapter Forty-Two

"Melinda, Melinda! Riders are coming!" Mrs. Sawyer called into the house.

Dropping the potato she had been peeling, Melinda rushed toward the barn where the guns were hidden. Quickly, she pushed back the hay to retrieve the strongbox. Grabbing the pistol, she slammed two bullets into the chamber. Out of breath, her grandfather reached Melinda. Without a word, she handed him the second gun she had loaded.

Stepping outside, Mr. Sawyer strained his eyes to see the riders. "There's three of 'em – one's hurt. It's okay; they're Confederates!"

Melinda pocketed her gun in her apron just to be sure there was no trouble. She joined her grandfather outside.

"Are you the Sawyers?" the young enlistee called from his horse.

"Yes, son, we are."

"Lieutenant Summerville here asked us to bring him here. He's been…."

"Oh, my God! Granddaddy, it's Nathan!" Melinda's eyes filled with tears as she rushed over to the body slumped across the horse.

The two young Confederates dismounted. "Where do you want us to put him?"

"In the house!" Melinda ran ahead as the young men pulled their commander down from the horse and positioned him for carrying.

Inside the house, she threw the folded clothes from the settee, readying the spot. Carefully, they placed him on the couch, and Nathan groaned as he teetered between consciousness and unconsciousness. Blood had seeped through what was left of his uniform jacket.

"He took a couple of bullets in his side. We were ambushed – only the three of us survived. Before he passed out, he drew a map to your house and asked us to bring him back to you." The young man's voice trailed off, not knowing what else to say.

Grandfather Sawyer patted the young man on the back. "You did the right thing. Now go water your horses and feed them. The women folk will fix you something to eat. Plan to stay with us until we see how Mr. Summerville does."

When the young men left, Mr. Sawyer suggested, "Unbutton his jacket, Melinda, so I can see how bad it is."

Her fingers flew to the task; soon the right side of the jacket was folded back. Two holes were evident amid the gory, bloody tissue.

"If I don't get those bullets out, he'll die of infection. He's already got a fever."

Over his shoulder he called, "Boil me some water, Sudie, and bring some clean sheets to tear in strips. Melinda, run to the barn and get my pliers."

Two days later, Nathan opened his eyes for the first time. He thought he was dreaming – Melinda was there beside him. "You had us worried, Nathan, but the fever broke last night. I knew then that you would be okay!" She leaned forward to kiss him. Nathan tried to touch her face, but a sharp pain stopped his arm in midair.

"Mama!" Melinda called loudly. "He's awake! Bring the whiskey!"

Gently, she caressed Nathan's face. "I prayed for your return each day, Nathan!" Then she laughed, "But, I certainly didn't want you to be wounded so that you could return to me." She smoothed his hair back from his face lovingly. "Thank God, you're safe now."

Her mother came bustling into the room with the whiskey. "Let's use a pillow to sit him up a bit so he can take a big drink." Gently, she shoved a pillow little-by-little behind him. Nathan didn't say anything, but the movement caused spasms of pain to shoot through his side. Gratefully, he took a big slug of the brown liquid.

At that moment, Grandfather Sawyer ambled in the room. "So you decided to wake up, huh? Melinda here," he jerked his thumb toward his granddaughter, "never left your side, night or day. She's a good nurse, she is!" He gazed fondly at Melinda.

They chatted back and forth, exchanging news about the war. Nathan was never quite sure whether the whiskey gave him the strength to say it, or whether his close brush with death had loosened his tongue. "Mr. Sawyer, I'd like to ask your permission to marry Miss Melinda."

Her grandfather laughed out loud. "You mean right now?" he teased.

"No, Sir. I mean in a few days when I have recovered enough!"

"Oh!" Mr. Sawyer's voice trailed off. He scratched his arm; then he shifted his weight from one foot to the other. The silence was pregnant with suspense. Finally, he spoke, "You were mighty good to us when we first met you, letting your men help us out on the farm. You musta been mighty good to Melinda, too, for she has talked about your return every day since you left. And you're fightin' for our way of life, so I guess I have no objection to the marriage. I wish her father was here to make the decision, but he's not."

"Thank you, Sir!" Nathan shook hands with Mr. Sawyer, sealing their bargain.

Then in a move that surprised everyone, Nathan reached for Melinda's hand, "Miss Melinda, I love you with all my heart. Will you marry me?"

A hot tear fell on Nathan's face as she bent over to kiss him. "I will, Nathan! I will be glad to marry you!"

Sudie and her mother smiled at Nathan. "We'll be glad to welcome you into our family." Then they both embraced Melinda, happy for her new love.

Five days later, the veranda had been polished to perfection and decorated with candles and fall foliage. Nathan's uniform had been cleaned to remove the bloodstains and grime. Melinda's mother's wedding gown had been re-sewn to fit Melinda, and Mr. Sawyer brushed up on wedding vows as he was to be the stand-in preacher.

Nathan's two enlistees proudly represented Nathan's side of the family, and Melinda's family, dressed in their pre-war best, rejoiced in their happiness.

"Dearly beloved, we are gathered here today. . .

A hunting lodge on the edge of the property was their honeymoon residence for a few days.

"I hope that I have gotten pregnant," Melinda cooed as she lay in Nathan's arms.

"Well, we've certainly given it a good try, haven't we, Melinda!" Nathan laughed.

"How long can you stay?" Melinda asked, afraid to hear the answer.

"A few more days. I haven't had a day off before this in a year. I don't have a regiment anymore -- I don't even know where the front line is -- but I'm sure the war's not over. The boys and I will have to head out soon." He stroked her hair and touched her face as he talked, memorizing every facet of her beauty. Nathan hated the thought of leaving her, but he knew that the Cause came first. Plenty of men hadn't been home in three years, and plenty weren't coming home at all; he knew he had to honor their sacrifice.

Melinda's next question took him from his reverie. "Tell me about the place where you live." Melinda sat up in bed and shyly pulled the sheet up to cover her nakedness.

"I live about seventeen miles west of Wilmington, North Carolina, which is a large seaport. Like your family, we had a plantation with slaves before the war. Thanks to Mr. Lincoln's Proclamation, I'm sure the slaves exist no more. I guess when we go home, we'll have to find some tenant farmers. You'll love my mom and dad. They never had any children but me, and my mom always wanted a girl. When I bring you home, she'll want us to start having babies right away! And – speaking of children, don't you think we ought to try to have a baby again?" Nathan teased.

"What a great idea!" Melinda laughed as she slid back down beside him. "Practice makes perfect, I've always heard!"

Chapter Forty-Three

The war officially ended on April 9, 1865, with Robert E. Lee's surrender, but there was no end to the work that needed to be done to restore the South. The war had changed everything: the societal structure, the economic conditions, the population, and the modes of transportation. Yet, the time-honored traditions of the South, the importance of their friendships, family, chivalry, and values remained in tact.

McGilly's Tavern had survived the war, but the saucy barmaids and dimly-lit gentlemen's atmosphere had gone with the winds of change. Windows had been added across the front and on the sides to let in much needed light. The wait staff now consisted of young people, clad in simple black pants and white shirts. McGilly's Tavern had become McGilly's Restaurant and Bar, catering to families.

On this beautiful Saturday morning in May, John, Nathan, Thorn and their wives, met for lunch as planned four years earlier. John, fluent in Robert's Rules of Order, rose to make the opening remarks. "In our day, we were called 'The Fabulous Four,' but in light of our marriages and babies, I think 'The Sensible Six' would be a better name. Thus, I declare the first meeting of 'The Sensible Six' called to order. The first order of business is to recognize McGilly's Restaurant and Bar as our watering hole once more."

"Here, here!" the others called, clinking their mugs.

"The second order of business is to recognize our beloved, departed member. . ." John was surprised that his voice broke and that his emotions gave way. Natalie patted him on the arm, and John wiped his tears away. Thorn and

283

Nathan did the same. Finding his voice once more, "To Ahab McGee, who is probably as we speak, no doubt charming the robe off of some unsuspecting angel."

"Here, here!" All mugs clinked in unison.

"The purpose of this monthly meeting shall be to celebrate our friendships and our love."

"Here, here." They all clinked again.

"Finally, we are here to give a salute to the South which shall rise again!"

"Here, here."

Sitting down, John continued, "And now the Chair yields the floor to Nathan Summerville."

"Thank you, John. Here's our news. My Dad and I have now secured twenty tenant farmers so that the plantation can get up and running again. The best news of all is that Melinda and I are expecting our first baby in November." Congratulations were given all around, and Melinda grinned from ear-to-ear.

"And now, the Chair yields to Thorn."

"Well, our news is that Angel and I officially moved into our new house here in Wilmington last month, and the housewarming will be held soon. Angel is managing her father's political career and our two children, and I am trying to manage our new business, McAllister's Lumberyard."

"Here, here!" The mugs clicked again.

"And you, John, what's your news?" Thorn questioned.

"Our news is that Natalie and I are expecting our second child, as all of you know." John gestured to the basketball size lump that Natalie was carrying around – "and I am trying my damnedest to keep the carpetbaggers from cheating our citizens and the newly-freed slaves."

"Here, here!"

"And now, there being no further business to come before this meeting, I declare the meeting adjourned, and it's time to order some lunch."

McGilly's Restaurant still offered great food, and "The Sensible Six" enjoyed the food and the fellowship.

An hour later when they walked outside, Nathan kissed Melinda goodbye through the window of their buggy. "I'll be home in a week to ten days, Honey."

"Love you," she called as the driver clicked the horses and off they galloped.

"I wish you guys luck. I know bringing Lieutenant Gage home means a lot to you," John commented.

Both Nathan and Thorn shook hands with him. "Thanks, John."

John took Natalie's arm protectively, and they strolled in the direction of their home.

"Let's go," Thorn called as he grabbed Angel's arm, to help her into Nathan's wagon seat.

"I hope you'll like our new house," Angel teased. Within minutes, the trio arrived at 522 South Nunn. "My God, Thorn! You bought the Sprunt place?"

"Well, the bank and I have bought it," he laughed. "Have you got the maps?"

"Oh, yes. Right here in my pocket." He patted the pocket of his shirt with a smile. The wagon had been packed with all the necessary supplies the day before. Thorn pulled Angel into his arms, "I'll miss you, my love. I'm glad you'll be with your dad while I'm gone. And, when I come home, maybe we should start thinking about our next child."

"Sounds good to me," she laughed, giving him a big kiss. Thorn climbed in the shotgun side, and Nathan giddy upped the horses. The pine coffin in the back of the wagon gave the symbolic gesture of their mission: Lieutenant Gage was coming back home to North Carolina to be buried with honors.

Not too long after they rolled out of town, Jeff arrived to pick up Angel. "Are these the only bags, Angel?"

"No. I have a few more in the house. Be very careful, Jeff. They're portraits."

"Okay. I'll put them up front with me."

Angel was looking forward to going home. She had a surprise for her dad.

Chapter Forty-Four

After making the final adjustments with the picture hanger, Angel hung the oil portrait of her mother that she had commissioned as her father's surprise birthday gift. Her new portrait of Thorn had just been hung beside hers a few minutes before.

Stepping back, she scrutinized her mother's portrait. The skill was certainly there in portraying her delicate features, but unlike Sarah's portraits, her mother's soul essence had not been captured. Angel loved the fact that all the family members now hung together in the entry hall: her mother, her father, her second mother Sarah, her own portrait, and her husband, in that order. The Madison family was now complete.

As she turned toward the study to retrieve her dad, she stopped quietly at the door. Looking over at her father, she noticed the graying around his temples and the "love handles", as he referred to them, around his waist. Despite his aging, Tom still cut a very handsome appearance.

Two month old Sarah was cradled lovingly in the crook of his arm, and Patrick, their two year old, rolled his wagon in and out of the legs of the chair. Some things are constant; some things never change. Angel took heart that their family's love was still strong despite the hardships of the last few years.

"Could the Senator from North Carolina put down the baby long enough to come out into the hall? I have a surprise for you!" Angel teased her father with a big smile.

Tom rose carefully, so as not to awaken the sleeping baby. Lovingly, he placed little Sarah near the back of the

287

settee, and as an afterthought, he placed pillows around her. Satisfied at last that she was safe, he crossed the threshold out into the hall.

"Look, Dad!" Angel called invitingly and pointed toward her mother's portrait.

Awestruck, Tom could only mumble, "Oh, my God! It's Rachel!" He moved forward and lovingly touched the creaminess of her skin. He marveled at her beauty once more. Hot tears crowded the corner of his eyes as the memory of the sweetness of their love came flooding back. How well he remembered that smile. For a few seconds, he basked in the joy of the love they once shared.

Finally, Tom turned to Angel and spoke past the lump in his throat, "Thank you, Angel, for bringing your mother back to life so that she can occupy her rightful place beside me."

As Tom wiped his eyes with the back of his hand, Angel enveloped him in a big hug. "I'm so glad you like the portrait. Happy Birthday, Dad!"

Only then did Tom notice the other addition to the wall. "Oh, Angel, what a wonderful likeness of Thorn! I love the touch of his Cavalry uniform." Walking closer to the portrait, he commented, "He looks just like he could speak, doesn't he? Has he seen this yet?"

"No, I picked the two portraits up the morning he left. He can see it when he returns with Lieutenant Gage. I think the painting will be a wonderful surprise for him."

Tom slid his arm around Angel's shoulder as they proudly gazed at the five portraits.

"What a wonderful daughter you are, my Angel. I love my birthday present."

They smiled at each other and once more looked back at the legacy of love that they were leaving behind for Patrick and Sarah's generation.

After awhile Angel broke the companionable silence, "Dad, I have been thinking that you will need to add a new line to your 'Greatness Thrust Upon Us' speeches."

Tom turned away from the portraits so that he could give his full attention to Angel. "I would like to hear what you have to say," he responded simply.

With a serious look on her face, Angel began, "There has been so much devastation to our lands, our way of life, our homes, and our families in the last five years that I believe we will have to rise to a new level of greatness to survive. But this time the greatness must come from another source. Our new level of greatness must be to ask God to give us the strength to endure, the grace to forgive, and the power to carry on."

"What a beautiful concept, Angel!"

Tom didn't know what to say. It was a defining moment. Tom realized with sudden awareness that the legacy he would be leaving behind would not be his political success, but that the legacy would be to leave Angel to carry on the Madison tradition of leadership."

"Well, well, well! I guess we know who the next Senator from North Carolina will be, don't we?" Tom announced proudly.

"I promise to do my best when my time comes!"

Tom lovingly draped his arm across Angel's shoulders once more as they turned back to admire the family gallery.

Even though Tom never told a soul, he would swear until the day he died that both Rachel and Sarah smiled at him from their portraits. For after all, they were part of the legacy of love, too.

FOOTNOTES

FOOTNOTES

Footnote 1

"Remember the old saying," Tom offered, accentuating his words with his fork. "Every cloud has a silver lining."

Have you ever remarked to a friend –
> "You know at the time I thought it was the worst thing that had ever happened to me. But now, a year later, I recognize that it was for the best!"

As adults we have all recognized that hindsight is 20/20 and that sometimes things happen for a good reason. Yet, it is our job to find the silver linings in our life problems instead of just complaining about them.

In our story Miss Lizzie could have become a bitter old woman because of her inability to have a child and the death of her husband. Instead, she took the two strikes against her and turned them into a plus. If she couldn't have a child of her own, she would start an orphanage for other people's children. Pretty ironic, isn't it?

Find your silver lining in the problem you are presently experiencing and enjoy life more!

Footnote 2

"There was no doubt in Tom's mind that there was always a divine plan, but sometimes it took years to figure out the plan."

Tom states his belief that we are part of a divine plan that expands to universes, galaxies, stars, planets, animals, trees, flowers, and every person on earth. There is an all knowing life force that runs through every part of creation from the smallest atom to the largest universe, and this is our Divine connection.

However, each of us must travel our own path by seeking out the teachers and the doctrines that are right for us. Strangely enough, everyone serves as a teacher in some form, to help and benefit other people. Our heavenly Father and His Angels are there to push us into the right place at the right time so that we may connect to important people and events that are destined to change our lives and to keep us moving forward on our life plan.

Footnote 3

Perfect timing – was that the chief criterion for the call of fate?

The term "fate" actually came from Greek mythology. The Fates were three sisters who were created even before Zeus became the King of the Heavens. They were just always there, and they controlled the fate of humans on earth by weaving threads. When a person was born, one sister made the threads of life; then the next sister spun the threads, and the third sister after many years, cut the thread. The idea was that when a person was born the thread was created, and it was spun for many, many years as the human processed his life on earth. When it came time for the human to die, the last sister simply cut the thread, and his life diminished.

The word fate also refers to a predetermined course of events. This concept is based on the belief that there is a fixed natural order to the cosmos. In some cases, fate is viewed as an outcome determined by an outside agency acting upon a person to determine a course of events. Therefore, there will be coincidental happenings that will propel someone exactly where he needs to be for something wonderful to happen.

Thus, in the story, Thorn just felt <u>compelled</u> to come to the meeting, he wondered if there were a <u>guiding spirit</u> who pushed men to their destiny. Every fiber in his being <u>knew</u> that he had to come to this meeting.

Sounds like fate, to me.

Footnote 4

Thorn wondered if there were people who were half-angel and half-human. If so, he knew from the depths of his soul that he had just met one.

Angels are immortal beings created by God to serve as the intermediaries between the heavens and the earth. Interestingly, the early Christians believed that human beings could become angels when they had perfected themselves.

Hollywood even joined in on this belief of the angel in disguise in the classic movie <u>Miracle on 34th Street</u>. Do you remember Clarence who was trying to "earn his wings" by looking after Jimmy Stewart?

Thorn, however, was taken by the beauty of Angel's face and hair, similar to the stained glass portrayals of angels in church windows. Whatever she was, she was the most beautiful creature he had ever seen.

I bet that Cupid, the mythological god of love, shot his arrow into Thorn's heart at the moment he saw her!

Footnote 5

"We know that your parents are in a wonderful place now called heaven, don't we Thorn?"

In a recent survey in the <u>AARP The Magazine</u> we find that in people fifty and over 73% believe in an afterlife. 86% say there's a <u>heaven</u> while 70% believe in a <u>Hell</u>. 46% say

<u>Heaven</u> is a place while 47% say it's a state of being. However, there were some survey respondees who believe that we live one time and that's it.

In the story Angel is reassuring Thorn that his parents are in a better place, free of earthly concerns and problems. But where does this Heaven exist and does everyone get to go there upon death?

What do you think?

Footnote 6

How often do you dream about her?

The ancient civilizations all believed that dreams contained very important information sent by the gods.

The Greeks even built Sleep Temples for citizens to use when they needed specific guidance. The citizen would come to the temple and sleep on the altar floor after petitioning the gods to visit him in his sleep. The next morning the Priest would interpret the message of the dream the gods had sent.

Angel relates to us that after her mother died, she would dream of her mother often. I'm sure the dreams were a great comfort for a ten year old child.

Some people spoof dreams and declare that they have no meaning; however, scientists do not agree. Dream researchers have actually categorized the most common types of dreams: solutions to problems, ideas for inventions, artistic expression, prophetic vision, and wish fulfillment.

My clients often tell me about their dreams, and the most common dream seems to be the visitation from a deceased relative. From their reports, I have realized there are four common components:

1. The loved one appears to look much younger than he/she was at the time of death.
2. The dead relative is usually wearing an article of clothing or piece of jewelry that my client remembers.
3. The relative usually has a message for my client or someone else in the family.
4. They all report that the dream seemed so real; "I felt like he/she was right there with me!"

Perhaps we should pay more attention to our dreams.

Footnote 7

Angel sat up abruptly and turned to look at her father. "Why that's just the way Sarah explained it to me – as a guardian angel."

Sarah and Tom were both referring to a special creation of God called the Guardian Angel. While the Archangels reign over the whole planet, the Guardian Angels guard and protect the inhabitants of the earth. Each person on earth has a Guardian Angel assigned to him at birth, and that angel is responsible for the spiritual growth of that person.

Our Guardian Angel takes a direct and personal interest in our lives, often sending the right people, right books, or right interests at a time when we need them. We can call on our Guardian Angels in prayer anytime we want to when we feel blocked in our lives. They love and accept us unconditionally, and they will answer our prayers as long as the requests are in alignment with our life's path.

Have you ever thought about your Guardian Angel? The Catholic Church teaches about them, and I personally think that the knowledge of a Guardian Angel would be a comforting thought to young children.

Footnote 8

"Thank you, God!" She remembered to be grateful and to express her thankfulness over and over again.

Angel remembers her father's teachings on gratitude, and she is careful to acknowledge this wonderful, unexpected twist in her life of Thorn resurfacing so soon.

Gratitude is a way to thank God. The word "gratitude" comes from the Latin stem "gratis", which means to satisfy or to please. On our earth, there is instant gratification abounding. There is instant oatmeal, instant muffler replacement, and instant fax messages. Everything must be done right now, which has lead us to the misguided belief that there are "quick fixes" to every situation. To really appreciate what we have, we must work for it, and then the feeling that we have in our hearts is thankfulness for the completion of the task. This thankfulness is what the higher thinking plane refers to as "gratitude".

When you recognize that God IS working in your life by sending the people or books or events to you, thank Him. Thank Him verbally or thank Him by extending the same courtesy to your neighbor. Your neighbor may need a surprise visit, or he may need some home-cooked bread. **Any act of kindness that you extend to someone is a thank you to God Himself.** The wonderful point about gratitude is that it comes back to you tenfold. God gives lovingly to you, you thank Him by giving lovingly to two or three others, then they get inspired and return the favor to you and to two others. You see, gratitude is like the ancient saying, "The more you give, the more you receive."

Footnote 9

Thorn always trusted his intuition, whether in business or friendship, and his gut told him now that John was serious.

Gut reactions or clairsentiences are very common in our daily lives. How often do we carelessly comment:

To tell you the truth, I just didn't trust him, but I don't know why.

or

I just knew something was wrong so I went over to Natalie's school, and sure enough the nurse wanted to send her to the Emergency Room.

or

You can say what you want, but my intuition tells me not to do it.

To be able to trust our inner wisdom is absolutely essential to our lives if we don't want to be sorry later. Trust can make such a difference in evaluating the experiences of our lives. Just listen to this event that happened to me.

One day I was riding with a friend of mine in heavy traffic when suddenly her car cut off. Luckily we were in the right lane, and she just steered the car over onto the side of the road.

"Oh my God, my car has never cut off before. What is wrong? I hope we aren't broken down because we are ninety miles from home?" she shrieked.

I didn't say anything, but my thoughts went in another direction. "All things happen for a good reason" was a fact I had totally accepted in my life. Quickly she turned the ignition again, and her car cranked perfectly. Checking for traffic, she eased back onto the highway. As we rounded the tree lined curve ahead, I saw the wreck that had occurred just seconds before and I knew why we had been delayed. Without the intervention on the side of the road, we would have been in that wreck.

"Thank you, God!" I muttered.

Only by listening to our inner wisdom can we see beyond the strange coincidences that happen in our lives.

Thorn knew by trusting his inner wisdom that John was smitten by Natalie with love at first sight and there was no talking him out of marriage.

Footnote 10

I've had one of my premonitions. I believe there is a new child at the orphanage.

A premonition is a type of prophecy similar to a prediction which involves advance notice of a future event.

How did Tom know that the orphanage would have a new kid? Scientists have researched many people gifted with extra sensory perception or a sixth sense, and the only explanation they can give about the ability of predicting future events is that time is not linear but exists in an ever present now.

Dr. J. B. Rhine and his wife Louisa established the first Parapsychology Department at Duke University in Durham, NC. The couple devoted their lives to researching gifted people, and they coined the terms: clairaudience, clairvoyance, clairsentience, and claircognizance.

Their research indicates that every person has extra sensory perception, but that some people are born more gifted than others.

Haven't we all had a "gut reaction" to someone upon meeting them? Have you ever said, "I had a hunch that he was up to no good?"

If so, you were using your higher perception skills.

You might remember that the famous Washington psychic, Jeanne Dixon, had a premonition that President John F. Kennedy would not be safe if he went to Dallas to campaign. When she tried to call the White House, they would not put her through to warn the President of her vision. Sadly, the future that she saw came true; John F. Kennedy was assassinated on November 23, 1963 as he rode in an open air convertible on the streets of Dallas. How did Jeanne Dixon know that he would be killed? The only answer is that she had the gift of extra sensory perception in the form of a premonition.

Footnote 11

"Yes, Ma'am. You's my Angel of Mercy."

The small, shoeless man was in danger, and without a moment's hesitation Sarah had showed mercy to him.

As Sarah reflected on hiding the runaway slave, she realized that she had acted from her heart – not her head.

Do we ever have times when we need to be Angels of Mercy to others? All the time!

- In Prayer work – Oh God! Please be merciful to Vivian; she has been in a terrible car accident. Don't let her die. Be merciful by praying for others.
- Forgiving a transgression – our innocent five year old child makes a mistake. We accept his apology – "And I won't do it no more", and we do not punish him. Be merciful to innocent children.

301

- Overlooking a broken promise – under great pressure at the office, your husband forgets to bring home the milk. "That's OK! I'll just order pizza." You smile. You don't make a scene, thereby showing mercy to the overworked man.

Yet, have you ever taken into account the fact that God shows mercy to us each and every day? We need to begin to notice the small and subtle occurrences in our lives:
- an unexpected card from an old friend just when we are feeing so down
- a wonderful compliment given to us from our boss even though the deal wasn't made
- a thank you note arrives just when we thought nobody noticed all the time and effort we spent on the party

We must pay more attention in our daily lives to the ways that God shows mercy to us; so that we, in turn, will want to show mercy to others.

Who in your family or circle of friends could use a call or text right now? It will make you feel so good to be an "Angel of Mercy" for someone today!

I have included a list of thirty possible acts of mercy.

ADULT ACTS OF MERCY

1. Write a letter to someone you've been meaning to write but somehow put it off
2. Return something you borrowed from your neighbor and either say "thank you" personally or attach a note of thanks
3. Share some home baked goodies with a friend or neighbor
4. Xerox an article that you know your friend is interested in and mail it to him or her

302

5. Send a card to cheer up someone
6. Remember a former friend with a phone call just to say hello and catch up on their lives
7. Send some flowers with a "just because" card to your mom, daughter, secretary, or girlfriend
8. Order a surprise from a shopping catalog for someone you love
9. Call your mother, father, wife or husband to see if they need anything from the store before you drive home
10. Call the friend who has called you three times to play golf, tennis, bridge, or whatever, and make a date with him or her
11. Cut some flowers from the garden and bring them inside for the family to enjoy
12. Surprise your child with a new book or toy
13. Surprise your teenager with a new CD
14. Write a note to your parents or to your spouse to say "thank you" for some act of kindness they did for you
15. Give someone a "mini" back rub
16. Visit a shut-in in the neighborhood
17. Call an elderly aunt or uncle to cheer them up because you know that they have few exciting times in their lives
18. Assist a stranger who dropped something in a store or on the street
19. Offer to carry something for an overloaded co-worker
20. Speak pleasantly to someone you've never taken the time to get to know in your office
21. Cook your husband's or your children's favorite meal
22. Surprise a family member with a gift for no reason at all
23. Send a floral arrangement to a shut-in or elderly relative
24. Compliment your neighbors on their pretty lawns or gardens
25. Take your child out to a restaurant for dinner for some one-on-one time
26. Call someone who has been on your mind lately
27. Give some volunteer time to a charity you love

28. Make it a point to give a compliment to your spouse/lover everyday for a week
29. Buy yourself a little luxury. Remember, self-love is an important new perception, too
30. Call a friend to congratulate him or her on a new promotion, marriage, or achievement that you read about in the paper

Footnote 12

Angel looked over at her father, and as Tom began speaking, pinpricks suddenly traveled up and down her spine, and for a moment the room faded away.

Past life recall can occur spontaneously or can be induced through hypnosis, bodywork, or yoga. Whether the memories are of actual historic past lives or whether they are subconscious mind projections is a matter of controversy in the scientific community.

Remember that when Angel had her past life recall, she was in a very comfortable state with the relaxing fire, satiation from food, and the comfortable bond of a loving family. All of these factors could have helped to move her conscious mind aside and allow the subconscious memories to surface.

The French have a word for these quick remembrances, *déjà vu*. Other words for this state are *vision, waking dream,* and *intuitive flash*.

I'll bet you have had your share of *déjà vus*:
- vacation spots
- daydreams
- meeting a person and feeling like you have known him/her all your life
- tears of joy for no reason when visiting a place
- feeling of overwhelming sadness when you visit a certain place

- just knowing how to navigate in a city you have supposedly never visited

Your dreams are a great place where past life recall occurs! Sweet Dreams!

Footnote 13

After all, the call from the "Angel of Inspiration" did not come everyday.

Creativity is a God given gift from our Soul who desires to express its authenticity. In the average person, creativity can take many forms, such as the way we dress, landscape our yards, decorate our houses, or live our lives. However, the most recognized form of creativity is expressed in the Fine Arts of painting, sculpting, dancing, singing, and writing.

What Sarah has illustrated to us is that the most important part of creativity is the art of surrendering to the creative flow and not questioning it. When a singer has a big hit, magazine writers always ask:

This has been your biggest hit yet climbing all the way up the charts. How did you get the inspiration for this song?

The typical response from the artist usually goes like this:

I don't know. I just picked up my guitar one day, and the words and music just came tumbling out. Within an hour the whole song was completed!

The same is true with painters and their creations:

I didn't have anything particular in mind, but the painting just took on a life of its own. The images just flew onto the canvas, and I was using colors I don't normally use. The whole process was amazing!

Neither the painter nor the singer tried to stop the creative flow. They went with the creative drive just like Sarah did. That's the secret to creation – surrender to its power.

Unfortunately our society completely blocks creativity. We are constantly bombarded by cell phones ringing, TV's blaring, radios broadcasting, dogs barking, children screaming, and neighbors arguing. We never take time to be still. How do we think the Angel of Creativity can contact us if we are in a constant whirl of chaos and distractions?

Deep inside us are unique forms of self expression that would love to manifest themselves as gifts and talents, but without stillness and quiet pursuit, the power of creation cannot bubble to the surface.

What did you love to do as a child? Draw? Sketch? Write? Make doll clothes? Create new hairstyles? Train your dog?

With fifteen minutes of stillness and an intent to connect to our uniqueness, we might rebirth an old passion for creative expression.

We won't know what will happen until we try! Why don't you call on your "Angel of Inspiration" today?

Footnote 14

"You're a lucky young man in many ways, Thorn, yet I've always said that we tend to make our own luck."

Tom refers here to the belief that "like attracts like." The Holy Bible even expresses this in the verse:

"Whatsoever ye sew so shall ye reap."

The concept is that by sending out positive thoughts and actions into the world, one will attract positive happenings back into his life.

If you are experiencing a string of bad luck, maybe the universe is sending you a wake-up call that you are putting out more negative thoughts and actions than positive.

This is an interesting concept, isn't it?

Footnote 15

"My dad is teaching me about the importance of service and giving back to the community. This is my first project!" she proudly announced.

Service is a very important spiritual principle. A person who is of service has a deep need in his soul to help others find more happiness in life. These purpose filled individuals take great satisfaction in the fact that their deeds make a difference in the lives of others, and they think nothing of the countless hours they spend in volunteer work.

We have been told many times that it is more blessed to give than to receive, but we must also understand another principle. *What you sow is what you reap.*

It is hard for servers to be receivers – think about it! Yet, the bottom line is that servers must learn to be gracious when others try to help them:
- Servers must accept a compliment with graciousness and not try to deny their worth
- Servers must feel worthy enough to accept the wonderful gift they have been given in thanks
- Servers must learn to graciously accept monetary rewards or tips for their extra efforts

In essence, we should be of service to others, but we must be able to receive graciously when someone wants to be of service to us!

Footnote 16

"Holding the lantern high, the leader boomed, "Well, lookey here who we got! Why, it's Mr. Ahab McGee, traitor to the South!" With that, he threw the corpse of the scout toward Ahab. "And here's your Jezebel," he sneered. "But this time, Ahab, it's your head that's gonna roll."

This quote references two Biblical characters in I Kings, King Ahab and his wife Jezebel, who were considered traitors to the Israelite God.

Footnote 17

"Give me a sign, Lord. Give me a sign that Nathan is still okay."

Thorn is echoing a belief that God communicates with us through nature. Ancient people were more in touch with birds, seasons, and animals than we are today because we have migrated to city life. It was commonplace for preceding generations to ask for a sign from God that would verify that some statement, some revelation, or some message was accurate. Therefore if a bird, rainbow, or animal was seen in a place out of its normal habitat, their appearance was considered a confirmation from God that the message was true.

The appearance of the cardinal was the confirmation Thorn needed. Cardinals are one of the most recognized birds because of their brilliant red plumage. Unlike other birds which migrate, cardinals are year round residents. Did you know that these birds are named for the Cardinals of the Roman Catholic Church with their bright red robes?

The symbolic meaning associated with cardinals is renewed vitality. Thus, to Thorn, the appearance of the cardinal affirmed the message that Nathan was still alive and well. In his deeply grieved state of losing Lieutenant Gage, the man who had become his "second father", Thorn needed a reassurance that life does indeed continue on.

Footnote 18

Find a way to let me know that you are okay. Please come back to me in some special way. That's all I ask.

When Tom made his statement, he indicated that he believed that there was another existence after death that Sarah would go to. All Eastern Religions uphold the doctrine of Reincarnation which teaches that the soul must continue to return to the earth until it has perfected itself. Our Catholic and Protestant religions teach that after death the soul will be resurrected, but they disagree when and where this will happen. Even though the various religions hold different views about what happens after death, they all agree on one point – there is an existence after death.

When my clients have lost a loved one, they always want to talk about the soul's existence after death. From these discussions and experiences, I have realized that there are three commonalities related to communication from deceased relatives:

1. The most common report about dead relative visits I hear from my clients is that the dead relatives come in a dream to let them know that they are OK. Sometimes other family members will have the visitation dream and tell the dreams to the bereaved; either way, communication is established.
2. Occasionally, my clients will report that a family member seems to be still around. People report seeing something out of the corner of their eye, but when they look, nothing is there.

309

3. Probably the most common occurrences involving visitations are lights that suddenly blink on and off and radios or TV's that seemingly turn on by themselves.

Who knows? But I can tell you one thing; everyone is always relieved to know that the deceased made it to the "Other Side" safely.

NAME SYMBOLISM OF THE MAJOR CHARACTERS

Have you ever thought about the fact that most writers carefully select the names of the major characters? If the concept is new to you, you may enjoy the explanation of how and why I chose the specific name for each of my characters.

SYMBOLIC NAMES OF MALE CHARACTERS

Tom Madison

Since Tom is the protagonist of the story, his name had to be very symbolic.

Last name – Madison

Tom needed a name that was connected to an important political person. Since there were many similarities in their lives, I chose Madison as Tom's last name after James Madison, Fourth President of the United States 1809-1817.

Like Tom, James Madison's first job was that of being a lawyer, and he was very devout in his religious beliefs. While attending the Continental Congress, Madison became the prime drafter of the Constitution and the Bill of Rights. All of Tom's speeches are closely tied to what is in those two documents.

The War of 1812 occurred while Madison was in office and, in like manner, the Civil War occurred while Tom was in his political involvement.

First name – Tom

"Uncle Toming" was a derogatory term used by the Negroes in the Civil War South. All Negroes were

311

against enslavement by plantation owners and hated them behind their backs. When a Negro was seen bowing and smiling to a white man's face to curry favor, the other Negroes called that act "Uncle Toming" and hated him for it.

I used the phrase "Uncle Toming" to derive Tom's name. The Unionists were a faction of North Carolina's population who wanted to stay in the Union, and they hated Tom and other political leaders who advocated secession from the Union. To the Unionists Tom was a traitor to his kind, and they despised Tom for his actions.

Thorn McAllister

Last name – McAllister

I chose the name McAllister to represent the Irish immigrants who located in Wilmington.

First name – Thorn

The name Thorn was chosen to represent a symbol of irritation. We are all familiar with the phrases

thorn in my side
or
a thorny issue.

Thorn was caught in the middle of political upheaval. He had no slaves so he was not a Pro-slavery believer. Unlike Ahab, he was not an Abolitionist, who had very strong anti-slavery feelings. The whole political confusion was a "thorn in his side" for he was going to have to get involved whether he liked it or not.

Tom, of course, finally makes Thorn understand that the issue is freedom and that everyone, the North and the South, is being asked to rise to the occasion to defend the Bill of Rights. After that night, Thorn was ready to step into his greatness.

Nathan Summerville

Last name – Summerville

Nathan's last name Summerville was the name of one of the plantations in the South.

First name – Nathan

I chose the name <u>Nathan</u> because of a historical character whose name was Nathan Hale.

Nathan Hale was a soldier for the Continental Army during the American Revolutionary War. He volunteered for an intelligence-gathering mission but he was captured by the British. He is probably best remembered for his purported last words before being hanged:

"I only regret that I have but one life to give for my country."

Nathan Summerville was the only one of the four friends who served the entire time in the Confederate Army battles, even heading his own regiment near the end. Thus, his patriotism had to be linked to another great American patriot, Nathan Hale.

Ahab McGee

Last name – McGee

McGee was chosen to represent the large Scottish immigration in Wilmington at that time.

First name – Ahab

Ahab was in the story to represent the faction of the population, the Abolitionists, who wanted to free the slaves and who went to great lengths to smuggle slaves to freedom. Therefore, the name Ahab had to carry a symbolic relationship with being a traitor to the Southern Cause. I chose the name Ahab from a Biblical story which involved a traitor.

Omri was the Israelite King of Samaria, which was in the Kingdom of Judah. To strengthen an alliance with his neighbors, the Phoenicians, Omri married his son Ahab to the Phoenician Princess Jezebel, who worshipped a foreign god Baal.

When Ahab became King, Jezebel persuaded him to build a temple to Baal in the middle of the Israelite territory. This act, of course, was against God's First Commandment: Thou Shalt Have No Gods Before Me.

Ahab and Jezebel were viewed as traitors to the Israelite religion. In like manner, Ahab and his scout (who was referred to as Jezebel in the beheading scene) were viewed as traitors to the Southern Cause.

John Thompson

Last name – Thompson

The name Thompson was chosen to represent the British immigration to Wilmington.

First name – John

The name John was chosen from a famous Biblical character John the Baptist.

John the Baptist was an itinerant preacher who lived in the hills around Judea spreading the good news of a coming Messiah who would deliver the Jews. He had a movement of baptism at the Jordan River, and Jesus of Nazareth was baptized by John in the River Jordan.

The two John's are similar in many ways. John Thompson left his home of New Bern, NC to move to Wilmington to establish a law practice. In like manner, John left his hometown to move to Judea where he began preaching and baptizing at the Jordan River. John the Baptist's job was to communicate the news that a Messiah was forthcoming while John Thompson's job was to handle all of the Confederacy communication.

Historically, John the Baptist was associated with a very important person, Jesus, the Christed One while John Thompson was associated with Jefferson Davis, President of the Confederacy, who was also a historical figure.

SYMBOLIC NAMES OF THE FEMALE CHARACTERS

Angel Madison

Last name – Madison

> Angel, of course, bore the same last name as her father, Tom Madison. With that name came involvement in politics, a role which she filled admirably.

First name – Angel

> I chose the name Angel for Tom's daughter for several reasons.

> First, the word <u>angel</u> always relates to God's heavenly creations. An angel's job is to help God carry out any and all tasks needed to make the Divine Plan run smoothly. As Tom's Office Manager, her job was to keep his law practice running smoothly. Angel also helped with Tom's political advocacy as we witnessed in the story.

> Second, the connotation of the word angel implies that the qualities will be close to Divine; such as, unconditional love, steadfastness, and devotion. The female protagonist certainly had these qualities.

> Finally, Angel was Thorn's "angel" who helped him understand the higher truths her father talked about so that he could emerge as a wonderful soldier, son-in-law, father and husband as the story unfolds.

Sarah Royster

Last name – Royster

Edgar Allan Poe is one of my favorite poets. <u>Elmira Royster</u> was Poe's first love, and they became engaged. Unfortunately, her father prevented the marriage, and both went on to marry other people. After the death of their spouses, they rekindled their romance. Sarah and Tom have a similar situation; they are greatly in love, but societal views of her being Creole prohibited their marriage. Like Edgar and Elmira, both married other people, but at a later date they were able to keep their love alive even though they were unable to marry.

First name – Sarah

> The name Sarah was chosen from a well known Biblical story about another woman who was barren.

> Abraham, the patriarch of the Jewish race, was married to Sarah for many years, but they were unable to have a child. An angel appeared to them to tell them that, despite their age, Sarah would still conceive a child. Miraculously, at age 92 Sarah gave birth to Isaac. In our story Sarah was barren, but in a miraculous way, she became the second mother for Angel when Rachel died in childbirth.

Miss Lizzie

Last name – No last name was given.

First name – Lizzie

> I'm not sure if you are aware that being a barren woman in the 1800's was an embarrassment; women showed their "worth" by producing large numbers of children to work the farms. The blessing, of course, was that Miss Lizzie turned her deficit into a positive.

> To me, Miss Lizzie became the Godmother to all the children who came through the orphanage. An old

custom still practiced today is the choosing of a Godmother by the parents when a child is born. The main purpose of a Godmother is to take the responsibility of raising the child should the parents be killed or severely injured, which is exactly what Miss Lizzie did for the children who were entrusted to her.

The name Miss Lizzie was chosen because my own Godmother's name was Lizzie.

ABOUT THE AUTHOR

Pat Robertson Rice lives in Wilmington, NC. She has two wonderful daughters, a very talented son-in-law, three delightful grandchildren, and two grand-dogs.

For thirty years Mrs. Rice was a high school English teacher, who was passionate about helping her students reach their maximum potential through the art of creative expression. Now in her retirement years, she is enjoying the luxury of writing for pleasure.

Her first book, <u>Bringing In The Light</u>, was nonfiction, and it was designed to be the textbook for her classes on spiritual growth. Two years ago she decided to try her hand at writing fiction, and she researched Wilmington and its role in the Civil War. <u>Greatness Thrust Upon Us</u> is the result of the research.

Presently she offers spiritually-based counseling and courses related to spiritual development.

8/29/12
3:00 p.m.